BY M. O'KEEFE

Everything I Left Unsaid

The Truth About Him

WRITTEN AS MOLLY O'KEEFE

THE BOYS OF BISHOP NOVELS

Wild Child

Never Been Kissed

Between the Sheets

Indecent Proposal

CROOKED CREEK NOVELS

Can't Buy Me Love

Can't Hurry Love

Crazy Thing Called Love

THE TRUTH
ABOUT HIM

THE TRUTH
ABOUT HIM

A Novel

M. O'Keefe

Bantam Books • New York

A Bantam Books Trade Paperback Original

Published in the United States by Bantam Books,
an imprint of Random House, a division of
Penguin Random House LLC, New York.

BANTAM BOOKS and the House colophon are registered trademarks
of Penguin Random House LLC.

Library of Congress Cataloging-in-Publication Data
O'Keefe, Molly.
The truth about him : a novel / M. O'Keefe.
pages ; cm
ISBN 978-1-101-88450-8 (softcover : acid-free paper)—
ISBN 978-1-101-88451-5 (eBook)
1. Man-woman relationships—Fiction. I. Title.
PS3615.K44T78 2015
813'.6—dc23
2015023223

Printed in the United States of America on acid-free paper

randomhousebooks.com

9 8 7 6 5 4 3 2 1

Book design by Karin Batten

This one is for Andy, Allycia, and Pillen.
For the sun-soaked Florida days. For the card games.
The Margaritas. The walks on the beach.
This week every year fills my soul.

Acknowledgments

I THOUGHT A LOT ABOUT COMMUNITY WHILE WRITING THIS book, and I have three very large communities that I could not live without.

The Truth About Him would never have been written without the parents of my kids' friends, who took my kids away on weekends and picked them up from school when Adam and I couldn't get there. Who fed me wine and dinner when I needed it, and who have become my very dear friends. Thank you to: Jenny, Eedit, Leslie, Lizzy, Emmi, Lorna, Leanne, Shawna, Tory, Sarah, Jennie O, Elaine, Alaine, Katy, and Ginette.

And to my writing community. The authors who inspire me, who keep me honest, who push me to try new things, to write better and harder. Who have provided hours and hours of reading pleasure. Whose books are on my keeper shelf, who I'm just so privileged to know. Thank you.

And to the readers who blog and tweet and review, and those who don't, but pass their favorites on to friends and family. Thank you for sharing so enthusiastically your enthusiasm about romance novels.

PART ONE

1

ANNIE

ANNIE MCKAY CAME TO SLOWLY. AWARE IN PIECES OF HER SUR-
roundings.

The pebbled linoleum of the trailer floor dug into her cheek.
Her ankle was twisted, wedged against something hard.

The hot copper smell of blood made her stomach roll and
she gagged.

"Annie, I'm sorry."

That voice . . . *oh God.*

It was Hoyt. Her husband. Standing over her.

For heartbeats, lots of them, she wasn't sure he was real.
Perhaps she'd tripped and fallen, hit her head coming back into
her trailer. She was hallucinating. Pulling Hoyt out of old nightmares. That made much more sense.

Because there was no way he could have found her here.

I was careful. I was so careful.

Two months ago, she'd run from him. Taking only the
bruises around her neck and three thousand dollars from his

safe. Desperate and scared, she left in the middle of the night and made her way in circles to this place, a patch of swamp called the Flowered Manor Trailer Park and Camp Ground in North Carolina.

Hundreds of miles from Hoyt. From Oklahoma. From the farm where she'd lived her entire life.

And she'd been happy here. The happiest she'd ever been. Not even two hours ago, she'd left Dylan and his magical house. Her body had been flush and alive and *pleasured*. And her mind had been clear.

She'd had plans, real plans, for her *life,* not just panicked and terrified reactions.

Everything had been about to get better.

"Annie?"

This is not a hallucination.

Be smart, Annie. Think!

"You hear what I said to you?"

She lay there silent. Hoyt hated her silence. Apologies were to be met with immediate acquiescence, his guilt promptly assuaged.

But she said nothing. Because *fuck him.*

"Get up."

She kept her eyes closed, because she wasn't ready to actually *see* him. Not here. Not in this trailer. Her home.

Hoping to feel her phone still in her back pocket, she rolled onto her back.

Please, please, she prayed, *please be there.*

But there was nothing under her butt. The phone was gone.

"There you go. It ain't so bad, is it? Get yourself up off the floor." He said it like she'd fallen, like she'd landed on the floor through her own clumsy, stupid means.

Despite her best efforts to restrain them, hot tears seeped under her lashes.

"Come on, now." His hands touched her hip and her armpit

to help her up and she flinched away, her body screaming in pain. Unsteady, she got herself to her feet. She opened her eyes and the world swam. She grabbed the edge of the table, landing half on, half off the cushion of the settee.

"You're getting blood all over the place." His familiar hands, with their small scars and close-clipped nails, held a pink washcloth toward her. It was the washcloth from her bathroom. He'd probably gone through everything, touching all of her things. Everything was contaminated now.

There was no way she could take the washcloth. Not from his hand.

"Fine," he muttered, tossing the washcloth on the table. "Do it yourself."

Pissed, he stomped off to sit in one of the captain's chairs at the front of the trailer.

The reality of Hoyt in this previously Hoyt-less place was shocking.

She forced herself to look at him. Really look at him.

He was a big man. Over six feet tall, and he used to rodeo when he was younger, so his legs and arms and chest were thick with muscle. He had white-blond hair that made his eyebrows and eyelashes nearly invisible, which gave his face a terrible expressionlessness. A vacancy. She'd never ever been able to tell what he was thinking.

Sincerity looked like deceit. Anger looked like forgiveness.

She used to think he was calm. Other people did, too; at the very beginning of their marriage that's what everyone said about him.

He's so steady, they'd said. And she'd clung to that. With both hands and all her fear after Mom died. She'd clung to the version of him she wanted to believe in.

But it was a lie. Everything about him was a lie.

And Annie had been a fool.

That he was so totally the same, wearing what he always

wore—jeans, his brown cowboy boots, and the dark blue West-ern shirt with the pearl snaps, his bone-handled knife in its sheath on his belt—made it even more surreal.

New place. Same nightmare.

Her missing phone was balanced on his knee. He'd taken it from her, gone through her pockets, while she lay unconscious on the floor.

Because he was an animal.

"I'm sorry," he said with utter and terrifying sincerity. "I know at home, you were scared. What I did . . . that night in the kitchen?" He said it as if she might have forgotten. "It was too much. I understand that."

An incredulous laugh she could not let out stung her throat. *Do you? Do you understand that?*

"It won't happen again. I swear it won't."

"How did you find me?" She tried to clear her vision, get her brain to focus.

"Do you believe me?" he asked. "That things will be differ-ent?"

No. Not in a million years.

"I believe you," she lied, putting her heavy, throbbing head in her hand. "Just tell me how you found me."

"It was actually pretty cool." He smiled, with what she guessed was modesty, like she was about to be real proud of him. "The *Bassett Gazette* has this widget thing—that's what they call them—on their website and it shows a map of the United States, and on that map are little pins that track the places where people are logging onto the website. The gal I talked to at the office was real excited about it, said it showed that there were people all over the state reading their newspaper online. And there was this one dot . . . this one little dot that I started to follow. You know where that dot went?"

Sick to her stomach, she nodded. She thought she'd been so clever.

"It went around in circles for a while. And then it went north to Pennsylvania and then back south. And then it just stayed in Cherokee, North Carolina. Over and over again. Cherokee, North Carolina. Every week. Once a week. Tuesdays. That's the day you liked to go shopping." He said it like he was offering her proof of his affection. A nosegay. A dead bird dropped at her feet from his bloody jaws. "You thought I didn't notice. But I did. You liked to shop on Tuesdays. So, I drove out here. I saw where you signed in for computer time at the library—Layla McKay. That's your cousin, right?"

In one of the historical novels she'd read, there was a character who had a falcon. And Annie had loved the descriptions of how the guy flew his falcon and cared for it, the bells and the gloves and the little pieces of meat in a bag attached to his belt. And she'd thought, reading it, how great it would be to control something so barely domesticated. Something so very nearly wild.

But at this moment she realized how the falcon must have felt. So free one minute, wings spread, the world a retreating landscape below. The next, hooded and chained. Captured. Freedom a memory.

"I stayed there for a week, hanging out at the library. The grocery store. Driving by all the motels, and . . . nothing. I heard about this trailer park out here and came out to investigate and I ran into this man, Phil, at a gas station. He told me all about the park. And when I described you, he told me he thought you might be here. You're like his wife's friend? I'm afraid Phil doesn't like you much."

God, brought down by Phil. How pathetically fitting.

"What do you want?" she asked, unable to pretend any longer.

He looked at her like he was surprised, his mouth gaping open, his translucent eyebrows halfway up his forehead. "I want you to come home," he said. "I want you to be my wife again."

"What does that even mean to you, Hoyt? Your wife? You don't love me—"

He stood up from that chair and she shrank back in her seat.

"I apologized for what happened before you left. I can't do any more than that. It's time for you to come home now. You've had your fun. People are asking about you and I'm getting tired of the sideways glances. Everyone thinks I've done something to you. The police came out to the house two weeks ago. *The police*, Annie. It's too much."

He touched her hand before she could jerk it back. It was worse when he pretended to care. Or maybe he did actually care and he just didn't know how to do it right.

"We can go back to church."

Annie blinked up at him, unsure if he'd actually said that, or if she was hearing things.

"Annie? Would you like to go back to church?"

"Yes . . . of course," she breathed. Three years ago she would have wept in gratitude. But she was not fooled now. He would let her go to church once, maybe twice, and he'd find a way to take it away from her all over again.

"And then we've got to talk about selling that land to Encro."

And there it was. That was really why he wanted her home. The land sale to Encro for more windmills. He couldn't do it without Annie's approval. That's why this little scene was happening. "It's time, don't you think, that we thought of our future?"

My future is as far away from you as I can get.

"I forgive you for stealing from me, Annie. The money, the gun. It's forgiven."

Oh my God.

The gun.

The gun in her bedside table.

Did he have it? Was it still there?

She tried to show him nothing. Not one thing.

"I . . . I need to change my shirt." Her splattered and torn sweatshirt was ruined with blood; it would never come clean. She'd had a few shirts like that at home. Clothes that made their way into the rag bag or the garbage because the truth of her life was sprayed all over it.

Annie got up on shaky feet, her hand braced on the wall as she walked down the short hallway to the bedroom.

Please. Please be there. Please be there. That gun was her only chance.

She closed the door behind her and then, sweeping her dizziness and headache aside, she nearly leapt over the bed to the small bedside table and yanked open the drawer.

It was empty. Sobbing, she searched it, pulling it all the way out, but everything was gone. The books. The gun. The article about Ben. Everything.

She collapsed against the wall and fell to the floor.

The bedroom door creaked open and Hoyt stood in the doorway. A blond devil. Her gun like a toy in his big palm.

In his other hand were her books. The sticky notes from Dylan. The artifacts of her rebellion. Of her entire life here.

Silent, he tossed the books onto the bed. The article. The notes.

She wanted to gather them up, out of his reach. Out of his sight. But it was too late. Everything she owned he'd ruined with his touch. She tipped her head so she couldn't see them. Like a child, if she couldn't see them, they weren't real.

They never happened.

All she had left was getting out of this.

"Who is Dylan Daniels to you?" he asked.

"No one. I don't know who he is." Annie got to her feet without any idea why she was bothering to lie when she was doing it so badly. All she knew was that she could not put Dylan in the middle of this nightmare.

"Stop." He held up the phone, the screen showing all of their text messages. The picture she sent of her nearly naked body. Her breasts and her tummy, the pale white blur of her thighs.

Annie had been unfaithful to a man who smacked her around over chicken potpies. Strangled her over windmills. She could not imagine what he would do over adultery.

"I know about it all. So you need to stop lying. For your sake."

He was going to kill her. A gasping sob cleared her throat.

"Don't look at me like that," he whispered, his face creased with agony. "I'm not going to hurt you."

Annie nearly laughed. But terror had squeezed her body.

"I don't like it, Annie, but I . . . I guess I understand." He tilted his head like the old yellow Lab they used to have. "What I did to you made you . . . act out like that. I know that's not you. That picture, those notes. That's not the Annie I know."

The Annie he knew was a rag doll. A scarecrow. An animated reflection of him. The Annie he knew was gone.

But Hoyt was still talking. "We can go back home and just forget it. Forget this Dylan Daniels. Start over."

That was impossible. There was no forgetting Dylan Daniels. He was burned under her skin. Into her bones.

Move, she told herself, *keep moving. Don't just sit here and let him ruin you again.* As long as she kept moving she was alive, and as long as she was alive, there was a chance.

Annie pulled a clean shirt out of the dresser. "You mind?" she asked, when he just kept standing there. That gun held so casually in his hand as if to mock her fear.

A muscle twitched in his jaw and he glanced down at the books on the bed and the phone in his hand, silently asking if she really thought she deserved modesty now. But then he bowed his head and walked out of her room as if granting Annie privacy was a favor. A silly, stupid wish by a silly, stupid woman.

Once he was gone, she pulled off her dirty shirt and slipped on her clean one. The windows in here were all too small to climb through, but she pushed open her curtains hoping Ben was still in his garden, hoping she could catch his eye. But his garden was empty. Joan's trailer was still dark.

As lightly as she could, she stepped to the door, listening for sounds from the rest of the trailer so she could try to tell where he was. But it was silent. Eerie and silent and awful.

Shaking, she cracked open the door to see Hoyt back in the captain's seat. He was eating a cinnamon roll from the bag she'd brought down from Dylan's. If Annie was careful and if she was quick, she might get to the door before he did.

Acting as if she were still dizzy, she leaned her hand against the wall as she made her way into the small kitchen. Four feet. Three. Two. The door was right there. She paused for a second, holding her head as if she could barely stand. He needed to think she was weak.

"You want to pack up?" he asked. "I'd like to get home. We've been gone too long." Like they'd been on a trip. A fun excursion.

"Can we have some food first? I need something to eat. It might make me less dizzy."

She turned herself around, getting her body between him and the door, and then made as if she were reaching for the paper bag but instead of the bag she reached for the door, pushing it open, cold air rushing toward her as she threw her body down the steps, but Hoyt grabbed the back of her shirt and then a handful of her hair and yanked her back into the trailer.

And then slammed the door shut.

Annie screamed so loud and so hard her throat ached and he backhanded her, tossed her on the floor of the trailer and got down on top of her, squeezing the air from her body. His hand closed over her mouth. His knife had slipped forward and the leather tip of the sheath touched the bare skin of her hip, where her shirt had ridden up.

She tried to flinch away from it, but he was too heavy.

Every breath she took, that knife rubbed her. Scratched her.

"Look at me, Annie," he said in that calm voice. "I found you and we're together again. There's nowhere for you to go. And you need to realize that."

She shook her head, trying to buck him off with her hips.

"This Dylan man, he's not for you. And you know what? I forgive you for having an affair with this man." His voice said otherwise. His voice and his narrowed eyes and the vicious, disgusted curl to his lip, they told her she would be paying for these sins. "Some kind of dirty affair. Sending a man who is not your husband a picture of your naked body. You—"

He shifted over her and she felt, to her utter horror, that he was hard under his zipper. This man who'd so rarely had sex with her was aroused. She closed her eyes against this new, awful terror.

The sheathed knife and his erection dug into her.

"This man you were screwing, did he know you were married?"

Annie did not respond. Would not. He was playing some sick game. He touched her hair just above her ear and she could have screamed.

"You smell dirty. Like sweat and sex." He sniffed her. Over and over again, his nose in her hair. Her neck. "I want you to spread your legs, Annie."

Whimpering, she clenched them together.

I am going to die this way.

There was a sudden knocking on the door and both of them stilled. She opened her eyes in time to see a momentary flash of panic on Hoyt's face. But as soon as it was there it was gone, replaced by that terrifying vacancy.

"Annie!" It was Ben. Old, frail Ben. "You all right? I heard screaming."

"Who is that?" Hoyt asked.

"My neighbor." Ben Daniels. Dylan's father. And . . . quite possibly, her only friend.

"You don't want that man to get hurt." The menthol smell of Hoyt's breath flowed over her face. He ate Halls cough drops like candy. "And if you say one word to him, give him one reason to think you aren't okay, he'll get hurt. We'll still be going home together, Annie. You cannot change that. No matter what you do."

This whole situation was made worse by the fact that Ben was a former motorcycle gang member and convicted felon. Cops would take one look at her face, and Ben's record, and they'd believe whatever Hoyt said.

Hoyt was very believable.

Bit by bit Hoyt got off Annie, watching her every second to see what she would do. Annie's reactions had become unexpected and she took some strength from that, from no longer being underestimated.

Shaking, she slowly got to her feet, grabbed the pink washcloth from the table, and held it to her head. Hoping Ben would believe the lies she was about to tell him.

Hoyt got out of sight and Annie pushed open the door to her trailer and stepped outside, the door closing quietly behind her.

I could run. Right now.

But Hoyt would come after her. And Ben would get hurt.

"You all right?" Ben asked, looking worried. He wore the familiar clean white shirt, pristinely ironed. He'd been sick recently, and he'd lost weight. No matter how tough he'd been years ago, now he was frail and he was old.

And he could not help her.

"Fine," she lied with a smile. "There was a snake and I screamed and jumped and smacked my head on the cupboard."

"I get those king snakes all the time," he said. "You want me—"

She got in his way as he leaned to the side as if to see into the trailer, or worse, try to come in. "I'm fine."

That lie didn't sound at all convincing and he pointed up to his own eye. "You smack your eye, too? Your lip?"

"Please," she breathed, unable to pretend anymore. "Please, Ben, just go."

"Annie—"

"For fuck's sake, old man. I'm fine. I'm exhausted and I just want to get some sleep. Leave me alone."

His dark eyes missed nothing and she had no idea what he was thinking but in the end he surrendered, holding up his hands and going back to his trailer. Taking all hope of rescue with him.

Annie was going to have to do this herself.

2

DYLAN

IF HOPE WAS HARD FOR ME, FAITH WAS IMPOSSIBLE.

Growing up Dylan Daniels among the thieves and killers and rabid animals disguised as humans that were my family, faith didn't stand a chance.

But goddammit—I was trying. I clutched hope and faith in my scarred hands. Hands far too used to shoving those things away.

I leaned back against my kitchen counter and read the text Annie sent me two hours ago. I knew it by heart. Could probably recite it on my deathbed. But still, I looked at those words, as if reading them again would help me actually believe them.

I know about jail. I know what happened. It doesn't change anything for me. It doesn't change who you are. When this is done, when I am done . . . I'm going to come back to you. To hear the story from your lips. To finish what we started.

If you'll have me.

My life since the fire five years ago had been about control. Letting no one in or out, including myself. I lived in a fortress on top of a mountain I owned. The headquarters for 989 Engines, the company I started with my only friends, was here; the garage was here. I worked with the same guys I'd been working with since the moment I'd gotten out of jail nine years ago.

I worked. I made money. More than I could spend in my life as a recluse.

I wasn't lonely. I didn't *want*.

Or at least I thought I didn't.

Until Annie McKay came out of nowhere. Right out of my blind spot, crashing into the center of my life.

And I never saw her coming.

It had taken years for me to kill all the feelings I had about my family. But I'd done it. The memories had been bound, chained, and dropped to the bottom of the ocean. My brother. My mom. Pops. It had been hard. Harder than most things, and I was the better for it. I knew that.

But Annie had left my mountain two hours ago and the place was crowded with her ghosts. The air thick with memory and scent and the fading echo of her voice.

There on my couch was where she'd let me into her body. Tight and wet and small. I could still feel her breath breaking against my shoulder as she worked to accept me.

On the chair, there, beside the couch, Annie had sat with her legs spread, her busy fingers beneath that blue underwear, her heavy-lidded eyes watching me.

She was drinking Champagne at the table. Lying about the cheese she didn't like. Wearing that black silk robe I never used.

The bathroom was haunted by her sitting up on that counter, leaning back against the mirror, her body laid out before me, pink and white. That surprising thatch of red hair between her legs. Annie had dyed her hair white blond and I should have suspected something staring at those red curls. But I'd been so hungry for her. I'd been so . . . compelled, those clues meant nothing to me.

In the bedroom her ghost was curled up on her side, telling me—shattering me—with her secrets.

I am married, she'd said after I fucked her. Twice. After weeks of a relationship of sorts over the phone.

I didn't have a whole lot of rules, but I didn't fuck married women. And I was pissed, sure, but it was fleeting. Both of us had been keeping secrets. That was hers.

Mine was . . . *fuck,* mine was worse.

And she said she knew, that Pops told her.

But did she really?

Someone knocked on my front door, and only two people would do that. My business partner, Blake, or his mother, Margaret. And I didn't want to see either of them. I didn't want to see anyone. I just wanted to be here for a few minutes, in the quiet. With Annie's ghost.

"Go away!" I yelled.

But the door opened anyway.

"You deaf?"

"I'm not." It was Blake walking into my house, and I quickly picked up the robe that was still draped over the table and the condom wrapper on the edge of the couch. "But maybe you are?" Blake asked, coming to stand in the kitchen. He wore one of his expensive suits and a silk tie and you couldn't see any of our garage in him. As the money guy, he'd had the grease manicured right out from under his nails.

He wore pink ties. *Pink.* And no one gave him shit about it.

Because he owned it. Made it work.

That smile he was flashing me was familiar. I'd seen it plenty of times before, right before he eviscerated someone. Blake had a well-played charm card and it suckered a lot of people. "That would explain why you haven't answered my calls."

He watched me with eyes exactly like his father's, the green of old glass Mountain Dew bottles. But unlike his father, Miguel, Blake's eyes judged me.

They always judged me. Even when he was trying not to.

And right now, he could fuck himself with that judgment.

"I've been busy," I hedged, dumping some of the leftover food in the garbage.

Blake leaned against my table, grabbing an olive and tossing it into his mouth. "So I've heard." He smiled as he chewed and then spat the pit into an empty champagne glass. There weren't a lot of people who could get away with talking to me like this. But Blake's father, Miguel, and his mother, Margaret, had taken me in after jail. Given me a second chance.

It gave Blake the right to bust my balls.

But only so much.

"What do you want, Blake?"

The charm fell away and Blake pushed off the table.

"Everybody is down at the garage running final tests on the transmission, including me, I might add, despite the twenty other things I need to be doing. Because we're behind schedule, because other engine builders are trying to replicate this shit, because all our very interested and very rich buyers are getting antsy, and you're cleaning your house?"

"The guys can handle it. I've put in more hours than anyone else on that transmission. I'll be down there when I'm ready."

"Is this about that woman?"

My hackles rose at his tone, the smear his voice put on "that woman."

"Her name is Annie."

"Whatever. I thought she left."

"She did."

She left a few hours ago, somber and decided. Unwilling to take more from me than my lawyer's phone number. She wouldn't take my offer to stay up on the mountain. Or to stay in my house in Charleston. Or my offer to drive her down to the trailer park myself. She left and she was going to divorce her husband. Get back her land and her freedom and her life.

I need to do this myself, she'd said with the kind of implacable courage I understood.

And I let her go because I believed her when she said she needed to do it on her own. I admired her for it.

"Thank God, man," Blake said. "Maybe now we can actually get some work done. You've been walking around this place for two months like your phone was attached to your dick." That was truer than he probably even guessed. It had gotten so bad in the last month that every time my phone rang my dick got hard.

"She's coming back."

Because when she asked if she could come back, I'd said yes. I'd said I would be waiting.

"Coming back? Here?" I understood Blake's incredulousness. People . . . women . . . didn't come up here. "Did you tell her—"

"No. I didn't."

"Dylan," he sighed. "You've got to tell her. Prison and what happened there—you can't keep that a secret."

"She knows."

"How?"

"Pops must have told her when she got to the trailer park. She texted and said she knew and she didn't care."

"Your dad is involved now? Holy shit, this gets better and better. You think he told her . . . everything?" Blake asked. Which, frankly, was the same damn question I'd been asking because there was no way she knew the real story, or the whole story, because a woman like her, a *human* like her, would care once she knew what I'd done.

"I don't know," I said.

And maybe the right thing to do was to let her go, free and clear. No ties. Nothing but memories.

But I wasn't ready for that yet. I still wanted more of her. All of her.

"And you trust this woman?"

Oh man, if Blake knew she'd lied to me—from the beginning and over and over again—he'd lose his shit.

"I want to," was all I said.

Blake laughed, but it was bitter. Hard. "I've known you nine years, man, since your family dropped you on our doorstep and walked away when you got out of jail. I've worked side by side with you. Made a shit ton of money with you and for you. My mom practically saved your life after the fire. My dad loved you like a son—"

"What's your point?" I snapped.

"My point is that after all that, I'm not sure if you trust *me*. You don't trust anyone."

"You sound jealous." I tried to make it a joke. But it wasn't funny. Not at all. Because he was right. I didn't trust anyone past a certain point. And that point was a shallow one.

My family had done that to me.

"No. I'm pissed. Because you're trusting some woman—"

"She's not 'some woman,'" I snapped at him.

"They're all some woman," Blake said. "The cute ones, the smart ones, the ones that suck your dick. The ones that don't. And now your dad is wrapped up in this. When has that ever worked out in your favor?"

Never. Not once.

There was a faint buzzing and Blake dug his phone out of the jacket of his suit.

"Hold on, man," he said to me and then turned and walked away toward the shadowed foyer, his phone pressed to his ear.

My weak hold on faith was breaking. I didn't want to listen to Blake. I didn't want his words to be true.

But so many of them were.

I had the Champagne bottle in my hand, the bottle Annie

and I had drunk just before we had sex. Just before she told me about being married.

I wanted to smash it into the sink.

I wanted to smash that person Blake was talking about—that version of myself. Break him into a thousand pieces. I wanted violence and blood, or speed and the roar of engines. I wanted every distraction I could get from being myself. Being trapped in this wrecked body with all this goddamn damage.

"Hey, man," Blake said, coming back in the room. "We got a problem."

I turned, and Blake held out his phone. His face had that still, quiet, damage-control look on it that I'd seen hundreds of times, in the minutes before he gave me bad news. "The call is for you. It's my brother . . . Phil. Down at the trailer park."

"What the fuck is he doing there?" I'd fired Phil not too long ago, the final straw in the fragile relationship between Blake and his brother.

"Apparently that's where he's living."

"My trailer park? Did you know that?"

Blake shook his head. "Phil keeps everything a secret. Everything. He's paranoid as fuck."

Oh Jesus. Now I have to worry about Phil living next to Annie.

"But he's saying some old man has a knife and is demanding to talk to you."

There was only one old man down at the trailer park who might be able to connect the dots between Blake, his shithead brother, Phil, and me.

And that was Ben.

Pops.

That part of me that was so attuned to karma prickled with sudden awareness. Sudden dread. I could feel forces out there moving around, events I could not avoid starting to take shape.

Inevitable.

"I'm sorry, man," Blake said, because he knew anything having to do with my father and Phil could not be good. Blake handed over his phone before slipping back outside to give me privacy.

"Hello?"

"Dylan?"

I'd had Pops looked in on for years, but hadn't once heard his voice. Not since that day he visited me in jail and asked me to give up my life so my brother could have his.

And hearing it now—that old pack-a-day voice, the rasp and the drawl—was like having a boulder dropped on my chest, pushing out all my air. I was twenty-nine and nine all at once. Distance shrank to nothing, and the years and the memories collapsed inward.

That first night in Duval, when my door rattled open in the middle of the night . . . *God,* I would have done anything to hear Pops's voice then, telling me to get my fists up because a fight was coming.

"What do you want?" I asked.

"Son—"

"Don't." It came out unbidden. My hand came up, too, as if I could fend him off from miles away. Years away. *Don't call me "son." You lost that right long, long ago.*

When I was a kid, I kept wedging myself into impossible cracks in his life, Max's, too, just so we could be close. Just so we could be together. After jail I let Max and Pops go. But only so far. I still had Ben watched, because the old man was dangerous. And the old man's mistakes had a way of coming back to bite me in the ass.

But Max . . . Max was long gone. Max left me alone at that party with a replacement brother and replacement parents and never looked back.

"Why are you calling?" I asked. Why now?

"It's Annie," he said, and my entire body, my whole life,

sharpened. "Some guy's in her trailer. Roughing her up. I think it's her husband."

Jesus. Fuck.

"Can you get her out?" I asked.

"I tried. She kicked me out. I'll keep an eye on things, but you need to get here, son. And you need to get here fast."

Ben hung up and I gave myself one second.

One second for the fire of my rage to blow through me. And then I grabbed my keys off the hook by the door and stepped outside into the cool twilight. Blake was there, leaning against the rough wood of my house. In my adrenaline rush I felt everything. The air. The gravel beneath my shoes. The sharp bite of the key in my palm.

"Everything okay?" Blake asked, and for all his tough words in there, I could see his worry. The guy was a dick, but he was the good kind of dick.

I threw Blake his phone and he caught it with one hand. "Is Annie—"

I shook my head, unable to speak, panic in my throat like rats in a pipe. Fear was a tidal wave heaving me up and I started to run for the car.

Faith, that weak rebellion, slipping from my fingers.

3

ANNIE

ONCE ANNIE GOT BACK INSIDE SHE MADE A BEELINE FOR THE
bathroom.

"Annie?" Hoyt asked but she ran past him, shut the door,
and barely made it to the toilet before throwing up. Whether it
was because of a concussion or fear or being so awful to Ben or
the belly full of Champagne she'd had not too long ago in
Dylan's kitchen, she didn't know.

Hoyt knocked on the door.

"Give . . . give me a second," she cried. She took her time
standing up, brushing her teeth, looking at the jagged cut over
her eye. And slowly, she came up with a plan. Not a great one,
but the only one she had.

"Annie?"

Fury curled her lip, but showing him that would only get her
beaten. Possibly raped.

Be smart, she told herself.

She opened the door to the bathroom only to find Hoyt

standing there with a sandwich. A peanut butter and jelly sandwich he'd made for her.

"Come on, now," he said, leading her over to the settee. "You've gotten too skinny, that's the problem."

Right. Too skinny.

"Eat up and then we'll get going." He sat down with his own sandwich. "Annie?"

"Thank you," she breathed, toying with the sesame seed on the edge of her crust. He liked manners, and Annie was all out of petty mutinies. Her molar was loose from her last uprising.

"You gonna eat?"

"I have an idea." Her voice was barely a breath. It was all she had. Her breath. Her pounding heart. Her shaking hands.

"You are not really known for those." He said it like a joke. Like one of those teasing things married people do.

My wife, the little dear, she keeps forgetting to close the garage door. What an airhead!

Oh, his stupid, careless little barbs, how they used to wound. But there was nothing left in her to wound.

"I will give you all the land," she said. "I will sign over everything to you—you can sell it to the energy people, you can rent it out for grazing. You can build an amusement park on it. I will give you every inch."

"That's not what I want—"

"You can have the land. But I won't come with you. We can have the deal drawn up, as well as a divorce, and I'll sign it all. It's yours."

"No."

"Hoyt, let's be honest. You don't care about me. All you care about is the land. It's all you've ever wanted."

"I promised your mother I'd take care of you."

The mention of her mother blew her back a second. "What?"

"Before she died. She came to me, asked me to make sure that you'd be all right. I think it's why she hired me."

"That's . . . that's ridiculous."

He shrugged. "Your mom was kind of ridiculous."

Of course he would think that. Everyone in town thought Mom was ridiculous.

And truthfully, it made sense that Mom had been trying to match-make. She'd been dying and terrified of leaving her alone. Alone meant unloved. In her mother's paranoid world, it was better for Annie to be with Hoyt, no matter what, than to be alone.

"She'd want you on that land, Annie."

"She'd want me alive," she snapped back.

For five years during her marriage she'd allowed herself a kind of powerful delusion. Not hope. But . . . pretend. A thick layer of lies she told herself. And that was all gone now; she could not hide from reality anymore.

Sooner or later Hoyt was going to kill her.

"It's gonna be different when we get home," he said, watching her from beneath his nearly translucent lashes.

Yes. So much terrifying, awful sex to look forward to.

Anger was losing ground inside of her, surrendering in great swaths to the old terror.

That was what he did. That was his power. Magical and awful. He was a black hole of hope. Sucking it in, neutralizing it. Turning it into fear and self-loathing. And she didn't understand how that happened to a person. How someone became that way.

"What was your mom like?" she asked.

He blinked those icy blue eyes like he didn't understand the question, and she wasn't totally sure why she was asking about his mother now. Maybe she was stalling. Maybe she was trying to figure out why he was the way he was.

"You . . . you don't talk about her much."

"There ain't a lot worth talking about. She died when I was young. I don't remember much."

"What do you remember?"

"Annie? What the hell is this?"

"I'm just talking. You know about my mom; I just thought I should know something about yours."

"She was pretty. And she smoked. That's what I remember."

"But didn't your grandparents talk about her? I would think they'd tell you stories—"

"They were my dad's parents, not my mom's."

"What were they like?"

"They were old. And they worked. And they made me work. No school. No friends. No birthdays. No church. Just work." He shook his head. The few times he'd talked about his childhood it sounded lonely. Cold. But was that enough to make Hoyt this way? Maybe the horror of Hoyt was that he just happened. There was a glitch in his chemistry. His cruelty was in the way he was wired. He was simply born this way. "And you know something, in the end it didn't even matter. They died broke. I had to sell the land just to pay the back taxes. That's it. That's the story."

"Were they kind, at least?"

"Kind? What the hell, Annie?" he yelled, his face getting red. "They're dead. All of them. Mom. Dad. My grandparents. All gone. All I have is you, Annie. We're alike that way, ain't we? No parents. No one else to look after us. To care about us."

"Smith." She dared to say a name she hadn't said aloud since Hoyt demanded Annie fire him years ago. "Smith would have taken care of me."

"That old fucker?" Hoyt laughed.

"He was my friend." They never talked about this. About what she did to Smith, about the things Smith said about Hoyt. She pretended it never happened just so she could sleep at night. Sleep at night next to her husband.

"He was a criminal, Annie. He went to jail for seriously fucking up some couple in a bar. Took out his eyeball or some shit. Punched out a woman. He was a drunk and he was dangerous. The whole town knew it. Everyone. Except your crazy mom. Or maybe she knew and she just didn't care."

"Don't . . . don't call her that," she said.

"Crazy? That's what she was."

"Don't call her that!" she yelled.

His hand snaked forward and grabbed hers, pressing the bones of her fingers together until the nerves screamed and then went numb. She hung her head, breathing through the pain.

"Your mom was a crazy old woman living alone. Putting her only child at risk because she had a crush on a violent dirtbag."

Annie thought of Dylan and those things Ben had said about him. That he was a criminal. That he killed someone in jail.

The apple doesn't fall far from the tree.

She'd known Dylan had secrets, painful ones. That he had a violence . . . an anger that simmered just under the surface. Annie had thought it was about the car racing accident, about having his life changed so irrevocably. But no . . . his secrets were much worse. Much more painful.

But she wasn't scared of that. Of who he was. Of what he'd done.

She was proud of him; she admired that he was a survivor. She liked it.

She was *attracted* to it.

So, what did that make her?

People threw the word *crazy* around like it didn't mean anything. But her mother had not been well, and worse, she had not been strong enough or did not care enough about Annie to take care of herself. To stay on her meds. To make better choices.

And she'd definitely had feelings for Smith.

Was Annie like her mother? Was there something dark in her drawn to that kind of violence?

Annie's head pounded and she could not hold on to her thoughts. They kept slipping through her fingers.

Dylan.

The farm.

Mom.

Getting free.

Giving up.

"If you ain't gonna eat," he said, "let's get going."

"It's getting dark," she said without much urgency or conviction. Annie used to be a much better liar. An excellent placater. In the months she'd been hiding, she must have lost the knack. Fallen out of practice.

Hoyt stood, looming over her. His shadow stretched across the entirety of her home.

"You don't have to drive," he said. As if she could.

Somewhere he must have learned at least some small measure of socialization. How to act as if he were human. And Annie's job as his wife had been to wait . . . to try to help him keep that mask on and then to brace herself when he could no longer pretend.

I can't go back to that. I just can't.

"I'm not going," she breathed.

"What did you say?"

He was going to hit her. There was no pretending otherwise.

"I said I'm not going."

"Stand up," Hoyt said, radiating terrifying stillness. An electric horror.

"No."

When he grabbed her arm, all that fear shattered. It fell to pieces around her, revealing only a bone-deep rage. A fury so hot she thought her skin might smoke.

Annie resisted. Not looking at him, she put everything she had, all her weight and grief and hate, into it. She kicked and punched and pushed and smacked. But he was big and it was over almost before it started. He cuffed her once, the heel of his hand catching her lip, and it split, blood pouring into her mouth.

"You done?" he asked. Like she was a child throwing a tantrum.

Annie spat a mouthful of blood at him.

His pale eyebrows and eyelashes stood out against the bright red flush of his skin. She'd never seen him this angry. Not even the night he put his hands around her neck.

"You should kill me now," Annie said. "We both know that's how this is going to end."

"It's going to end with you coming home where you belong. And us being a family again. Like we're supposed to."

"We're never going to be family." He didn't know the meaning of the word and frankly, she didn't, either. Mom had not given her that kind of vocabulary.

"Get up." He pulled Annie up by her upper arms, his fingers digging into the tender skin near her armpits, pushing those nerves against the bones so that sparks radiated into her fingers. "Is there anything you want to take with you?" he asked. "Them dirty books?"

Annie shook her head. She wasn't going to take anything with her, not even the romance novels she'd loved so much. Because she was only going to run again. She would run and run until he was forced to kill her.

"We're going to be okay, Annie," he said. One of his hands touched her hair and she flinched away. "I like this. Your new hair. Did I tell you that? Looks real nice."

She spat blood onto the floor near his boots.

He huffed a long breath and she braced herself for another smack. More pain. More blood.

"Come on," he said, grabbing his denim coat with the shearling collar from where he'd thrown it over the driver's chair of the old RV she'd been calling home. "We're leaving."

The outside world was a shock. Cool and dark. The trailer

park was quiet and still, as if everyone was gone. Or maybe just cowering, like they knew that something evil was here and they didn't want to attract its attention.

That instinct was honed to a bright edge in the Flowered Manor.

Annie had kept her head down her entire marriage. She'd never asked for help, and the people who would have helped her, who looked at her like they knew what was happening in her home—she pushed them away. Hard and fast.

That was over—as of right now.

"Help!" she screamed. "Help me!"

4

ANNIE

NOT EVEN A TWITCH. NOT EVEN A DOG BARK.

"The hell you doing, Annie?" Hoyt demanded, shaking her. Annie's brain sloshed against her skull and there were little explosions of light behind her eyes.

She spat more blood out onto the grass, leaving a trail past her trailer. *Like anyone is going to follow me,* she thought with dark despair. The lights were on in Ben's trailer and it glowed like an aluminum jack-o'-lantern.

But she couldn't see him anywhere. There were no shadows behind his blinds.

"Ben!" she cried and Hoyt began to run, pulling her toward the front of the park where he'd parked his truck in the shadows behind the main office. She hadn't even noticed it before. She barely noticed it now.

She'd pushed Ben away too well, apparently.

This is it, she thought. *The beginning of my end.*

Those thoughts she'd refused to have before about Dylan— she opened herself up and let them flood her. Every memory.

Every moment. How everything he asked her to do was some-how exactly what she wanted, but could never ask for. The strip club and the skinny-dipping. The gifts. Touching herself until she figured out what she liked and how she liked it.

It was as if he'd seen inside the dark corners in her head and found every secret desire and then had put a voice to them, made them real.

More real than most things in her life had ever been.

No one ever touched her the way he did. And it wasn't just his hands on her body. In her body. It was how sure he was when he touched her, like what he gave her, she deserved. And like the thing she wanted so much it was a fire in her blood, running under her skin, he deserved. He touched her like everything be-tween them was exactly the way it should be. No shame. No regrets.

Just a hunger.

And care.

Annie's breath sobbed in her throat. Really. He'd been so kind.

And all her reasons for leaving him, which had seemed so real, and so valid and so important—they were stupid now. And she wished she'd never walked away. Never left that mountain-top. And the promise of him.

I'm sorry, Dylan, she thought. *I'm so sorry.*

Hoyt opened the passenger-side door and she resisted again, digging her heels into thick mud and puddles, sitting back until her ass almost touched the ground.

"Get in the goddamn car, Annie."

"No."

God, where was Joan when she needed her? Joan would stop this. With her badge and her gun and her fuck-you fearlessness.

"There a problem here?"

It was Kevin coming out of the office, and Annie sagged with relief. "Annie. You all right?"

"No."

"We're fine," Hoyt said. "You need to mind your own damn business."

"Call the cops, Kevin. Call—"

"I'm having a conversation with my wife," Hoyt said.

Annie jerked her arm away and turned, trying to run, but Hoyt caught her around the waist.

"Hey!" Kevin jogged toward them. She'd never seen him move so fast. But just as he got close, a black car screeched into the entrance of the trailer park, spitting gravel everywhere, its headlights cutting across the whole of them, making everyone freeze as if they'd all been caught stealing something.

The car was barely stopped before the driver's-side door was open and a man was hurtling toward them. All Annie saw was a black fleece and a pair of jeans but she knew, under her skin where she was attuned to this man, it was Dylan.

Relief crashed over her.

"Get the fuck away from her," he bellowed before exploding like a cannonball against Hoyt. The two of them hurtled against the side of the truck and Hoyt held on to Annie's arm just enough that she got pulled with them, smashing into the car as well. Her head bounced off the side of the truck. Hoyt dropped her arm and she collapsed onto the ground. Behind her, she heard the terrifying animal sounds of a fight and she knew just enough to crawl away, as fast and as far as she could.

Her hand hit something hard and cold in the dirt. The gun. Her gun. It must have fallen out of the back of Hoyt's pants where he'd shoved it.

She grabbed it and kept crawling.

Arms caught her. Rough hands that were gentle against her skin.

I won't hurt you, they promised as they lifted her from the ground and Annie sobbed for breath, blood still spilling from her mouth.

"Hey, hey, girly."

"Ben," Annie sighed.

"Yeah, come on, now, let's get you out of the way."

He led her to the darkest shadows near the office. Kevin was there, too. She didn't realize he had a bat in one hand, a cellphone in the other.

"You all right?" he asked, sparing Annie only the quickest glance before looking back at the men locked together against the side of the truck.

Annie sank back down onto the ground, onto her knees. Her head spinning.

"How did Dylan get here?" she asked, watching the fight. He was smaller than Hoyt and the two of them fell to the ground. Rolling over each other. Dylan smashed fists into the side of Hoyt's head and Hoyt shot back against Dylan's ribs.

"I called him," Ben said. Annie would try to make more sense of that later. That Ben had talked to his son, that his son had come down off that mountain like a berserker.

For her.

I am saved, she thought, not even for a moment imagining the cost. Unable to foresee what everyone would pay for her rescue.

"You need to stop this," she whispered, trying to get to her feet, but very suddenly and all at once, she couldn't do it. She landed hard back on her knees. "Kevin, please call the cops. Please—"

"No," Ben said. "No cops."

"I can't let them kill each other on my front lawn," Kevin muttered.

"It's Dylan's front lawn," Ben said. "I figure it's up to him. And he would not want cops here."

The fight had changed. Hoyt was bigger but Dylan was on top of him, his fist wrapped in the neck of his shirt, his other fist smashing across his face. Blood splattered across his shirt, into the dirt. Over and over again. His face in the shadows was awful. Terrifying. Something different had slipped into his skin. A creature, violent and vicious, that she only recognized as trouble. As dangerous.

And mine.

That vicious creature was *hers.*

Annie watched him beating Hoyt and his violence gave her an awful thrill. A visceral, nameless pleasure. That he could meet Hoyt on this particular battlefield and crush him. That he had the guts and the will and the strength to do what Annie could not.

Dylan will kill Hoyt for hurting me. For touching me.

Because I am his.

And only his.

In a matter of a few minutes it would be done.

And she wanted that.

Was attracted to it.

Felt powerfully *cherished* by it.

"Stop!" she cried. The thought, the guilt, all of it was overwhelming. His violence, her thrill of its use on her behalf. It put a magnifying glass up to the worst of herself and she was horrified.

I'm not this person, she thought. *I don't want to be this person.*

"Please, Dylan, stop."

He did not listen and he was dodging Hoyt's hands as they came up trying to grab his throat, his face. His ears.

"Please. Ben!" Annie looked over her shoulder at Dylan's father. "Please make him stop."

Ben's face was impassive and she didn't know if he was on her side or not. She began to crawl forward.

"Dylan!" she cried again and he stopped. Her words called a halt to his muscles, his bloodlust. His fist remained cocked over Hoyt's face but he glanced over his shoulder in her direction.

Blood ran down his face from a cut over his forehead and his lips were curled back from his teeth in a snarl.

"Stop," she pleaded. Tears ran over her lips and stung, but she barely felt it. She just wanted this to be over. Her vicious glee in the violence to be washed away. She couldn't use this man like a weapon. Like a beast. "Please, Dylan. Stop."

She'd forgotten about the knife. Hoyt's knife. There on his belt, where he always kept it.

And Hoyt used Dylan's distraction to unsheathe his knife. It gleamed in the light from the office. Its long, lethal blade ran like silver before he sliced it across Dylan's side.

The world screamed. Time dragged.

Dylan fell sideways, his hands clutched to his side, blood trickling over his fingers, his eyes wide with shock. Hoyt staggered to his feet, looking for Annie.

Ben grabbed Kevin's bat and swung it back, rushing across the grass aiming for Hoyt, but Ben was old and Hoyt was young and he just shoved Ben aside, into the cab of the truck.

"You see what you do?" Hoyt screamed at her, his anger a physical force, and she fell back on her ass, her hands brushing against the cold steel of the gun she'd stolen from his safe months ago.

Hoyt still held the knife in his hand, only now it ran with blood. Slick and red.

She didn't think about what to do.

If she had—at all—she would never have done it.

But because she didn't think, because she was acting on instinct and fear, she lifted the gun with both hands, elbows soft, body prepared for the recoil. Just like Smith taught her.

Annie must have closed her eyes, because she didn't see him coming toward her. She only heard him telling her how she would pay.

You're going to hurt for this, Annie. You're going to hurt real bad.

Annie pulled the trigger. Once. The explosion ripped the night, tore it to pieces.

And then she did it again.

And again, until the gun was empty, but she kept pulling the trigger until someone touched her shoulder. Annie screamed and tried to scramble away.

"Annie." It was Dylan.

He was on his knees beside her. Pale. So pale. His tanned skin bone white. And the trickle of blood over his hands was thicker now.

A river of it. Black in the twilight.

He was bloody and torn up. Bleeding. Dying. Mortal and human, and minutes ago, she'd wanted to use him as a weapon. She'd wanted him to kill Hoyt for her.

But she'd pulled the trigger.

Who have I become?

"Hoyt?" She tried to see over Dylan's shoulder but he got in her way. She could see Ben there, standing over something. His hands were red with blood.

"It's okay, he's not hurting you anymore," Dylan said in a quiet voice.

"What—? Are you—? Oh . . . God . . . oh my God." She was suddenly freezing and she couldn't get a breath.

"Come on," he breathed, "let me—"

He reached for her and she flinched away from him. She flinched so hard, she fell back, her hand up like he might hit her. She cowered from him.

He stopped. On a dime he stopped.

"I'm not going to hurt you," he said.

She knew that and she didn't. At the same time, both those things were true. The world was hurting her.

"Is he dead? Did I kill him?"

"Annie—"

Again he reached for her, but she screamed this time. *Look at us,* she wanted to say, but the scream didn't have any words. *Look at what we've done to each other.*

He fell sideways, his eyes blazing but unfocused.

"Dylan!" she cried and tried to force her body to get to his, to reach for him, but she was so cold. Her hands and feet numb. Blocks of ice. And it was spreading up and over her skin. Through her chest. Her heart. Her brain.

"I've called an ambulance," Kevin, behind her, said. The world was spinning. So fast.

"Good," Dylan breathed, his eyes drifting shut. "Baby," he sighed, smiling at her. "It's going to be okay."

She wanted to believe him. She did.

But the world went dark and she fell, alone, onto the cold earth.

ANNIE

ANNIE'S MOTHER USED TO SAY SHE DIDN'T DREAM. ANNIE BE-
lieved her when she was young, because that's what young kids
did. They believed their parents. But as Annie got older, she
heard her mother in her room, crying out in her sleep. Annie
would creep to her mother's doorway and watch as she twitched
and moaned, fighting off whatever nightmare plagued her. Annie
would wake her up, calm her down. But the dreams always
came back.

Night after night.

Annie's mother dreamt. She just chose not to remember. It
was an act of will.

Complete self-preservation.

Annie had no such skill. And her dreams roared through her.

In them, Hoyt was over her, telling her to part her legs. She
could feel the hard length of his body, and the awful thrust of his
erection.

"Do it, baby," he whispered. "Let me in."

And then, in the way of dreams, between one moment and

the next it wasn't Hoyt. It was Dylan over her. Dylan's hands on her.

"It's okay," he kept saying. "It's okay." And she let him in. All the way in. Because she trusted this man. And her hunger for him, for the pleasure he could bring her, for the mindlessness and ease, was nearly painful. It went past craving. It was a need she felt in her blood. In the fibers of her muscles. The hidden recesses of her heart.

His body was wet and hard, sliding into hers. She licked the sweat off his neck, put her teeth against the tendons there and bit. Bit hard. So hard she tasted blood.

"Yes," he breathed and he reared up, his eyes dark. Violence and desire thrummed between them.

He was bleeding, where she'd bit him. A red drop slowly making its way over the muscles of his shoulder. *I did that,* she thought. *I made him bleed.*

In the dream she turned cold.

"Do it again," he said, and she shook her head. Pushing against him. She didn't want that. Didn't want to want it.

"Baby, it's okay," he said in that dark voice. "I like it. You like it, too."

She shook her head. "Dylan—"

"You wanted this," he said. That smile turning into a sneer. Hoyt's sneer. "You like this."

No. She didn't.

"Deep down," he whispered, licking her lips. She could smell cough drops on his breath. "Deep down you want this."

He put his hands against her neck. Not enough that she couldn't breathe, but enough that she was scared. Scared of Dylan. Or Hoyt. An awful monstrous mash-up of the two.

"Dylan! Stop!"

She sat up, her hands at her neck, the scream raking nails across her throat

The room was dark. The bed she was sitting up in was a

hospital bed. On her body was a green hospital gown, damp with sweat.

A hospital? How did I get here?

The night, pieces of it, sharp fragments, memories like knives, slipped into her. Hoyt. Dylan. The fight. The knife.

Oh God! The gun!

A garbled cry squeaked out of her throat.

"Hey!" said a soft voice in the shadows. "Hey, you're okay."

"Ben?" She sobbed his name, grateful and terrified all at once.

"Right here." He stepped out of the dark side of the room, where he'd been sitting in a gray vinyl easy chair.

"Where am I?"

"The hospital in Cherokee."

"Where is Dylan? Is he . . . okay?" *God. Please don't let him be dead. Please.*

"Doctors patched him up. He lost a bunch of blood but he's fine. Real worried about you."

Annie pulled her legs to her chest and blocked out the shadowed room by putting her head down on her knees.

She tasted blood from her lip and she pressed the collar of the hospital gown to the split. Beneath the thin cotton of the gown, she felt the heavy silk of stitches.

That dream . . . she pushed it away from her. Away from her thoughts. Her memories. She would pretend it didn't happen to her. And the further away the dream got, the colder she got. Until she was ice. Ice all over.

It felt very good to feel nothing.

"What time is it?" she asked, finally lifting her head.

"Eight a.m."

"Hoyt?" The name, the question, hung in the air.

"You shot him in the leg, that big artery there. He bled out in the ambulance."

Bled out. She knew what that meant.

"I killed him."

Ben looked at her for a long time, like he would spare her this. Like if he just didn't answer, it wouldn't be true. And she wished she could tell him that it wouldn't hurt her.

Annie was ice. She was going to be ice forever.

"Ben?"

"Yeah. You killed him."

Her breath shuddered. Her mind was blank. Ben put his hand on Annie's shoulder but she shrugged it away.

There could be no touching. The ice would melt under someone's hands and she knew in the depth of her frozen bones that she needed to stay this way. Cold. Unfeeling. Removed.

"The police have got some questions for you."

"Am I going to be arrested?"

"I don't think so. Dylan's lawyer is pretty good." "Pretty good" was undoubtedly an understatement.

"Did you talk to them?"

"We all gave our statements."

"Dylan?"

"Yeah. He answered the questions."

But did he tell them? she wondered. *About us.*

"Terrence wants you to tell the cops the truth. About you and Dylan," Ben said. "Don't lie. It will only cause more trouble for both of you."

"Is he in trouble?"

"There is some big blond cop who isn't a fan, but it's nothing Dylan can't handle."

She made the sound of something wounded low in her throat.

"You got nothing to worry about, Annie. It's a rock-solid self-defense situation."

"Nothing to worry about?" She laughed.

There was a hard and terrible seed growing in her chest. Something that felt like relief.

Relief that Dylan and Ben were okay.

That Hoyt couldn't hurt anyone anymore.

Behind her eyelids she saw the flash of that knife, the way it disappeared into Dylan's body. She imagined she'd be seeing that for the rest of her life.

So, yes. That hard and terrible seed was relief.

"Doctor says you got a concussion and some stitches in your lip and on your forehead," Ben said. "And there are a bunch of bruises. He . . . Hoyt knocked you around pretty good."

"He's had some practice."

She turned and stretched her legs out, putting her bare feet against the hard ground. The cold didn't register.

"Where you going?" Ben came to her side and she was suddenly swamped with gratitude. That he hadn't listened when she pushed him away outside her trailer. That he'd been watching her just as much as she'd been watching him. All along.

"Thank you," she breathed.

"For what?"

"Being here. Bringing me here. Keeping me safe."

"Not that safe," he said, looking over her face. "I should have taken you outta there."

"You couldn't," she said. "He would have come for both of us. And that . . . I couldn't—" her voice broke.

A sound humphed out of him, something like grief, but he cut it off quickly and nodded, this gruff old man with the garden of regrets.

"Let's not get sappy, girly."

Her internal wasteland brightened at his familiar crustiness. And she would have thought it was impossible a few minutes ago, but she smiled.

Slowly, she pushed herself to her feet and stood on shaky legs.

"Going for a walk?"

"I need to talk to Dylan."

"You . . . you sure about that?"

No, she wasn't sure of anything.

"You were dreaming a few minutes ago about him and it didn't sound good."

"It wasn't." Tears clogged her throat. "But I need to see him."

"And people call *me* stubborn," he muttered under his breath. He lifted his hands and it looked like he might try to help her but she jerked away from his touch, nearly falling back over on the bed.

His look told her she was acting crazy, but she didn't know how to stop. Finally, he took a step back, giving her some distance.

"Be careful," he said at the door.

"He . . . won't hurt me."

"He won't mean to, girly. Just like you won't mean to hurt him," he said. "But love is a knife that really only cuts one way, and that's deep."

I wouldn't know, she thought. *I am battered and bruised. Adulterous. Scared.*

A killer.

But love had never touched her. Not really.

"He's three rooms down," Ben said as he pulled open the door, and she stepped into the dark and quiet hallway.

There wasn't a cop outside her door.

And Dylan wasn't three doors down.

He was sitting right there, in the hallway outside Annie's room on a chair against the wall. His head in his hands, his arms braced on his knees. He wore a hospital gown, just like hers. Mint green with some kind of checker design on it. He'd been cleaned up. The burns on his neck and the side of his face were red and inflamed, the fragile skin split in places, all of it shiny with ointment.

There was a small white bandage at the corner of his eye and his knuckles were taped and wrapped.

He looked like a boxer after a hard fight.

"Dylan." The word barely got past her heart pounding in her throat.

"Annie!" His head popped up. He winced and pressed a hand to his side, where she could see the outline of a thick bandage. A dark spot beneath the green fabric. "You're awake." His eyes were bright with relief, and he stood, reaching for her.

He gathered her fingers in his hand, all at once.

His heat was searing and Annie gasped. She gasped in pain and pleasure and the . . . shock of it.

"Annie?" he asked and she jerked her hands back. Out of his touch.

His face went stone-like.

"I just . . ." she stammered. "I don't . . . want to be touched. Right now."

Twenty-four hours ago she'd begged for his touch. Sobbing and wet, she'd lain across his bed and begged him to fuck her. But there were no bridges that she could build to get them back to where they'd been yesterday.

She'd burned everything to the ground.

"Are you okay?" she asked.

"Just a bunch of stitches."

"It's not. It's not just a bunch of stitches."

"Barely a scratch, Annie. I've had worse." He said it with a smile, but he was lying. His lips were white and he carried himself like a man in pain.

"I'm sorry." What stupid words. What a shallow sentiment.

"Don't—"

"He stabbed you." The words were sticky. Awful. "He could have killed you."

"But he didn't." His eyes traveled down her face and she didn't know what she looked like, but she could imagine. The stitches on her lip, and over her black eye.

Annie looked down at his hands, the bruises and cuts. His

knuckles were swollen, and those that weren't covered in tape were red and raw, wet with fluid.

"Look at us," she sighed.

"Annie—"

"I wish I'd never picked up that phone, Dylan."

"Don't say that." He stepped closer, and she stepped back until her body hit the wall behind her. And still he came, closer and closer. A wall of heat. Of intention. Until she could smell him. Sweat and blood and hospital. Until she could feel the heat of him through their thin gowns. Too much. It was too much.

She put her hand up to stop him.

"You don't mean that."

"I do. I really do. Go," she whispered. "When you're discharged, I want you to leave. And don't look back. Forget about me, Dylan."

"No." He shook his head, flat-out refusing. "Not going to happen."

Footsteps coming from the other end of the hallway broke the moment open and Dylan turned to look over his shoulder.

"The cops are back," he said and stepped back. "I'll call Terrence. He's around here somewhere."

A black woman was walking toward them in a pair of jeans and a blazer. She exuded authority, the kind of capable assurance that made some knot in the back of Annie's neck loosen. She was reminded, somehow, of Joan.

This woman was going to make things okay.

Next to her was a police officer with a camera. A man Annie recognized. It took her a second for the pieces to click together, but then she realized he was the blond police officer from the library.

"Grant!" The name sprang from her lips.

Everyone in the hallway looked at her.

The black woman looked between Annie and Grant. "You two know each other?"

"We've met," Grant said, giving Annie a nod. All business. None of that puppy-dog eager flirtation from a few weeks ago. "At the library."

He didn't say anything about asking her out, and she didn't, either.

"I'm Angela Roberts," the woman said, coming to a stop a few feet from them. Annie could feel Dylan's apprehension. His prickly unease. He glared at Grant and Grant glared right back. "Chief investigator for the District Attorney's office. Glad to see you're awake. How are you feeling?"

"A little foggy, but okay."

"You feel up to answering a few questions?"

"Not until her lawyer gets here," Dylan said.

"It's fine," Annie said. She would have said anything to cut the tension in the hallway. She would have cartwheeled down it naked to get Dylan and Grant out of this hallway. "We can get—"

"No." Angela shook her head, her smile wide and effective. "Mr. Daniels is right. You should have your lawyer."

That seemed terribly ominous and she must have blanched, because Grant gave her a comforting smile. "Don't worry," he said. "It's going to be all right."

People had been saying that to her all night and it really wasn't working out that way.

Within a few minutes, a short black man in a sleek suit with intense eyes behind glasses came up behind Dylan.

"I'm Annie McKay's lawyer, Terrence Marshall. I didn't realize the District Attorney's office was already involved."

"I am called in on a lot of domestic abuse situations," Angela said.

Terrence nodded. "Perhaps we can do this where my client will be more comfortable."

There was no place on this earth where Annie would be comfortable with any of this.

"Go," Dylan said. "The cop is right—everything is going to be okay."

Everyone was going into her hospital room. A cop. Two lawyers. One of them hers. They were all going in there and she needed to go, too. But she couldn't get herself to move.

"Annie?" Dylan said.

"What?"

"I'm not going anywhere."

She wished it were different. For his sake. Maybe for her own. But his words pushed her forward, gave her the strength to put one foot in front of the other and walk into the terrifying unknown.

6

DYLAN

Leave? Not look back?

Forget about her?

Did she honestly think that was possible?

It was the shock. The concussion. She wasn't thinking clearly. Because if she were, she would know there was no way I could just . . . walk away.

I sat back down in the molded plastic chair outside her room. I had just enough experience with the law to know what they were going to do. The questions they would ask about the gun. About the night she ran away. About the nature of her marriage. The nature of her relationship with me. And for her, all of those questions would be hard to answer.

In the world I grew up in, those guys, the cops and the lawyers—they were the bad guys. The ones not to be trusted. But I didn't lie to them about Annie and me. Because I knew that when they asked her, she'd tell the truth.

The door opened a few seconds later and my head snapped

up, like a hunting dog on a scent. But it wasn't Annie coming out.

It was Pops.

Once upon a time he was the scariest person in my life. Well, perhaps the second. Mom had him beat some days.

But right now he was just a tired old man. A gray smudge against the brown door behind him. He was shorter than I remembered. Smaller. Balder.

Last time I saw him was in jail. Max and I had just gotten arrested for illegal street racing and a bunch of other shit. He came to Duval to tell me Mom had left, for good this time, moved out to Arizona with her sister who hated us and that I needed to take the rap so Max wouldn't get tried as an adult.

When I got out four years later, having paid in full for my sins and the very worst of his, he'd vanished.

I never saw him again. Not even after I was rich. Not even after the fire.

He just lived in that fucking trailer park. And I paid people to keep an eye on him.

That was the extent of us.

"What are you doing out here?" he asked. "You should go to your room. You look like you're about to fall over."

I said nothing.

Pops looked into the room through the window, craning his neck like he couldn't quite see what he wanted to see. "I hate that Hero Cop."

"You hate cops period."

"True." Pops backed away from the window, leaning against the wall. "She's not doing so well."

"Yeah, well, she killed a man tonight. Song and dance might be expecting too much."

"Someone should throw her a goddamn party for putting that animal down."

"She's not like you. Or me." This wasn't something she was going to be able to just shake off. Shove to the side and pretend like it never happened. That kind of denial was a Daniels specialty. "You should go home."

Pops's laugh was dark. "Really bothers you that she likes me, doesn't it?"

"Yeah, well, you haven't known her long enough to ruin her life."

"Son—"

"Go," I said slowly and clearly.

After a long moment he nodded. "I'll be around," he said. "If she needs me—"

"She won't," I told him and he shuffled down the hallway. A beaten dog.

Walking past Pops, coming toward me, was the nurse who'd been on my case ever since I took a seat out here. She looked like a strong wind could blow her over, but she was tough.

She reminded me of Annie. Of Margaret, too, in the way she kept yelling at me.

"Mr. Daniels?" She stopped next to my chair, her hands on her hips. "I really must insist you go back to your room."

"I'm fine."

"Your wound would say otherwise," she snapped.

I glanced down to see a red blotch on the green hospital gown. I'd bled through the bandage.

"You've already lost a lot of blood," the nurse was saying. "We need to get you stitched back up."

"Just a minute." I could hear the rumble of voices behind Annie's door. Mostly Angela, with Annie's quieter voice answering. But every once in a while there was the authoritative snap of Terrence doing his job.

"Mr. Daniels—"

"In. A. Minute."

The nurse had the good sense to leave.

The door opened and Terrence came out with that blond cop that I didn't like. Hero Cop gave me one unreadable look and then headed down to the nurses' station.

"What the hell are you doing out here," Terrence demanded, his sharp eyes narrowed.

"Everything okay in there?" I asked.

"Better than it is out here. You're bleeding all over the place."

Hero Cop came back with the nurse who was pissed at me and she gave me a sour look before going into the room.

"What's she doing?" I asked. The world was getting a little fuzzy at the edges.

"A witness for photographs." Terrence stuck out a hand and I ignored him. Annie was getting photographed right now. She was going to shrug off that gown and reveal her bruised body to their eyes, the sharp glare of a camera.

It was all I could do not to beat down that door and stand between her and their eyes.

"You know you're not going to help her bleeding to death outside her door." Hero Cop crossed his arms over his chest. He had a thing for Annie, I could feel it. He was trying not to show it, but his eyes followed her everywhere. And he was throwing me some serious aggression.

"Yeah, you'd like it if I left," I said.

Hero Cop nodded. "You're right. I would. She's a sweet girl and she's got no business getting mixed up with you and your family."

I lurched to my feet.

"Come on, man." Terrence got in my way. "I'm gonna get testosterone poisoning out here and you're going to bleed out."

I let Terrence turn me around and lead me to my room, but I could feel Hero Cop's eyes boring holes in my back.

Terrence closed the door behind us. "Maybe you don't want to get into it with the local law enforcement."

"Maybe," I said with zero intention of stepping back.

He pulled the blinds over my window.

"You gonna tuck me in, too?" I asked, climbing into my bed.

"You don't pay me enough," he said. He reached out and hit the call button for the nurse. He hit it a couple of times. "You don't pay me enough for this shit right here, either. Why are you so hell-bent on dying for this woman?"

My eyelids closed despite all my efforts to keep them open. I'd do anything for her. Go to any length to make her safe.

"You met her," I whispered.

That was all it took for me.

I didn't know what this was, this thing we had between us. But it was powerful. And compelling. And both of us had spilled blood over it.

I'd walk into hell for Annie.

ANNIE

THAT NIGHT, HOURS AFTER THE POLICE AND THE DOCTORS LEFT, Annie startled awake, the dream that woke her gone before she could hold on to it. Moonlight fell across her bed from the windows. She could tell by the silence and the stillness in the room that she was alone.

What time is it?

She rolled to her side to look for a clock on the table, but there was only a cellphone. It wasn't hers from before. That one was probably still in the trailer, or smashed underfoot in the parking area in the trailer park.

This must be Ben's, she thought.

She jiggled it, hoping for a clock readout.

10:08.

But there was a text, too.

DYLAN: Annie, plz call me

All the breath sighed out of her lungs. Dylan had bought her another phone.

In the dark and the hush, the sounds of the hospital muted through the door of her room, she wished she could pretend it was just a few weeks ago. And she was Layla in the trailer park. And he was in his mysterious house on a mountaintop. And she would call him and make herself come to the sound of his voice.

It had been so simple.

But you were lying, she reminded herself. *You were lying and scared and on the run.*

Things were awful now, but at least the truth was out. At least she wasn't running anymore.

This was awful, no doubt about it. But it had to get better.

She'd told Dylan to leave. To forget her. But right now, she was so glad he didn't.

She picked up the phone, curled up on her side, and called Dylan.

Through the hallway or perhaps the thin walls she heard the echo of another phone ringing. He was here. Three doors down.

"Hello?" he said, his voice rough with sleep.

"Hi."

"You okay?"

She closed her eyes, squeezed them shut.

"Annie?"

"Can I skip that question?" she asked. "Just . . . just until I have a concrete answer."

"I can wait for that," he said.

"You bought me a new phone," she said.

"I did. Had a nurse put it beside your bed."

She heard his breath. In. Out.

"Thank you."

"I'm glad you used it."

Across the room, illuminated by icy white moonlight, there

was a painting of a bunch of rabbits in a warren, deep under the ground. They were curled up together, a furry lump, washed out in the moonlight. All together. No one alone.

Dylan's voice made her feel that way. Not alone.

"I shot Hoyt in the leg. He bled out," she said.

"I heard."

"I killed my husband."

She tried out the words, felt them in her mouth. Tasted their bitterness.

"That's one way of looking at it."

"There's another way?" If there was, Annie was keenly interested in hearing it.

"You saved your own life. You probably saved my life."

She turned the phone away so he wouldn't hear her shuddery, panicky breath.

"Thank you," he said. "For what you did."

She shook her head, denying his thanks, even though he couldn't see it. "I should feel worse, shouldn't I? I killed a man. He had a life. A soul. He was a kid once. Innocent, once. Someone at some point must have loved him."

"You put down a violent sociopath. You did the world a favor."

"But that wasn't all he was? Right?"

"In that moment, it was all that mattered."

Breathing. In. Out.

Her thoughts, her mind, everything was twisted; there was no clear thread to follow. It all ended in the same knot.

How do I move on from this?

"I stopped thinking he'd come for me," she said. "I was feeling safe. I was feeling . . . happy."

You made me happy. Even that little bit that we had made me happy. Happier than I'd ever been.

"Are you scared of me?" His low voice broke under the

words as if they were too heavy to carry. "I mean, last night and then today in the hallway. You seemed . . . scared. Of me."

She didn't know how to tell him what exactly she was scared of. The combination of the two of them that in so many ways terrified her.

But him alone . . .

"No. I'm not scared of you."

"I mean . . . I know what Ben must have told you about me. About prison."

"You survived, Dylan," she said. "I'm not scared of that."

"But you're scared of something," he said.

"I watched you beating up Hoyt and I liked it, I was attracted to it. Attracted to you doing it." She thought of his brutal body and remembered the pleasure it gave her. "I felt in those minutes more cared for than I had in my entire life."

"And that scared you?" He didn't get it. She could tell.

"Yes. Because that's really scary. It's terrifying. I am scared of me. Of who I am right now. Of what I've become."

"Annie, you're a survivor. And if you can admire that in me, you can admire it in yourself."

Suddenly, that was a thought she could follow out and away from the knot in her brain. That was a comfort she could use.

"You're going to be happy again," Dylan said "I swear it. We can . . . we can get through this. You and me. I promise."

"We barely know each other, Dylan," she said. "We lied to each other for two months. I nearly got you killed. Why would you promise that?"

"Because you said you wanted to come back and I said I wanted you to."

"It can't be that simple. Not anymore."

"It is. For me it is. It's you and me. That simple."

Before she could think twice, or second-guess or tally up the potential disasters, she turned off her phone and slipped out of her bed. Her feet were bare against the cold floor as she crossed the wide blocks of moonlight and short bars of shadow to her door.

Three rooms down the door was cracked, and she really hoped she didn't have the wrong room as she pushed open that door.

But it was Dylan on the bed, staring down at his phone. The moonlight falling across his face. His scars.

She must have made some sound because he looked up at her. Concern and relief all across his beautiful face. And doubt. And fear. And worry.

Everything she felt was reflected in him and it comforted her. Like that painting. It made her feel less alone.

He put his phone down, and as if he'd read her mind, he pulled back the covers on his bed and shifted to the side to make room for her. Because he knew. He knew what she needed.

Him close to her.

She lurched toward him, threw herself across the divide, up into his bed, the sheets warm from his body.

He covered her with the blanket and she turned, pressing the whole of herself against him. His solid frame, filled out with muscle, hard under her cheek. Against her hands. His skin was hot and she could feel his heart beating against her palm, where it cupped his neck. It was an awkward, sideways hug. His elbow against her sore ribs. His shoulder beneath her lips.

"Baby . . ." Slowly, carefully, he turned until her chest, battered and sore, rested flat against his, equally battered and sore. And his arms, those wide hands, they covered her back, urged her impossibly closer to him. His breath whistled past her ear, lifting her hair and sending a distant quake through her body.

It wasn't sexual. She wasn't sure when those feelings would come back. If they could. But this was more than enough. This was all she could handle.

Not so frozen after all, she melted against him in seconds. Let him hold her because he could.

He was strong and steady and warm, and she breathed him in so hard she could taste him. In the back of her throat and on the tip of her tongue, she tasted Dylan. She put her head right there in his neck and wrapped her arms around his waist.

They were both careful. With their bodies. With the strength of everything they felt—with the whole of each other—they were careful.

7

ANNIE

"HAS ... HAS ANYONE SEEN THE OLDER MAN THAT CAME IN with me?" Annie asked the nice nurse pushing her in an unnecessary wheelchair toward the front door.

"Ben?" the nurse asked.

"Yes," Annie said, glancing back at her, though because of the angle she really only saw up the nurse's nose. She'd been in the hospital two days, they kept her longer because of the concussion and Ben hadn't come back. Not once. "Has he been around?"

"I haven't seen him, hon. But you tell him, we'll be ready for him on Friday. You gonna be picking him up?"

"For what? What's Friday?"

"Chemo treatment."

Her mind went blank.

"He never has anyone to pick him up, the poor guy. Driving home so nauseous I just can't imagine."

"How many times has he had the chemo?"

"Two. Friday will be three."

Ben was having chemo. On Friday.

The front doors opened with a quiet gasp and swish, and idling in front of the hospital was a sleek black car. Dylan sat in front wearing dark glasses, with the window down.

He was smiling at her. With that mouth, those lips—she loved that smile.

"That your ride?" the nurse asked.

"Yes," she said, slightly breathless at the sight of him. "He's . . . ah, he's with me."

"That fool man left yesterday against medical advice."

"What?" She spun around in the wheelchair.

"He lost a lot of blood and he's not being too smart about his stitches. But he wouldn't listen."

"I'll take care of him." Though she was not sure how she would do that. Or if he would let her. Or if she was even capable of that. But the impulse to try was real. And it made her feel good.

"Good luck with that," the nurse grumbled, and she took the wheelchair away when Annie stood.

Dylan opened his door, unfurling from that car and stepping out onto the curb. He winced slightly as he straightened. "I'm fine," he said, reading her concern.

"The nurse said you left against medical advice."

"They want me to rest and not get stabbed again. Both of which I can do at home. What did they tell you?"

"Take it easy, try not to get beaten up."

"Should be easy enough."

Annie smiled at him. As best she could with her lip. And he smiled back at her. As best he could with his lip.

"Hi," she said.

"Hi." His fingertips touched the side of her face, his thumb under her chin, his pinky by her ear. Little spots of contact, the warmth bleeding across her skin. "You look good."

She laughed and held out her arms, showing off her scrubs

and flip-flops. The pink hoodie with the brand name across the front that she'd never heard of. "The nurses dressed me from stuff in the lost-and-found."

"I've got a bag of clothes in the car for you. Margaret went a little nuts when she heard what happened."

"That's really kind—"

"I had to restrain her from coming down here herself."

"You've done enough. Really. I don't . . . I can't take any more from you."

He looked about to argue and this wasn't a day for arguing.

"Except," she said, "a ride home. That I'll take."

"Okay, you tell me," he said, tipping his head. "Where's home?"

"What if I said Oklahoma?"

Dylan glanced at his watch. "Then I'd say we'd better get moving."

Annie was pretty much an emotional ping-pong game. Bouncing between joy and grief and tears and laughter, and for some reason, him offering to drive her halfway across the country to that run-down farmhouse with the wraparound porch and all the framed embroidery samples hanging cockeyed in their frames made her laugh.

Home Is Where the Heart Is and *A Back Door Guest Is Always Best.*

It made her howl, really.

Like a crazy woman.

He grinned at her. "What's so funny?"

"The idea of you in that farmhouse."

"That's not what you want?"

What do I want?

Where exactly was home? Oklahoma was a journey too far to even contemplate.

That left the trailer park. The field and the work. The kudzu. Joan and Ben.

That strange place where she'd found happiness for the first time in her life.

"The Flowered Manor."

"Then hop in," he said.

It was warm out, the sun bright. If she were a kid, drawing pictures of today, the sun would have a big smiley face. Sunglasses maybe.

They got in the car and unrolled the windows, the breeze teasing their hair, the soft loose edges of their clothes. She leaned back against the seat, tired down to her bones.

"You get any sleep?" he asked.

"Not much."

"You heard from the cops again?" he asked, glancing her way.

"Angela came by this morning and asked me a few more questions. She told me I needed to stay in the area just in case . . ."

"In case of what?"

"In case they have more questions, I guess," she said. "That's what Terrence said."

"He didn't seem worried?"

"He said it was standard operating procedure."

He nodded as if satisfied by that.

"Thank you," she said. "For hiring him for me. I'll pay you back—"

"Don't worry about it."

"I'm not worried. I'm just saying I'm going to pay you back."

"Yeah, and I'm telling you not to worry."

"Dylan, I can't let you pay for everything."

"It's just money," he said.

"You're saying that because you have lots of it."

"No, Annie, I'm saying it because it's only money. We both could have been killed a few days ago. It's just money, and if it can buy you some safety, it's the least goddamn thing I can do."

She sucked in a quick breath, loud in the silence after his outburst.

"I'm sorry," he said.

Her instinct was to say that's all right, because she'd had a lot of practice pretending to forgive just so the person who was out of line would feel better.

And she had a lot of practice saying nothing, which never got her anywhere.

"Thank you," she said.

But the air was suddenly cooler and she rolled up the window partway even though she knew the chill had nothing to do with what was outside the car. It was them. It was all them.

He cleared his throat as if he, too, could feel the sudden chill. "What are you going to do about the farm?"

"Sell it."

"Really?" he asked.

"It's not home anymore," she said, and was surprised how much she meant it. Despite its years in her family, despite the blood, sweat, and tears she'd put into making it work, that farm was her past. It was not her future. "I want to sell."

"Maybe that's just a reaction to what's happened," he said. "You might decide to sell it and wake up in a month and wish you never had."

"You think it's possible I'll forget everything that happened there?" she asked. "Like I'll go in and paint the walls and hire a new crew and it will somehow be my place instead of the place where I got hurt. Over and over again."

"I think anything is possible," he said.

She scoffed low in her throat. "If anything is possible, why do you hide up on that mountain?"

He looked over at her as if startled by the question. And she was a little startled, too.

"I think anything is possible and that's *why* I hide on the mountain."

What a very Dylan thing to say.

As the drove, the tiny town of Cherokee gave way to country, random shacks selling boiled peanuts set back among the kudzu.

"The nurse said something to me as we were leaving," she said.

"Yeah?"

"Ben's been getting chemo done at the hospital. He has an appointment on Friday. He's already had two of them."

Silent, Dylan shifted gears and took a slow turn onto the highway on-ramp.

"Your dad has cancer."

Dylan was throwing up all kinds of signs that he didn't want to talk about this. And she knew if she kept pushing, what was left of the easy comfort between them would be shot to hell. It was so fragile, so new.

But she couldn't stop.

"Did you know anything about this?" she asked.

"Know?" He laughed, but it was sharp and awful. "Not really."

"What do you mean, not really?" She turned toward him, tucking her knee under her, careful suddenly that they didn't touch. The mood from minutes ago, that affection . . . it had turned so cold.

"I got a call a while ago from the hospital, asking if I was Ben's next of kin. I said I was and asked if he was dead. The woman said no. I hung up."

Incredulous anger bubbled up under her skin. "Just like that?"

"Just like that."

"She was probably calling to tell you about the chemo. That he needed a ride."

"That seems likely, doesn't it?" He glanced over at her. "Jesus, Annie, don't look at me like that. You don't know Ben."

"I know . . . I just feel bad that he's been going through this all alone."

"You know why he's alone? Because he's an asshole. Because he's hurt everyone who would have been there for him through this."

"He hasn't hurt me," she said.

"Yeah." Dylan laughed. "Give him time."

"Do you think people change?" she asked. The question had been a drumbeat in the back of her head for the last three days. A constant whisper in her ear.

"Ben has not—"

"Not just Ben. Any of us."

"Yes," he said.

"Because you changed?"

"Because *you* changed!" he said. "Do you honestly think you're the same person you were when you got married? You're not even the same person you were when you answered my phone for the first time."

"Because I killed a man?" she asked. The nail on her thumb was ragged, and she started to pull it off and tore off too much, until it hurt. But she kept pulling until the pain was sharp and burned and she wanted to stop. Wished she'd never started. But she was too far now; the cuticle was bleeding and tearing, and then it was gone. She held the ragged nail out the narrow crack of the window and let it blow away.

She put her thumb in her mouth and licked away the blood.

"Killing Hoyt was something that happened, Annie. I won't pretend it's not going to change you. But it's something that happened. Most change is a choice. It's long and it's slow."

She rested her head against the window and licked at the blood.

"I am different," she said.

"Damn right you are."

"You're different than you were, right? As a kid?"

"I don't know about that."

"Ben could be different." The words turned all the oxygen to crystal, unbreathable and hard.

"He's not."

"But he could be. You said it yourself—anything is possible."

"But it wouldn't matter, Annie. Do you get that? It wouldn't matter. The damage is done."

He took the exit off the highway and things were familiar again, yet somehow not. Like everything had been washed in a different color.

"I don't want to fight," she said.

"Me neither," he was quick to say. "And I'm sorry I'm not . . . softer."

She put her hand over his on the gearshift, lacing their fingers together. He squeezed. She squeezed back.

"I don't need soft," she said. "I need you to be who you are. But I need you to hear who I am."

Or who I am becoming, she thought. *Just as soon as I figure it out.*

They drove past The Velvet Touch, the concrete bunker surrounded by an ocean of parking.

"That's the strip club you went to?" he asked, watching it go by in the rearview mirror.

"The one and the same."

"It looks like a prison."

"I like it." It was the scene of her best rebellion. Forever she would love The Velvet Touch. Her fondness for that bunker knew no bounds.

And that night, what she'd seen. Those things she and Dylan had whispered to each other. Fevered and frantic. Alone, but somehow, somehow, impossibly together.

It had been one of the best nights of her life.

"You liked it, too," she said, and he grinned at her. That dirty, knowing grin.

Heat pulsed through her and she sucked in a startled breath.

This wasn't comfort, what she felt. This was excitement. Desire. She barely had a chance to recognize it before it was gone. Summer lightning in a dry sky.

Killing Hoyt had drawn a jagged line through her life. Before and after. And nothing on this side of the line felt familiar. But that . . . that lust. That curiosity. That connection. That had made it across the line, to settle under her skin. Warming her from the inside out.

Something survived, she thought. Something good.

A FEW MINUTES LATER HE PULLED UP TO THE FAMILIAR WHITE fence and the front office. It looked extra shabby in the bright sunlight. The storm damage hadn't been cleaned up yet, and the gravel and mud drive were littered with downed branches.

"Here?" he asked. He looked exactly like Margaret had when she dropped Annie off a few days ago. Like a rat had died on his foot.

"It's your property, Dylan. I just live here."

Dylan sighed and parked the car next to the office. Kevin was out the front door before she could get her body free from the soft leather of the bucket seat.

"Hey, Annie," he said in the kind of low, vaguely happy voice people saved for old folks or dogs they really liked. "How you doing?"

"I'm fine," she said, smiling as much as she could with the stitches.

"I'm really sorry," he said, dropping the tone of voice used for invalids. "I should have listened to my gut instead of Ben and called the cops."

Yeah, she thought. *That would have been helpful.*

"Come on," Dylan said, taking her elbow. His fingertips on her skin felt like bright points of light.

"I'll talk to you later, Kevin," she said, waving over her shoulder as they passed through the park. Tiffany's trailer was dark and the swing set was empty. Annie wondered where the kids were, on a bright day like today.

Tiffany apologized that night before Annie went back into her trailer only to find Hoyt there. And Annie wondered if she'd known he was there. If Tiffany had a part in the ambush. Hoyt had said as much about Phil. But had Tiffany been aware, too?

Annie didn't want to think about such betrayal.

"You okay?" Dylan asked, and Annie realized she'd stopped still in the dirt track, staring at the dark Christmas tree lights Tiffany had hung around their little fence.

"Fine," Annie said. Dylan followed her past the laundry room and the rhododendron until they got to her beige RV. The morning glories were out in full bloom. Little splotches of purple and blue against all the run-down grief of the RV. Those flowers made her happy. The trailer made her happy. The memories of past happiness made her happy.

Home.

"This is me," she said, giving the crap aluminum door a happy pat. "It's no mountaintop fortress but it's got a really great bed."

She tried to see it the way he must be seeing it, but couldn't. Every shabby inch of it was hers. More now than ever, because it was a choice made among options. Not a last-ditch effort to hide and stay hidden.

And that Hoyt had been there only made her angry. It did not make her love it any less.

She could tell by Dylan's face that he was not even in the ballpark of in love with her trailer. He did not see its beauty beneath the rust.

"Come on." She touched the hem of his red tee shirt with *989 Engines* across the front of it. It was warm from his body and the sun. Soft from a hundred washings, or maybe it just came that way. A rich guy's tee shirt. "I'll show you around."

Stepping inside the trailer, it felt like the other night had been frozen. The sandwiches were still on the table. On the banquet seating was the pink washcloth, covered in dried blood. There was blood on the floor, too, where she'd spat at Hoyt.

"Look," she said, throwing everything Hoyt had touched or broken into the garbage. "It's like he wasn't here."

Dylan bent down and picked up her old phone, cracks across the screen like a spiderweb. He pressed the power button but nothing happened.

"Did he . . ." He took a deep breath. "Did he do this to you because he found out about us?"

"He was going to do it anyway." She skirted the issue, knowing it was useless.

"Annie, did he find out?" His eyes were imploring and she couldn't resist that look. Even though she knew it would hurt him.

"He looked through my phone. Found the texts. The . . . picture I sent you."

He took a deep breath that rattled through him. His chest shuddered. "What did he do?"

"There's no point in picking this apart." She stepped out of the doorway toward the captain's chair in the front of the RV, but he grabbed her hand. Keeping her still. Forcing her to look at him.

"I need to know, Annie. If he hurt you because of me."

"He hurt me because he's an asshole."

"Annie—" He squeezed her hand and then dropped it, and she felt colder for it.

"He . . ." She swallowed. "He got turned on, I think."

His eyes opened wide. "Turned on?"

"Well, your dad knocked on the door so I don't know what he would have done, but at the time . . . he was turned on."

Silent, he looked away, but she could feel big, heavy, powerful emotions rolling off him and the trailer was too small. Way too small to contain him.

When he turned back toward her, his face was set in rigid lines. His lips were pressed tight. The pink burns stood out against his pale skin.

"How much time do you need?"

"For what?"

"To get your things. An hour? That will get us back to my house around six."

"I'm not . . . I'm not leaving, Dylan."

"If you don't want to go to my house outside of Asheville, we can go to Charleston or anywhere you want."

"I want to stay here."

"I can take you away," he said. "You never have to see this place again. Annie, you don't have to live with me. I get it—you want independence. You deserve independence. I don't have to be there. I just want you to be okay!"

"The police told me to stay here in case there were more questions."

"Terrence can handle the police."

"How will it look if I leave with you? If we both leave the area. We can't, Dylan."

The blood splatter on the floor held his attention like a magnet.

"If I could erase everything that happened, I would," he whispered.

"I don't want to forget everything," she said, stepping forward, her fingers touching his waist. "Some things that happened in this trailer were beautiful. Amazing."

"You masturbated, Annie," he scoffed, diminishing what they'd had. But the color was high in his cheeks. "You can do that in a new place. I'll buy you a goddamn vibrator and you never have to get out of bed."

"Don't." She knew what he was doing and she understood where his words were coming from, but they still hurt. "Don't be mean."

"I'm sorry. But I can't . . . I can't just leave you here, Annie."

"Then stay."

The second the words were out of her mouth, she knew they would cause trouble. Push him away. And they did. He looked at her with horrified, incredulous laughter.

"Here? Stay here?"

"Your father—"

"Don't call him that!"

Annie pulled herself back in. Reeled in the hope, that foolish wish. She clutched it all to her chest.

"I'm sorry," he said. "But that guy you like. The guy I like being, that version of me—he doesn't exist when Ben's around."

"How do you know? You haven't had a relationship with him in years."

"Well, the one we had was pretty bad."

"Then go. I absolve you of responsibility." This was a fight that had spun out of control too fast and they were both saying things they didn't mean.

They blinked at each other, held back by a thread that ran between them both.

"Is that what you really want? Is that what you think this is?"

Before she could answer, before she could say of course not, before she could do anything but shake her head, there was a knock on the door.

Swearing, Dylan leaned down and pushed it open.

Ben climbed up the top step and stood in the doorway. She imagined the walls of the tiny trailer bowing out with the pressure of the three of them and all of their drama. She could practically hear the metal stretching.

"Ben," she said. His arrival put all their damage in perspective. He was dying. That was another reason why she was here. "Are you—"

"What the hell are you doing back here?" Ben asked, his eyes bouncing between her and Dylan. He seemed wired. Angry.

"Ask her," Dylan said, pointing at Annie.

"He's rich, Annie," Ben said. "He'll take you anywhere. Anywhere you want to go—"

"What is wrong with you two?" she asked, taken aback by Ben's frantic energy. "This is the only place I want to be right now. Right here. It's my choice. Mine. Not anyone else's. Why can't you both respect that?"

"I respect it, Annie," Dylan said, shooting Ben a killing glance. "We get it."

"I don't!" Ben cried.

"It's not your business," Dylan said to Ben. "It's Annie's. We'll work it out."

"I need to talk to you," Ben said to Dylan. "Outside."

Dylan shook his head. "We got nothing to say to each other."

"You're going to want to hear what I have to say," Ben insisted.

"No—"

"It's about an old friend."

She didn't have any idea what Ben was talking about, but a chill ran up Annie's spine all the same. "Ben?" she asked. "Are you okay?"

"Fine. I just . . . I need to have a word with Dylan."

The panic in Ben's face that he was so clearly trying to contain must have registered with Dylan, because after a moment he said, "I'll be there in a second."

Ben nodded and stepped back outside the trailer. The door

shut behind him with a small click. She looked at Dylan and realized how they knew each other in theory, behind the safety and subterfuge of lies and phone calls. The dizzying haze of sex and desire.

But she did not know him in real life.

In practical terms they were still strangers.

And that look on his face was guarded and braced. Wary. He was realizing the same thing.

Now what? she thought.

"You look tired," Dylan told her. "Why don't you go lie down? I'll go see what's wrong with Ben."

She nodded and stepped up next to him, wrapping her arms around his neck. Sighed with relief when his arms came around her back, pulling her closer.

"I can't stay here with you, Annie."

She hugged him harder, trying to absorb the pain he had to be feeling. He could pretend all he wanted, but a man who spies on his dad for years doesn't feel nothing. But Dylan began to step away, taking her hands and removing them from his body. She could feel the whole of him retreating, pulling away from his skin, sinking deep inside himself where he'd been living for so long.

"You have the phone from the hospital?" he asked.

"Yes," she said, patting the front pocket of her hoodie.

"I'll call you," he said.

He kissed her lips, a soft kiss. A friend's kiss, without the breath and the bite of every kiss they'd shared before. It was a new kiss, ushering in a new version of them.

And then he was gone.

Leaving her alone in the trailer she called home.

8

DYLAN

I STEPPED DOWN OUT OF ANNIE'S TRAILER AND STOPPED, BLINKing up at the sunny world.

There were birds somewhere making a racket, and the swamp nearby made the air smell like dying plant matter. It was hot down here off the mountain. The air was soggy. Thick.

Ben came back around the edge of the trailer with a familiar look in his eye. I grit my teeth, not wanting to remember. I'd spent years killing off these memories, but now, with one look the old man brought them all back.

That look, it was panic. It was panic he was trying to hide. It was the look he got whenever he knew Mom was using again and he was trying to keep it a secret from me and Max. Or pretend it was no big deal.

But the old man had a shit poker face.

Growing up, I felt like our little family boat was full of holes and we were sinking into poison and I was the only one who bothered to say, "Holy shit, I think we're sinking."

And I was a goddamn kid.

Everybody else was busy pretending we were fine.

"What the fuck are you doing back here?" Pops spat, his voice low. I guess because he didn't want Annie to hear what we were talking about.

"This is where Annie wants to be."

"You need to change her mind. Fast."

"Yeah, well, I'm trying to be sensitive—"

"Fuck sensitive," Pops hissed, getting up in my face. "Both of you need to leave. Now."

I stepped back. "What the hell is wrong with—"

"Well, well, well," said a voice over my shoulder. "It's a regular family reunion."

Shit. Shitshitshitshitshit.

That's why Pops was so scared.

I didn't want to turn around. Turning around made everything real. Too real. Too dangerous. But there was no choice.

Because it was Rabbit standing there, leaning against the edge of Annie's trailer in his leather cut and his fucked-up teeth. His dirty-blond hair hung down to his shoulders. He wore his leather cut over a plaid shirt with the sleeves ripped off, revealing bone-thin arms covered in shitty tattoos.

Seeing him was like running into a wall at top speed, and I lost my fragile grip on happiness. On hope. On everything good that came with Annie. Everything we were reaching for—it vanished over the horizon.

And all that was left was a bone-deep dread.

My past coming back to bite me.

"Come on, Dylan," he said, lifting a can of Bud in his hand. "I got a case a beer, and me and your old man were just talking about the good old days."

Despite that smile, fucked up as it was. Despite the beer and the mention of good old days—of which there were very few with him—Rabbit reeked of menace.

Of danger.

Whatever this guy wanted, it wasn't conversation. And it wasn't good.

"Dylan was just leaving," Pops said. He was such a shit liar.

But I wasn't going to leave. Not while Rabbit was here, three feet from the door of Annie's trailer.

Oh God, please, Annie, don't look out your window. Don't come out your door.

"I got time for a beer," I said with a smile. The thing with Rabbit was to not show him anything. Not weakness, not fear, and definitely not ever happiness. You show that guy happiness and he'll find a way to take it from you. To spoil it. To turn it to poison while you still held it in your hand.

He did it to me over and over again.

"There we go." Rabbit laughed. "There's the Dylan Daniels I know."

He put an arm over my shoulder and I felt his gun in its holster against my side. His long knife pressed into my hip. And I would guess he had at least one more gun and probably one more knife hidden on his body.

He was armed and he was crazy.

And I could feel Annie, her tender flesh, her beating heart, behind me, through the walls of her trailer.

So, I let this asshole lead me toward a dirt track that ended at a big, long trailer with an awning off the back. Under the awning there was a cement pad with a picnic table and in the shadows, a brown recliner. There was half a stone oven built on the edge.

A few feet away from the trailer was a water spigot, and next to that a fenced-in garden.

"The old man is a gardener," Rabbit said. His arm over my shoulder weighed a thousand pounds and I wanted to shrug it off. Put my fist in the asshole's face. But no good would come of that. Instead, I counted each step away from Annie's trailer.

Hoping it would be far enough. But knowing there was no chance it would. "Can you believe that shit?"

"No," I said, because I couldn't.

We got under the awning and Rabbit took Ben's chair, dropping into the recliner with a sigh. He pushed the case of beer over toward me with his scuffed, worn boot. "Help yourself."

I reached into the ripped hole at the top and grabbed a lukewarm can. I handed the first can to Ben, who was sitting next to me. He shook his head.

"Come on, old man," Rabbit barked. "When a guy offers you a beer, you take one. Am I right, Dylan?"

Ben took the beer and I popped the top off mine. Foam poured out and I sucked it into my mouth. Warm and gross. It was the taste, in a way, of my childhood. Drinking beer with my brother on the beach, in the back of a car. After a race. Before we'd go on a car-stealing spree through parts of Jacksonville.

It reminded me of Max. Of happier days.

What does it say about my memories when the taste of shitty, warm beer actually makes me happy?

That I need better memories, probably.

Ben beside me popped open his can and held it out past his legs so the foam ran down over the brown grass and dirt.

Rabbit rubbed his forehead. His cut had a sergeant-at-arms patch on the left side, which meant he had moved up in the world in the nine years since I'd seen him. Back when we were racing, he was just a soldier for the Skulls. Unpredictable and brutal. But cagey. And a straight-up believer in the club. A wide-eyed convert to the life.

He'd worked a pretty good chop-shop network over the years, and Max and I had been two of his big producers.

"See now, this is nice, ain't it?" Rabbit grinned, revealing his yellow teeth. "How long has it been since we shared a beer?"

"Just before the cops raided that race," I said. We'd been drinking. Toasting my victory, again. Rabbit used to find the illegal races, on the edges of backwater towns or using the logging roads in the Florida Panhandle up into Georgia. He'd find them, Max and I would steal a car, and I'd drive and we'd split the winnings.

Because I always won.

We'd been talking about going legit, Max and I. Leaving Rabbit behind. Buying a car, fixing it up, entering a race at the local track. Getting some of the expensive NASCAR insurance.

But then we got busted and everything changed.

"Yeah, fucking shame about that," Rabbit said. "But you took that shit like a man, keeping your brother out of jail." He lifted his can toward me in a toast and I raised mine toward him. After a long moment, Ben did, too. "You took that shit that happened to you in jail like a man, too. Proper fucking Skulls business, right there."

He was talking about the kid that I killed. Proper fucking Skulls business, indeed.

"You know what your Pops told me?" Rabbit said.

"Couldn't begin to guess."

"That you like . . . made some kind of fortune building engines for race cars. You have like patents and shit . . ."

"I've done all right." I could feel the tension rolling off Ben and I refused to look at him. I refused to wonder how he even knew about the patents.

"Look at you being modest. Now that's a change—you used to be the cockiest fucking kid."

"I was winning a lot of money," I said with a shrug.

"And fucking a ton of pussy. Jesus, you were pulling left and right. I guess . . ." He winced, waving his fingers over his own face, indicating my scars. "Those days are over, huh?"

"I do all right," I said, keeping my smile on, though it hurt. It hurt to not put my fist through his face. "With women and money."

"Right. Money. See . . ." Rabbit tapped the side of his head.

"Makes me think, you never would have started racing cars if it weren't for me—"

I laughed, because that was what Rabbit wanted, for all of us to grin while he tried to slice us apart. "You want a cut?" I asked.

"That ain't fair?" He laughed, too, but nothing was funny.

"It ain't gonna happen," I said.

"I know, I'm just giving you a hard time." he sighed. "Too bad about the fire. You were on a hot streak for a while there. Thought we'd be seeing your name up in Daytona. That would have been something, huh?"

"Accidents happen," I said, looking right into Rabbit's dark eyes. I wasn't laughing anymore. I could barely keep down the warm beer and I wanted this over.

"Yes, they do," he said right back.

"What brings you up here?" I asked, turning the can in my hands.

"The North Carolina chapter closed down in '86," Ben said. "You guys opening it back up again?"

"Look at you." Rabbit grinned at Ben. "You can take the man out of the Skulls but you can't take the Skulls out of the man. But no, we're just up here doing a little business."

"What kind of business?" Ben asked.

"The kind I can't tell you about."

Sweat ran down my side into the bandage around my wound, which was aching. I shifted, trying to relieve the throb.

"I heard you got sliced open the other night," Rabbit asked, pointing his can at me.

"How'd you hear about that?" Ben asked.

"I have my sources," Rabbit said. "Sounded like you all had a real trailer park special the other night, some bitch shot her husband."

Show him nothing. Not one thing.

Because there was no telling what Rabbit knew.

Out of the corner of my eye I watched Ben take a drink of his beer, like nothing at all was wrong.

"You guys never lived in a trailer park, did you?" Rabbit asked.

I shook my head. "We had an apartment out on Olive."

"Yeah, I remember that place. Your mom threw some fucking raging parties there. You know," Rabbit said, draining the last of his beer, "my parents were nothing special. My dad was a drunk who liked to hit us and my mom was the fucking doormat he wiped his feet on, but they were better than the folks you had. That's for damn sure. That mom of yours—"

Rabbit took his empty can and stepped on it, the metal crunching under his boot.

Ben flinched next to me. "I gotta use the can," he said, and leaned hard on the table to get to his feet. Rabbit and I did nothing to help him, and he slowly shuffled into his trailer.

"The old man don't look so hot," Rabbit said. He reached into the case of beer for another can and offered it to me. "He used to be the toughest brother around. I watched him once, just fucking slice this dude open, balls to—"

"What are you doing here, Rabbit?" I asked.

"A guy can't catch up with old friends?"

"We weren't friends. So you can drop the act."

And just like that, the smile left his face. And those eyes, those hard, mean eyes, they got harder. "You know where your brother is?"

"I got no clue."

"See," he said, pointing at me again, "I think you're lying. I know Max was here a few nights ago."

"I didn't see him. Max stopped being my problem a long time ago."

"Well, I'm making him your problem." Rabbit leapt to his feet and I got to mine. Too fast and the world swam around me, but I kept myself rock solid. "He's been missing for three days.

Everyone thinks he's split. Like . . . for good. And we got this deal happening, and the bat-shit-crazy parties involved won't deal with anyone but Max."

"I still don't understand what this has to do with me."

"You're going to find him. Make him come back."

"I haven't talked to Max in nine years."

"Well, I figure there's no time like the present to get in touch." He took a piece of paper out of his pocket and pressed it against my chest. His touch made my skin crawl and I grabbed the paper, shaking him off.

"That's the last number I had for him," Rabbit said.

I looked down at the numbers. "And you think . . . what? I call him and he'll answer? Call me back? Come back here just because I ask him to? He forgot all about me."

"You better find a way to remind him or I will burn this trailer park to the ground. Starting with that trailer, right there." He pointed at Annie's trailer.

Breathe in. Breathe out. Show him nothing.

But I was out of practice, living up on that mountain, and I must have shown him something. Some facial tic I couldn't control gave me away.

"That's right, Dylan," he said. "I know about your girl-friend."

"Then you know she's the girl who shot her husband the other night. She's got cops watching her. The District Attorney's office."

He leaned down, his mouth and its fetid smell brushing over the side of my face. "I'll kill them all, Dylan. The girl, your old man. Your business partner. His mom. Get your brother back here or they're dead."

The trailer door opened and Ben was belched out onto the brown grass.

"You been hiding for a long time," Rabbit said to me. "But everyone that hides gets found sooner or later."

"Everything okay out here?" Ben asked, his cagey dark eyes shifting from Rabbit back to me.

"I was just leaving. See you around, old man," Rabbit said, lifting his hand. "The beer is all yours."

Rabbit started up his Harley. The rumble of the motor startled birds from the trees behind Ben's trailer, and they took to the sky en masse, getting the hell out of this place.

Smart birds.

Ben and I were stuck like that, frozen, until the roar of Rabbit's bike had faded into silence.

And then the old man sagged, bracing himself against the side of the trailer. "Jesus," he sighed, wiping his hands over his face. They were shaking, his hands. And I tried not to care. "What did he want?" Pops asked.

"Max has gone missing. No one has seen him since he was here that night. If I don't find him he said he'd burn this place to the ground, starting with Annie's trailer."

"Shit. How did he know you were here?"

"I saw Rabbit a month ago. He caught up with me outside of Charlotte. I was leaving a party and he . . . he must have been following me." It had seemed like a weird coincidence at the time and I'd been so crazy to get home so I could talk to Annie, so I could wrap my hand around my dick and come to the sound of her voice, that I didn't pay any attention to the fact that Rabbit had shown up out of nowhere. If I'd been in my right mind I would have known something was bad. Really bad.

That's how he knew about Blake and Margaret. I needed to call them. Warn them. Blake was going to lose his mind. Put the whole place on lockdown. "And my guess is he's been watching you for a while."

"I got a number for Max," Ben said, pulling his phone out of the pocket of his pants.

I lifted the scrap of paper. "Rabbit gave me one."

Pops looked at it and shook his head. "Different number.

Call them both." He tapped on the screen and then handed me the phone. "One of them is probably a burner; he might have ditched it by now."

Right. Max's phone might be in a shallow grave with a bunch of bodies.

With his own body.

But it was all we had at the moment. Two phone numbers. One missing brother.

How had this happened? I wondered. How was I somehow working with my father to find my brother? Nearly a decade of nothing from them, and I spend three days off my mountain and I'm pulled right back into their bullshit.

I punched the number Rabbit gave me into my phone and walked away from the awning out in front of Pops's weird garden. I paced for a little bit, like a dog picking his spot to lie down.

Calling my brother, wanting to talk to him, hear his voice, had been a hard habit to break. And one I never would have broken on my own without him making it clear for nearly a year that I was not welcome in his life.

Despite the years trying to yank it free, I could feel the pull of this . . . this *worry* over the never-ending black drama of my brother's life. The grinding knowledge that someday, somehow, my brother would get himself killed.

There was nothing I could do to stop it, and I knew that. I'd known it for a long time, but it didn't stop the small belief, fostered by nothing, not one thing, that I might be able to change the collision course of my brother's life.

Save him.

My heart was pounding. Hard. In my throat. In my gut.

My brother.

The phone rang and rang and then just stopped.

I called the number Ben gave me.

After three rings, a robotic female voice said, "Leave a message."

And there was a long beep.

"Max," I said. "This is Dylan . . . your brother. We need to talk. It's about Rabbit and this disappearing act you're pulling." I took a deep breath. "I don't know what's going on, but you need to come back here. Now. You owe me. And you know it."

I hung up and walked back toward Pops.

"Nothing?"

"Machine."

"He hangs out at The Velvet Touch."

"The strip club?"

The very same fucking strip club where Annie had been. I felt like my heart was going to explode.

"I'll go tonight," I said. Rabbit probably had the place watched, but I had to do something.

"I'll go," Ben said. "You look like you're going to fall over."

"No."

"But—"

"No. Max might show up here."

Ben nodded, as if accepting his bullshit assignment.

"We'll find him," he said.

I laughed. Right at him. "How the fuck did you stay an optimist?" I asked. "All those years with Mom, all the broken promises, all the rehab that didn't work. The cheating and the lying. The stealing. The club, your 'brothers' who—"

Ben blinked up at me, his dark eyes full of pain. So much goddamn pain. Enough pain that I shut up. Looked away. Stared at this weird exile my father lived in. And then realized it was where he was going to die. Rabbit or no Rabbit. This was Pops's grave.

Because he had cancer.

I took a deep breath and then another. Until they stopped feeling like they were digging me out from the inside.

"Nurse at the hospital told Annie you have chemo on Friday."

For a long time Ben didn't say anything, and I refused to look at him. "Annie knows?" he finally asked.

I nodded. Pops swore. For what it was worth, I had to give him credit for that. At least he wasn't trying to manipulate Annie with his illness. That she was manipulated anyway was still a problem.

"She's staying 'cause of you." I spat the words and all my scorn at the old man. "She hasn't said as much, but it's part of why she's staying. To look after you."

"I didn't ask her to."

"Oh, well, that makes it all right then. Pardon me for thinking you'd give a shit—"

"Watch what you say there, son. You have no idea what I give a shit about."

"No," I laughed. "You're right. I have never had any idea what you cared about."

Ben pulled a joint out of the chest pocket of his gray tee shirt and lit it up. He took a hit before handing it over to me.

"You're joking," I said. All the years between us and he thought I would just smoke up with him?

"It's medicinal." Pops shrugged and took another drag.

"So you really have cancer."

"I really do."

"Is it . . . bad?"

"No, son, it's great. It's the rainbows-and-blow-jobs kind of cancer."

"You know what I mean."

"No. I don't. I don't know what you mean." Ben looked up at me through a curl of smoke. "Maybe if you took the time to spy on me yourself instead of hiring other people to peek through their blinds at me, I might be able to figure out what you mean. But we're strangers, so you'll have to spell it out."

"Are you dying?"

"Yes."

My mind was blown totally blank and I could feel some kind of reaction to my dad's statement coming to life. Breathing fire. Grief. Anger. A hideous sort of righteous vindication.

Yes, part of me howled, *This is what you get.*

Immediately, I emptied my mind. I thought of nothing so I wouldn't think of Pops dying of cancer.

There was a white trailer between Annie's and Ben's. A white trailer with a porch. There were some white plastic chairs on it, a plastic table that had blown over.

"They figure I've got about six months. If the chemo don't kill me first."

"Why bother with the chemo?" I asked, staring at that trailer. As far as trailers went it was about a million times better than Annie's. "Seems like a shitty way to go out."

"I suppose it does," Ben said, taking another drag and then stubbing the joint out.

Six months. Holy fuck.

"Why was Max here the other night?" I asked.

"Because I reached out. Told him about the cancer."

Finally, I turned to look at him. "I thought you two weren't talking."

"Yeah, well, something about dying makes you want to get a few things off your chest." Ben pointed over at Annie's trailer. "What are we going to do about her?"

"We?" I laughed, not interested in the ways a dying old man was going to try to keep Annie safe. Just like fucking Hero Cop at the hospital, with his heart in his eyes. I didn't trust that guy to keep her safe, either.

Me, I was going to keep her safe.

"*We* aren't going to do anything. I will take care of her."

"Seems to me, a rich hotshot like you oughta be able to get her to leave. She deserves better than this place."

"No shit." Suddenly I thought of what Hero Cop said.

She's a sweet girl and she's got no business getting mixed up with you and your family.

That was truth made out of blood and bone and steel.

She deserved a whole lot better than my family.

I am not my family, I told myself, when I felt those dark thoughts start to turn that way. I worked really hard not to be my family.

But only because they sent you away, said a poisonous voice in the back of my brain.

"Who lives there?" I asked, pointing over at that white trailer with the nice deck. The white trailer right smack-dab between Annie and Ben.

"A woman named Joan," Pops said.

"The undercover DEA agent?"

Ben reeled back in his chair. "The fuck you talking about?"

"Annie said she was undercover DEA. She showed Annie her badge the night Max was here."

For a second I thought Ben might pass out. But he only closed his eyes and thumped his head against the back of his chair.

"The fucking bitch. Fucking cock-sucking bitch. Of course," he muttered.

"Something you want to let me in on?"

"No. But she ain't here no more," Ben said. "Haven't seen her in days. Since the night Max was here."

"So that trailer is empty?"

"Guess so."

So Max was in the area. Dad was here. Rabbit was hanging around. And I couldn't get Annie to leave.

With all those rotten pieces, something bad was inevitable.

I pushed the heels of my hands into my eyeballs until I saw sparks behind my eyelids.

"You want to sit down?" Pops asked. "You look like you're about to fall over."

"I'm fine."

"You ain't, and anyone with eyes can see that."

My father's concern made my skin crawl.

Where was your concern when I was in jail, getting beaten for your sins?

"Suit yourself, you stubborn cuss," Pops muttered.

I'd spent years getting rid of this anger . . . this hate. The boy I'd been, the man I would be if I stayed in my father's orbit. I'd shed that like a shitty skin.

And now it was back. And I was scared of it. Scared of what it would turn me into. Of how it would infect my life now.

How it would infect Annie.

But I didn't have a choice.

"I'm going to be your neighbor, Pops."

PART TWO

9

ANNIE

MAYBE I SHOULD TAKE UP SMOKING, ANNIE THOUGHT, STARING UP at the moon. The clouds were a sparse veil, moving fast in some unseen, unfelt wind.

Or knitting?

She needed a hobby. A distraction from her own thoughts.

Knitting sounded boring.

The night was black and thick. And she felt impossibly small inside of it. Like if she sat very still she would simply lose her edges and blend into the night around her. And when morning came she'd be gone.

Her moments of strength, of feeling like . . . herself . . . were too few and far between, and she didn't know how to gather them up to make something recognizable to herself.

Inside, where she'd always known who she was despite everything that happened to her. Where the concretes of her identity, of her existence, lived, now felt vacant. Missing.

She was sitting on her small stoop. The metal steps were digging into her thighs, but it was too hot inside her trailer. Too small, with all her thoughts.

Her fully charged phone was dark on the step beside her.

He said he would call.

Her longing for him was a physical ache.

Dylan. His voice in her ear. His rough capability. His dark past that matched her own dark present.

It was selfish—she knew that. He'd been exhausted the last time she saw him and he'd had to drive back to his house.

But she couldn't stop the feeling.

Her hands shaking, she picked up the phone and called him.

"Hey." Relief and pleasure at the sound of his voice shot through the darkness inside of her, creating little pinpricks of light. Just enough to see by. "You okay?" His sleep-rough voice was asking a question so familiar, so incredibly beloved, that she smiled.

"Yeah," she answered. "I'm sorry to call so late—"

"It's okay. I was awake."

"What have you been doing?"

He paused before answering. "Nothing, really. What about you?"

"I fell asleep like the moment you left the trailer. And now I'm wide awake."

"The dangers of naps."

"Have you slept?" she asked. "You looked so tired earlier."

"I'm fine. Why are you whispering?" he asked.

"I'm sitting outside. It's too hot in the trailer."

"I hear that."

"You've got central air. There's no such thing as too hot where you are."

He was silent for a moment, and she thought maybe they'd been disconnected.

"Dylan?"

"Yeah," he said.

She leaned back against the door and she heard something rustle on his end. She imagined him rolling over in that big bed of his, the purple comforter down around his waist.

"It's funny to be talking to you now that I know what you look like. And what your house is like."

"It's a little more disturbing now that I know where you live," he said.

"Don't speak ill of my trailer."

His laughter was a small sigh. And it filled her like air.

"I'm sorry we argued today," he said.

"I've been thinking about that."

"Yeah?"

"I don't have any practice being honest with someone. Showing someone how I really feel."

"You can show me."

"Sometimes . . ." She looked up at the moon, so clear in this moment she could see the craters on its surface. "Sometimes what I feel is scary."

"That's the stuff I want to see, baby."

"I want you to show me your scary stuff, too," she said.

"I don't know if that's a good idea," he said. "There are some things . . . some things that maybe should just stay hidden."

"I think if you and I are ever going to stand a chance, those are the things you have to show me."

She could hear his breathing, agitated now, as if he were running.

And had been for a long time.

She stood, her butt numb from the metal seat, and went back inside her trailer. It wasn't any cooler, but it was private.

She climbed onto her bed and stared out her window. Same moon as before. Same clouds. Different perspective.

"Do you think about that man you killed in prison?"

"Of course," he said. "Not as much as I used to. But I think about him."

"What do you think about?"

"Why do you want to talk about this?" he asked.

"Because we both have this thing. This big, awful thing in our lives, and you're the only one I know who might understand. Who I can talk to about it. This is the scary stuff, Dylan, that you said you wanted to see."

"You want to start some kind of murder survivors club?" She flinched at the words. At his tone. "Because that's some morbid shit, Annie."

"It's the middle of the night and I can't sleep and I feel pretty fucking morbid," she snapped back at him.

"Yeah," he said. "All the ghosts come out at midnight, don't they?"

"I understand Hoyt would have killed me and maybe you, too. But that doesn't erase everything that was good about him. And there were good things. He worked hard. Day in and day out. He was good to the crews. And he used to love corn on the cob, like he could eat dozens of ears, every August. No butter. No salt. Barely cooked, and he'd—"

"Shhhh," he breathed. "Okay. I understand what you're getting at."

And you're the only one that does. That's why I need you.

"So tell me," she said. "Tell me something about that guy you killed."

"He was a boy, really. Younger than me. His father was a part of a gang that had bad blood with the Skulls going back generations."

"Did you know his name?"

"Hector. Hector Vasquez. His dad was killed in that fire Ben set."

"Oh my God, Dylan."

"Like six months into my sentence he was on me. Relentless. And I couldn't avoid it. Couldn't keep my nose clean. My head down. It was fight or be killed. I took some serious abuse from this guy and his crew for two years and it just kept getting worse, and I knew the only way it was going to end was him or me."

"What happened?" she asked.

"Baby, you don't want to hear this."

"I do." She wanted to hear everything. All of his stories.

"They came at me in the shower—they'd bribed some guard to look the other way. But I had this fucking screwdriver I paid a guy to get for me and I'd been sweating over it for weeks. I had it sharp as a razor and I . . . I killed him."

"How?"

"I stabbed him, what do you think?"

"But where? How? Was it fast? Slow?"

He took a deep breath. "I'm worried about you," he finally said, his low voice cracked and dry with concern.

Stop doing this to him, she told herself. But she wasn't going to. No. She was in now and she was going to hear all his dark secrets. Burrow through all his dark places. She was greedy for it. Hungry for it.

"I'm worried that you want to hear this."

"Me, too," she said with a laugh. "But I'd be more worried if I didn't. We can't pretend these things didn't happen to us."

He was silent for a long time and she had no idea what he was thinking.

"It was fast," he finally whispered. "But it felt like a thousand years. I stabbed him in the neck. His boys scattered. The guard who had been paid to look the other way so I could be beaten or raped or killed, he charged in and put me back in chains."

A low moan of distress came out of her throat.

"Don't, baby," he murmured. "It was years ago; don't take that pain on, too. It's been a long time since I thought about him."

"I'm sorry," she said. "For asking."

"No, you're right. I can't pretend like it didn't happen. Like it's not this huge tear in my life. Everything after that was totally different. I was totally different."

"I feel completely changed," she said. "And I'm not sure if it's good or bad. It's just . . . change."

"You're scared."

She closed her eyes and pressed her face against the pillow. It wasn't a question. He just knew that truth about her.

"When we first started talking," he said, "you were this . . . I don't know, this, like, bright light. So fucking pure—"

"That's not true—"

"Hey, this is my side of the story. You don't get to tell me what I think is true." She smiled at his fond, rusty chastisement. "And everything I asked you to do, even as shit got a little darker, you stayed so bright. Even up at my place, even when you were telling me you were married and I could tell how awful you felt about making me a part of adultery, you were still bright and pure. You still are now. This shit with Hoyt, it didn't change you. Not where it counts. Not the way I see you."

It was so nice talking to him again. The tiny bridge between who she was now and who she'd been just a few days ago. He was the link. The line connecting the wildly scattered dots.

"You should talk to someone," he said.

"I'm talking to you."

"No, like a real someone. After I killed that kid, I got moved to Union to finish my sentence—"

"But it was self-defense, wasn't it?"

"Yeah. I mean that was the ruling, but when I was in juvie I got added time for fighting. So the two years I originally got for stealing cars and illegal street racing quickly turned into four, so I had to finish my sentence in Union."

"I'm so sorry."

"Yeah, well, I survived," Dylan said, downplaying it. "But in Union, this priest used to come in—"

"You're religious?"

"Fuck no. I just . . . I don't know . . . this priest kept coming in. And he seemed cool, like, badass. He had a pretty shitty history that was not unlike my shitty history, so I talked to him. And it helped. It helped a lot. I mean, I was surprised."

"I loved church," she said. She closed her eyes and remembered the feeling she'd had in those pews. The sunlight in the stained glass bathing the entire congregation—their praying hands, their upturned faces—in brilliant colors.

The sunlight at church seemed warmer than anywhere else.

Or maybe it was just the power of being surrounded by people when she was usually so alone.

"You should go back," he said. "Find yourself someone to talk to."

"I don't even know what day it is, isn't that funny?"

He chuckled. "It's very early Monday morning."

She'd just missed it. *Next week,* she thought.

How incredible it would feel to get back that part of herself. A piece Hoyt had taken away. Quite suddenly, there were a lot of pieces of herself she wanted back.

And maybe it was because of his voice in her ear, but she wanted her body back. She wanted those moments of pleasure. The long, rolling orgasms she'd given herself. The exploration and the thrill.

But more—she wanted the ones he gave her. And she wanted to give someone else pleasure. Oh God, not someone else, what a stupid lie. Him. She wanted to give Dylan pleasure, with hands that had just been learning how.

But her body felt dead. Heavy.

"Annie?" he asked. "You still there?"

"Yeah. Do you think . . ." She didn't know how to put it into words.

"What?"

"I just . . . I wish you were here."

"Why?"

"I want to feel my body again. The way you made it feel."

A week ago he would have groaned at her words, that dark, excited growl of his that traveled from satellite to satellite to settle in her belly, where the sound would reverberate through her whole body. And then he would have asked her to do something to herself. Squeeze her nipple. Her clit. He'd tell her to roll over onto her stomach and put all of her fingers as far inside herself as she could.

And she would have done it. Sobbing and wet and on fire with her own pleasure, her own ecstatic enjoyment—she would have done everything he asked.

There was a pulse, weak, but there between her legs. A brief ache, but then it was gone. The clouds back over the moon.

"You can do it yourself," he said, his voice cold and distant.

"It's not the same."

"You just need some time—"

"Stop," she cried, suddenly angry. "Stop telling me what I need. I know what I need and it's to feel something again. To feel good. To feel wanted and cherished and desirable."

"You are, baby. You are."

"Then where are you?" she demanded. "I need you, Dylan."

He blew out a long breath and then he said, "I'm in the trailer next to yours."

DYLAN

MONTHS AGO, WHEN ANNIE AND I FIRST STARTED THIS THING between us, when it was just phone calls and we were pretending to be other people, I told her that I would never lie to her. I wouldn't always tell her everything, but what I did tell her would be the truth.

Tonight she asked me what I'd been doing and I said nothing.

Because I couldn't tell her that I'd spent three hours in the parking lot of a strip club looking for my brother.

And when I got home from The Velvet Touch, I told myself when I collapsed face-first into this bed, in this crappy trailer, that just because I was staying here didn't mean we would rush into things. We would go slow, because she deserved that.

Because she'd experienced some fucking trauma.

Because my past had moved in with me and things weren't so simple anymore.

You need to keep her away from you and your shit.

Oh, that fucking voice. That angry, bitter voice that only served to keep me feeling small—I'd gotten rid of it after jail. I'd worked hard at silencing it and losing the dark doubts that came from how I grew up.

Of course it would be back now. Living next to Pops. Looking for Max.

I am not my family, I told myself. Except I was. Right now, I was rolled up and packed in tight with my family. I was shoulder to shoulder with their poison.

One fucking phone call from Annie and my plan was demolished. So much for keeping my distance. I could hear the fear and desperation in her voice and I would do anything to make it stop. Anything to make her feel better.

Ah, listen to you, you piece of shit, telling yourself you're going to fuck her for her own good. You are a regular saint.

I wasn't going to fuck her. I wasn't.

There was a knock at the door to my new home and I got out of bed to answer it. I could not deny my pleasure. My excitement. And if I were a better man I'd tell her to go back to her trailer.

Because she deserved better than me lying to her. She deserved better than the bullshit I had attached to my back right now.

I opened the door and she stood there, barefoot and bathed in bright white moonlight. She wore a tank top and shorts, all that alabaster skin so perfect.

Her intentions were obvious and my blood started to pound. My dick agreed with her intentions. The base part of me that just wanted to feel good, to make her feel good, got excited.

But the bruises on her face, her swollen lip—*fuck,* I couldn't do this.

"Annie," I breathed. "This is a bad—"

As she walked up the steps and into the trailer, I could feel her vibrating with tension. Her hands were fists. Her eyes bright and wide.

"I don't care what you think," she said, all upthrust chin and attitude.

Oh God, I tried not to smile. But I loved her like this. Unchained and furious. It was pure. A mess, but it was a pure mess.

"I'm not going to have sex with you," I told her, but her expression called bullshit. "I'm serious, Annie. It's a bad idea, and you'd see that if you weren't so charged up right now. You want to feel something good because there's been a whole lot of shit. I totally get it. I want it, too."

"Then why not?"

Because I'm lying to you.

"Because we're not in any shape for it, honey. Because you've been through something awful and sex isn't going to make that go away. Because there's a good chance neither one of us will like ourselves in the morning!"

She looked deflated, unbearably sad and still somehow pissed off, and before I could stop myself I crossed the small trailer and pulled her into my arms.

"I don't want to be alone," she breathed against my chest. Her hands, cool and shaking, slipped around my waist.

I didn't want to be alone, either. For the first time in longer than I could remember, my solitude chafed.

She stared back at me with haunted eyes. "Don't make me be alone," she whispered.

Oh. Jesus. I could not refuse.

"Come on." I led her into the bedroom. Which was so damn tiny. There was the double bed in faded and worn flowery sheets and there was us. She took a deep breath and her chest nearly touched mine. "Let's . . . let's try to get some sleep."

She crawled up onto my bed, and I looked out the window instead of at her ass in those little shorts. Her petite body curled up into almost nothing on one side of the bed.

"You cold?" I asked, and she shook her head. Her blue eyes piercing in the darkness.

Did I really tell her those things? About prison and the priest? Looking in her eyes, I couldn't see her knowledge of them. Or if not knowledge, her . . . reaction to them.

"Those things I told you, about the guy in jail . . . ?"

"Yeah?"

"Other than the priest I've only told one other person. A woman. The night I got out."

Annie blinked up at me.

"There was this guy who I used to race with, an older guy named Miguel. He was kind of a local legend when I was growing up. He'd done some low-level NASCAR stuff when he was younger. Margaret was his wife, Blake was his oldest son—that's how I met them. When I got out of jail they threw me a party. Max took me and I think he hired this girl."

"Like . . . a prostitute?"

This is you, asshole. Pretend all you want, but this is you. And she should know who you really are.

"Yeah. Like a prostitute. She was real sweet. Real kind, you know. And I was high from a blow job and weed and freedom and I told her."

"What happened?"

"She threw on some of her clothes, enough that she was decent. Grabbed the rest of it and got gone."

"I'm sorry she did that," Annie said.

"Yeah, well, Max probably didn't pay her enough to listen to my confession."

Tell her about the other whores, the voice said. *The ones after the fire. The women you paid to touch your skin and suck your dick, so you could try to feel like a man again.*

"Do . . ." Annie sat up, her eyes on her hands. "Do you want me to leave?"

"No." Fuck me, but that was the truth. I didn't want her to leave.

I crawled into bed beside her, making sure we weren't touching. Half my leg was hanging off the bed and my arms were behind my head. The bed was barely big enough for me and while she might be tiny, this thing between us was huge.

Tell her, I thought. *Tell her why you're here. Tell her what being here might cost her.*

But I couldn't. I didn't want to scare her. I didn't want to add to her worry; she had enough.

Bullshit, that voice said. *You don't want her to leave. You don't want her to leave you alone in this fucking trailer park with Pops and your brother and your past. Be man enough to admit that.*

Suddenly, she crawled toward the end of the bed.

"What are you doing?"

"This is worse than being alone," she said. "I'm lying here thinking about everything you asked me to do, everything we did together, and you're right here and I'm right here and we might as well be miles apart. It hurts, Dylan." Her eyes, her beautiful eyes, revealed it all, the width and breadth of her agony. "It hurts to be near you like this."

Hurting her was the last thing I wanted.

"I'm sorry," I told her. "Come on, come back to bed."

She eyed me warily but I put my arms around her, pulling her back into me. I shifted, rolling us to our sides, and pulled up my knees until they were right behind hers. Her back against my bare chest, her ass pressed into my groin.

Her head was right under my chin, my arms tucked around her, and I could feel every breath she took. After a few seconds, my breath started to match hers. Our chests lifting and falling at the same time. Our heartbeats, pounding against each other, started to beat in time.

I wasn't going to tell her about Rabbit, or my brother. She had enough bad shit spinning through her thoughts. I would handle my past. She would get better. Maybe in a few days it wouldn't matter. Max would come back, the deal would be done, and the threat would be gone.

The deep breath she took shuddered at the top and I squeezed her a little tighter.

"These beds are nice, aren't they?" she asked.

I laughed, and she was so flush against me it made her shake. "They really are."

The night was thick and lush around us. And I was trying hard not to feel everything, her skin and her weight and the air. But I was failing. Blood was beginning to pound in my dick. I knew she could feel it and I felt obscene.

Carefully I shifted away from her. "No," she breathed, her hand reaching back and curling over my hip. Her fingertips biting into the muscle of my ass. "Stay."

"Baby, this doesn't feel right."

"But it feels like something, doesn't it?" she asked.

I had to concede. And like an idiot I stayed there. My dick against her ass, getting harder with every breath.

My belief that this could stay innocent was going up in flames. It was a stupid belief anyway.

Her hand, surprisingly strong, clutched mine against her stomach.

"I hurt," she said.

"Where?" I sat up, thinking of her concussion. "That Joan woman left a ton of shit—I can see if she's got aspirin or something."

"No." She shook her head. Slowly she pushed my hand down her body and I buried my face in my pillow. Powerless to stop her.

She had our hands between her legs.

"I hurt here," she whispered, and moved our fingers until I was cupping her. "Make it better. Please."

10

DYLAN

WHO WAS I SAVING BY BEING NOBLE? SHE DIDN'T WANT NOBIL-ity. She didn't want reason.

She wanted some basic animal connection.

Fuck it. I did, too.

I pushed my fingers against her, feeling the thick folds of her pussy through the cotton. I found the seam between them and ran my finger along it.

"Like this?" I asked. She nodded, pushing back against my cock. Her breath came in harder. "Or like this?" I lifted my fingers so I could slip them down over her tummy, between her shorts and her skin. She wore no underwear, and so my fingers slipped right over her bare pussy.

I made a sound low in my throat. "I'd forgotten you'd shaved," I whispered into her hair.

"You like it?"

I kissed her head, closed my eyes, and slipped one finger between her folds. She parted her legs a little to give me access.

I'd never touched a woman so tenderly. I'd never been so careful.

I found her wet, but I wanted more. I wanted to be sure. So I rubbed the callused edge of my finger over the sensitive skin of her clit until it was hard as a bead at my touch.

"Dylan . . ." she whispered, her voice breaking.

"What?" I stopped touching her, pulled my finger away, but she pushed forward into my hand.

"It feels so good," she sobbed. "Thank you for bringing this back."

It felt good to make her feel this way. Healing, somehow.

I pushed one finger inside of her and found her drenched. I brushed my thumb against her clit over and over again, harder each time.

"More," she breathed, and I gave her another finger, burying my face into her neck. Inhaling the scent of her sweat and her skin and her arousal.

"There. Oh . . . God. Dylan. Right there." She clutched at my hand and jerked her hips against it and I let her do it. I let her use me. She rolled onto her back and threw her leg over mine, until we were a tangle on top of the bed. The sight of my hand buried between her legs, her own hands grabbing onto my wrist like she had to keep me there, like it was possible I could leave, was powerful.

Us. Together. As basic as it could be.

I shifted my hand until I had her clit between my two fingers and I squeezed it until her eyes flew open and looked right into mine.

"Good?" I breathed.

"So good."

Her hips were lifting and I could tell she needed more. Wanted more.

This pleasure of ours had been buried under the rubble of the last few days and we had to work hard to get it out.

I remembered what she said she liked, from the conversations months ago, and I rolled her carefully onto her stomach and braced myself over her, giving her just a little weight, a little pressure to push her pussy into the mattress. Her pussy and my fingers.

She braced her hands wide and pushed back into me. "Dylan," she whispered, frantic and wild, grinding herself against the mattress and against me.

Against my fingers she was hot and wet and against my chest she was small and sleek. Warm and alive. My cock was squeezed between her ass and my stomach and it hurt. Ached. I imagined coming on her back. How good it would feel to let go, how hot it would look. The mess of me all over the beauty of her.

Her hips were moving in small, tight circles, my hand was beginning to ache from the awkward position, but I wouldn't move. Not if the trailer was on fire. I was with her to the end.

Her hands grabbed the sheets, pulling them up off the edge of the mattress.

"Fuck, yes. . . . Dylan," she moaned. She was close, I could feel the tension of her body, every muscle taut as if she were wrestling the orgasm.

"Come on, baby," I breathed, "come for me. Let me feel you. Let me feel all of you."

She whimpered in her throat, excited by my words. She had a thing for filthy talk and I could get behind that.

I put my forehead against her shoulder and whispered how hot she was, how wet. How I remembered how she tasted, and she shook beneath me.

Close, I thought. She's so close and I held on until she stiffened and shook and cried out into the folds of that pillow.

When it was over, her body replete and soft against mine, her hair and part of the pillowcase over her face, I slowly eased myself away, careful not to touch where I knew she was sensitive.

My hand glistened in the moonlight and if this were just a

precursor, the beginning of a night of depravity, I would have held it to her face and told her to lick it. To taste herself.

My cock, hard as a rail, twitched against her. And I shifted away so I could press that wet hand against my cock, trying to get it to behave.

"Thank you," she said, pushing the pillowcase off her face and rolling over to face me.

The bruises and her lip were highlighted by the moonlight and I hated myself all over again.

I pushed harder against my cock until it hurt. But the damn thing was insistent.

Her fingers against my face made me jump.

She touched the bruised corner of my lip. The raw scrape against my cheek. The corner of my black eye.

Aren't we a pair, I thought and smiled at her weakly.

"I want to make you feel good, too," she said.

"You already have," I told her. I would have kissed her, but our mouths were a mess. And I was barely holding on.

Her hand slipped down over the fist I was using to try to control my cock. She pushed it away and replaced it with her own fingers. Small and nimble. Surprisingly sure.

"I'm not a child," she said. "And I'm not ill. I'm a woman. And I know what I want. I want to give you what you just gave me. Nothing in my life has ever been equal. Ever. I want this . . . I want us to be equal."

If there was a way to resist that, I didn't know it.

I fell onto my back and dropped my hand to my side. She curled up over me, her fingers slipping down into my underwear. I jumped.

"Does that hurt?" she asked, with wide eyes.

I could only shake my head. Words were gone.

She pulled down my underwear, and my cock, eager and hard, lay long against my belly.

She shifted on the bed and I knew what was coming, I braced myself for it, but her mouth—wet and warm, tight—still shocked me. Still made my entire body twitch. The stitches in my side pulled and I winced, pressing my hand against them.

The pain took a chunk out of the pleasure, but she took more of me. Inch by slow, hot inch. I lifted my head and watched my cock disappear into her mouth and everything but her and this pleasure vanished.

At my side I curled my hands into fists, refusing to touch her.

The way I usually fucked had no place in this trailer. No place with her and what we were giving each other, and so I dropped my head back on the pillow and closed my eyes and concentrated on her touch.

Her hand found a rhythm with her mouth, with her tongue, and she got faster and harder. She did something fancy, curling the palm of her hand over the head of my cock for a second before slipping me back into her mouth.

The stripper, I remembered. She learned that from watching the stripper give that guy a blow job.

Affection flooded me, running headlong with my lust, and it was over for me. I felt the orgasm building in the base of my spine, in the nerves at the bottom of my feet.

"I'm gonna come," I told her, curling my hand over her shoulder, giving her warning. She took me deeper, the head of my cock brushing the back of her throat, and I couldn't stop myself.

I came in wild, thick spurts into her mouth. Down her throat.

Slowly, sweetly, she milked me with her hand and I twitched in crazy aftershock. My entire body felt like I'd been electrocuted.

She sat back, her face beaming. Her beauty like a fist in my stomach.

"Thank you," I said to her.

"Felt good?"

"Felt fucking amazing."

She lay back down next to me, both of us on our backs, smiling up at the ceiling with our split lips like a couple of goons.

"Told you that was what we needed," she said.

I laughed and then groaned. The muscles in my stomach were sore. My side hurt. All the aches and pains came rushing back in the aftermath of that pleasure.

She held a hand to her lip and it came away with a little blood.

"Oh, shit," I said and stood up, pulling my underwear back up from my knees. In the bathroom I found a washcloth. I ran it under water and brought it back to her. "Didn't the doctor say don't give head until your lip heals?"

"Surprisingly, no," she said and pressed the damp washcloth to her mouth.

I didn't know what to do, how to rest in this tenderness we'd created. I had an instinct to smash it, because that was what I was good at. Because that was what I usually did.

That utter, bone-deep relaxation from minutes ago turned to cement in my muscles.

"Do you want me to leave?" she asked, watching me with dark eyes. The laughter draining from her face.

Yes.

"Remember when you said you weren't scared of me?" I asked her.

"I'm not."

I shook my head. There were still so many ways me being in her life could screw things up for her. My dad, my brother. Rabbit. My past. All those things could come back and hurt her.

"Maybe you should be," I told her.

As if to argue, she didn't leave. Or fight. She just curled up on her side, away from me, and I lay on my back, staring up at the ceiling. Listening to her breathe. The heat that had not been an issue five minutes ago was now suffocating and sweat gathered on the insides of my elbows. The base of my spine.

I counted her breaths as she lay beside me. Listened to them get deeper. Longer.

I spent the rest of the night watching the ceiling. Wondering what forces out there in the dark were going to fuck with me for this.

ANNIE

I THINK I GOT PITY-FINGERED.

And she did not like it.

Though, truthfully, what did she expect? She'd sort of forced herself on him last night. He'd said no, and she'd begged, and maybe . . . maybe pity-fingered is just what happens after that.

Annie lay on her side, her knees curled up, her hands under her cheek, and she watched a sleeping Dylan Daniels. He looked younger like this, relaxed and unaware. His dark hair flopped over his forehead, his boxer-brief underwear a little skewed on his thick body. Those lips of his, so full and pink, were marred by the bruise, the cut on his lip that he'd reopened in the night.

We didn't even kiss, she thought. Today they would kiss. Tomorrow. They had hours of kissing ahead of them.

She hoped. She hoped there was kissing ahead of them and not more pain.

Certainly no more pity. She was *waaaaaay* done with pity.

But she would be lying if she said that hope wasn't tinged with doubt. She could feel him pushing her away with the very same hand that he'd used to make her come.

"Why should I be scared of you?" she whispered. He'd told her about jail, killing that boy, sleeping with a prostitute, and none of it turned her head. None of it made her doubt.

What was making him doubt?

"What aren't you telling me?" she whispered.

He rolled away from her, and she stared at his back, the freckles scattered across the wide, smooth skin of his shoulders. She itched to touch him, but she kept her hands to herself, curled under her cheek.

The fact that she'd forced herself into his RV, forced herself into his bed, forced him to touch her—well, it was all starting to bother her.

But he'd stayed. Some instinct told her it wasn't only because of her.

Yet part of it was.

And she wanted to lean on that. She wanted to wrap herself in it and allow his feelings to give her worth. To dictate her own feelings about herself.

But that . . . she couldn't do that again.

She deserved better; she required more from herself.

In his sleep Dylan twitched. The muscles of his back and shoulders trembled.

What did Dylan Daniels dream of? Work, maybe? The fire? Prison?

She wondered if his nightmares would ever push him into her arms. For comfort. For care. For a pity hand job. In her heart, she knew the answer was no.

He was used to handling his grief by himself. Or not handling it at all.

Where does that leave me? she wondered. *Where does that leave us?*

No one said a relationship with Dylan Daniels would be easy, but she was getting a pretty good look at exactly how hard it would be.

And it's not like I'm a total treat, either, she reminded herself.

For a second the combined weight of their baggage seemed too heavy to carry.

But quickly, she pushed those worries aside.

Because the sun was just up, and the trailer park outside the window was slowly coming to life. Car doors were slamming as people went to work and got their kids to daycare before school.

There was a world out there that just kept spinning. A world that did not care about what she'd done. And that made her feel very small and oddly comforted.

And last night had returned something to her. Not just the sex, though that had helped more than she'd even thought. To pull herself back together, back into her body. Her own mind.

Dylan kept sleeping and twitching, dreaming his dreams.

You were this bright light. Pure.

That's what he'd said about her last night. And she liked that description. She would like to be that kind of person.

He'd told her she was brave once, too.

She scooped that idea up in her arms as well. Cobbling together a version of herself that she could admire. That she could aspire to be. That could build and sail her own boat out of the darkness.

Maybe that's how it began, this new life of hers. She'd decide who she would be.

Last night had been intense. And he was going to wake up soon, she thought, and he would try very hard not to show his worry. His pity. But it would be a lie.

And she would say that she was fine and she would pretend that she couldn't see his worry. Or his pity. And maybe his guilt. But that would be a lie, too.

I can't rely on him to make the ground steady for me, she thought. *I can't count on him to make me okay. I have to do this work on my own.*

Today she was a bright, pure light—just like Dylan had said—and she was only interested in finding more of that.

And perhaps, if he would accept it, pulling him into her boat with her.

Last night he said that he was worried she wanted to talk about the morbid and dark things both of them had in their lives. But she had to in order to move on, to move through it.

And she worried he lived in that darkness. Up on his hill, with people who let him be like that. Spying on his father from afar, pushing away the memories that hurt him. Building a new life on top of the still-breathing body of his old one.

She rolled over and opened the bedside table. There were packs of gum and books and condoms. A pair of handcuffs. Lube.

Despite last night and every night with Dylan before, she still blushed. She might always blush.

Underneath it all she found a notebook and a pencil.

Quickly, she wrote a note and tucked it beneath his hand.

He wouldn't like it, would undoubtedly resent her efforts to push him and his father together, but he was here. He stayed.

And there was power in that.

Power she never would have taken advantage of before. But these were new days. And she was a new woman.

Carefully, so she didn't wake him, Annie crept out of the bed and out of his room. She needed a shower in the worst way; she smelled like sex and sweat, and the day was already hot.

The trailer was set up exactly like hers, only slightly bigger. Slightly newer. And Dylan was right: Joan must have left in a rush, because a lot of her stuff was here. There was a pile of clean laundry on the driver's seat that had been turned around and what looked like a gym bag beside it.

Joan, she thought, with no small pang, and gathered those things up.

Maybe she'd go to the strip club and see if she was there. It seemed unlikely, but it was worth a shot. She really needed to be sure her friend was okay.

The wind blew and the breeze shifted a folded slip of paper across the counter, and she caught it before it fell off.

Annie.

That's what was printed on the front. Her name.

Kevin, if you find this give it to Annie.

She set down the bag and clothes and opened it.

Annie,

If you get this it meant you came back to the trailer park, in which case, you're even more of an idiot than I thought. I had to leave, sorry I didn't get a chance to say goodbye, but if you do get this and you are in the trailer park, we really need to talk. Call me.

Beneath the handwriting was a phone number.

Her heart suddenly pounding in her throat, Annie curled the note up in her hand, like a secret she needed to keep hidden.

11

ANNIE

It was strange using Dylan's phone for anything but calling him. But once she got in her own trailer, she dialed the number on the paper and got a man's computer voice telling her to leave a message. There was no name, no repetition of the number. Just *leave a message. Beep.*

"Ummm," she said, slipping the note into the bedside table. "I'm looking for Joan. Joan, this is Annie. I . . . uh, I got your note. Call me back when you can. I ah . . . oh shit . . . I don't know my phone number. Hopefully, it just pops up or something. I'll call you back tomorrow if I don't hear from you."

Annie took the phone into the bathroom with her when she showered so she could hear it if it rang.

And then slipped it into the back pocket of her cutoffs when she headed out of her camper. The air was cool against her skin and the earth smelled new—damp and dark. Mysterious. A new day unfolding.

She glanced up at Ben's trailer and saw him sitting under his awning. He lifted a hand in greeting and she walked over.

"Morning," he said. "Need some coffee?"

"I'd love some."

He began to rock himself up and out of his chair, but she stopped him. "I'll go help myself."

With a heavy sigh of relief he sat back down.

Inside, she poured herself a cup of coffee and noticed, lined up on the windowsill, a row of amber prescription bottles, glowing slightly in the morning sun. She turned the labels so she could read them.

Vicodin. Reglan. Decadron.

She had no idea what most of them meant, but it all sounded bad.

"How are you feeling?" she asked, once she was back outside and sitting on the splintered and weathered bench of his picnic table. She'd had to rearrange some pots out of the way to do it, but he didn't seem to mind.

"Oh no," he said. "We're not doing that."

"Doing what?"

"Starting every conversation with how I'm feeling."

"But—"

"I have cancer, Annie. I feel like shit. All the time. Move on."

She blinked at him, and at a loss, she took a sip of coffee. Thick as tar; somehow she wasn't surprised.

"Why didn't you tell me?" she asked. "About the cancer."

"Because I figure it's not much of your business."

She shook her head at him. "Are you saying that because you don't want me to know or because you don't think I care?" He blinked at her this time. "Because I care, Ben. And there's nothing you can do to stop that."

Clearly deeply uncomfortable, he shifted in his chair, turning away from her.

It was hard not to see Dylan in that gesture, the way he kept his face averted from emotion he did not want. Could not handle.

He'd learned it from his father, maybe.

Ben was losing his hair. She hadn't noticed it before, but the gleaming silver was gone in large patches, revealing a shiny, smooth scalp.

"Stop," he said, still not looking at her, but he ran a hand over his head, like he knew what she'd been looking at.

"Am I supposed to pretend you're not sick?"

"Yes."

"Ben—"

"You look better," he said, lifting his cup toward her face. Changing the direction of the conversation so fast she nearly got whiplash.

"Thanks. I feel better."

"That have anything to do with you coming out of Dylan's trailer this morning?"

While she wished she didn't blush, she couldn't control it. Ben smiled at her.

"He told me he's trying to get you out of this shit hole, but you ain't moving."

"I like this shit hole."

"He says you're staying because of me."

For you. For Dylan. For all of us. Annie nodded. "I am."

"That's the dumbest thing I've ever heard."

"So is driving home alone after chemo. Which, I will point out, won't be happening on Friday."

His smooth brow furrowed. "What are you doing, Annie? You got yourself a clean break. A brand-new beginning. No asshole husband chasing you down. A man, a rich man, living in a freaking trailer next to the father he hates, because he wants to keep you safe. You can go anywhere right now."

"All I want to do is go to the field. Maybe do some mowing."

"Oh lord, now *that* is the dumbest thing I've ever heard."

"No, Ben." She finished the last of the coffee and set the cup down on the table before standing up. "The dumbest thing *I've* ever heard is you, sitting in this trailer park for years waiting for Dylan to come down off that mountain to deal with you—"

"I ain't been waiting—"

"Bullshit, Ben."

His eyes opened wide at her tone.

"He's here, Ben. Dylan is here. Now is the time."

"No, Annie. Listen to me, girl. If you're staying here thinking that me and Dylan are going to have some kind of big reconciliation, you're wrong. Ain't nothing ever going to change between me and Dylan. And if you want a chance with him, at having something real and lasting, then you need to leave. You need to get him out of here. Right now."

"You don't know that."

"Ask him why he stayed here," Ben said, rocking back and forth in his chair. "Ask him why he really stayed."

Something pinged in her chest, a sharp pain that spread. She'd been right this morning—his reasons for staying were not just about her. There was something he wasn't telling her.

"It doesn't matter."

"If he tells you the truth it will."

He was sucking away her good mood, adding weight to those misgivings she did not want to have. "I'll talk to you later. And I'm driving you on Friday. No argument."

"You're going to be stubborn about this?"

"I'm a farmer from Oklahoma—you've never seen my kind of stubborn." That was a total lie, complete bullshit, but she liked the idea of being stubborn in this new life of hers. So she was going to try it on for size.

He chuckled, once, a little heave of his chest. "You're going to be good for him, girly. If you can get him out of here. But you ain't taking me anywhere in that shit-box car of yours."

"Then fix it for me," she said. The name Ben called her as she walked away was said with such fondness she actually smiled.

The bell over the front door rang as she walked into the meat-locker chill of Kevin's office.

"Hey, Kevin," she said, and miraculously he turned in his chair to face her.

"Hey, kid, you're up."

She winced at the nickname.

"You don't like that?" he asked and she shook her head. "Can I call you killer?"

Her mouth literally fell open.

"Too soon?"

She couldn't help but laugh. "I'm here to work."

"No way." He shook his head, and his long ponytail snaked back and forth across his back.

"I won't do anything crazy. I'll just mow. I'm sure with the rain and me being gone, the campground field is totally overrun."

"It is, but I'm guessing you're supposed to be resting."

"I *will* be resting, on top of a riding lawn mower. Trust me, I'm a big girl."

"I feel like I should get a doctor's note or something."

"You get a note from me. Telling you I'm fine." Stubborn was really working for her today.

"Okay," he said, slowly. Reluctantly. "You still got your key to the shed?"

She lifted up the dinky key on the rusty key ring and leaned back against the glass door, opening it with her butt.

She was alive.

The sun was shining.

Dylan was here. For now. And her body was back under her keeping.

And she was safe.

And if that note from Joan and all of Ben's warnings made her nervous, made her feel scared, she could chalk that up to paranoia.

It was just paranoia.

There was nothing to be scared of.

DYLAN

I WOKE UP ALONE, IN A SWEATY MESS OF A BED, HOT SUNSHINE beating down on my skin.

In that thin place between asleep and awake, I thought I was back in my parents' apartment in Jacksonville. Sleeping in the bottom bunk in the little room off the kitchen. Listening to my brother fart and snore in the bunk above me.

The memory made me smile.

But I wasn't in Jacksonville, and I definitely wasn't in my king-size bed outside of Asheville.

Annie.

In this sweet spot, half awake and half asleep, I didn't allow myself to feel anything but satisfied.

The ways she was different from any other woman in my life could not be counted. I didn't want to say she was sweet, because that seemed to negate all the ways she was fierce. I didn't want to say she was generous, because it would deny the ways she was selfish.

I'd never had a woman in my life show me so much of herself.

I reached out into the empty side of the bed, just to feel where she'd been.

Something crinkled under my hand.

I opened blurry eyes and read the note stuck to my palm.

I'm mowing. Ask your father where the field is.

Ask my father . . .

So much for satisfied.

I grabbed my phone and saw that I had two missed calls from Margaret and four from Blake. I also had a missed call from an unknown number.

Max.

Quickly, I called it back and it rang twice and then, again, a robotic woman's voice said to leave a message.

"Max?" I said. "Call me back."

I hung up and then called Annie, thinking she'd just gone back to her trailer at some point this morning. But when she answered, there was the heavy grind of a motor for a few seconds before it went silent.

"Hey," she said. I could tell by the tone of her voice she was smiling. And that made me smile.

"What are you doing?"

"Mowing the field. Didn't you get my note?"

I looked down at the Post-it she'd attached to my hand.

"Come find me," she said. And hung up.

I closed my eyes. I was going to have to tell her that she needed to be careful. Annie thought the trouble was gone with Hoyt dead, but there were men on the sidelines who were a whole lot worse than Hoyt.

My own brother among them.

I stood up too fast and I got hard-core dizzy, so I sat back down before I fell over. The doctor had said I'd lost a lot of blood and that the only way to recover was to rest. Take it easy.

Not to spend half my night in a strip club parking lot and the other half with my hand buried between my girlfriend's legs.

And frankly, not here—this trailer park, with Pops, with Max and Rabbit on the periphery. This was the last place I would take it easy. Here, I needed to be vigilant.

More slowly this time, like a freaking invalid, I got up out of the bed and threw on my jeans and tee shirt from yesterday. It was time to face the music. In this case, the wrath of Margaret.

I dialed her number and she answered before the first ring was over.

"You'd better have a good reason for not calling me last night," she said.

"I'm a grown man, Margaret."

"Who just got stabbed in the side and left the hospital against medical advice. Blake and I thought you were in a ditch someplace."

"Well," I sighed. "You're not far off. I'm at the trailer park."

"The what now?"

I laughed. "The Flowered Manor Trailer Park. Annie wanted to stay here."

"And you couldn't convince her otherwise?"

"Not with all my money. She's happy here."

"Yeah, well, she'd probably be just as happy in Tahiti—she just doesn't know it yet. What about you?" she asked, knowing me better than just about everyone. When Miguel and Margaret took me in after jail, I was feral. Grateful, yes, and eager to start fresh and race and work on engines. But I snarled and bit anytime she tried to get close to me. She kept trying, though; I'd give her that. I just didn't know how to let her get close.

Bodes real well for you and Annie, doesn't it?

"I'm fine," I said, putting my watch on.

"How long are you staying?"

"I don't know. So, I'll need you to bring me a few things." I rattled off a list of the necessities.

"Does Blake know you're not going to be back at the garage?"

"I'm calling him next."

"Well, then, I'll know to stay out of his way."

Blake was not going to appreciate me moving down to this trailer park for some unknown amount of time.

"I'll be down there after three," she said and hung up. She hung up even though I knew she wanted to grill me. She wanted to talk about my feelings. And what Annie meant to me and what I thought was going to happen between us.

All questions I didn't have answers for.

I looked through the bathroom and found that Joan had left behind some toothpaste, which I squirted into my mouth. She also left behind a package of condoms. I thought of Annie's body under my fingertips last night, the strange and sad desperation between us, and I didn't know if the condoms were a blessing or a curse. But they were here.

It was just past ten. I hadn't slept that late in years. Blood loss and a blow job really took a guy down. I tried not to smile, because smiling felt sacrilegious now that I was awake and looking around this dump of a trailer. Smiling seemed like the opposite of what I should be doing.

But I couldn't stop it.

Outside, it was already humid and sticky. I cleared the edge of my trailer and looked right, toward the end of the dirt track where Pops lived.

He was sitting in that recliner, slowly rocking back and forth. A smoke in one hand, a coffee cup in the other.

He caught my eye and didn't do anything.

I didn't, either.

We just stared at each other for a long moment.

"You heard from Max?" I asked.

He shook his head. "You?"

"I think he called sometime last night. I got a hang-up from that number you gave me."

"That's good."

Ben didn't say any more; he just rocked back and forth.

"You looking for Annie?" he asked.

"She's in the field," I said.

He pointed to the far side of the trailer park. "Follow the path through the trailer park—about a hundred meters past the

last trailer there's a little bridge. The field is another hundred
meters past that. You'll find her."

I turned without a word and walked away.

"You're welcome, son!" he shouted after me.

I gave him the finger over my shoulder and he laughed.

I walked past the laundry block and then the playground
across the street.

There were two blond girls in pretty dresses with their hair
tied back in clips on the swings, and they slowed to a stop as I
walked past. Their eyes wide as saucers, tracking me as I walked
toward them.

Right. The scars.

Truthfully, I was not used to being stared at.

Everyone in my life was used to my scars. Used to my moods.
Used to the beast.

Everything was different down here.

And the staring was part of the reason why down here
sucked.

A woman came out of the trailer next to the laundry and
jogged across the street toward the kids, watching me out of the
corner of her eye like I was going to eat those girls.

The mom was pale and wan, her blond hair pulled back in a
ponytail revealing the sharp ridges of her collarbones, the fading
edge of a bruise around her wrist.

I was scaring them and I didn't know exactly how to stop.

I nodded and lifted my hand in a half wave that I tried to
make as nonthreatening as I could.

One of the little girls, the younger, lifted her hand and waved
back with her whole arm, her jack-o'-lantern smile revealing a
bunch of missing baby teeth.

It was impossible not to smile back, but I turned away before
the mother saw me.

With my scars, my smiles were not . . . friendly.

Past the last trailer, I kept walking until I crossed the small wooden bridge and saw Annie riding a red mower toward me, a straw hat tipped back on her head, big black gloves on her hands.

My heart surged with more emotion than I could name. Worry. Admiration. A heavy, hard kind of desire. She was pretty freaking cute in that hat.

Perhaps it was because we were out of the hospital or because of what we'd done last night—that tender, heartbreaking act that had been not at all like any sex I'd ever had—but the thought of something happening to her was devastating.

It was devastating and not out of the realm of possibility.

Because my father was here. My brother nearby.

She could get hurt by my family's bloody past.

And I felt a powerful urge, a need to get her out of here. Away from me.

I had to tell her.

She yelled something at me.

"I can't hear you!" I yelled.

"What?" she asked with one of those little smiles of hers. She was joking. This was funny to her. "I can't hear you!"

When she was close, I reached over and cranked off the key. The sudden silence echoed.

"Hi," she said, with a wide smile. "You got my note!"

"I did. And I don't like what you're doing."

"Mowing?" she asked, pretending to be obtuse. Behind her, half the field was light green and stripped, the other half dark green and wild. "But I am super good at it. Years of practice."

"Didn't the doctor tell you to rest?"

"I am. I am resting on my lawn mower."

Cute, she was so damn cute.

"I don't need you pushing me and my dad together."

"Well, you are neighbors—"

"Annie," I said. "Let me deal with Ben."

"You still want me to spy on him for you?" she asked, a mad twinkle in her eye. "I'll call you every night with updates."

The urge to kiss her was insane. Literally magnetic. So, I took a step back. She noticed, and that twinkle in her eye diminished.

Good, I thought. She needed to be realistic. She needed to look at this place and these people—me—with eyes stripped clear of rose-colored glasses.

I wanted to fuck her and protect her all at the same time. I wanted to keep her and push her away. I was everything in opposites, and I felt torn apart by her.

"I need to talk to you," I told her, and the wattage behind that smile dropped.

"About last night?"

"No. Well . . . in a way." She stiffened, her cheeks red, and those bold eyes of hers didn't quite meet mine. She was ashamed. Somehow. Some way.

And what I should have done was wrap her in my arms, tell her that I wasn't talking about what happened in my bed, but I didn't.

And the distance between us slowly grew.

"Annie—"

"No." She shook her head and then looked right at me, her eyes stormy, her jaw set. I blinked, taken aback by this sudden ferocity, though I wasn't sure why. She'd shown me her fierceness. I worshipped at the feet of her ferocity.

"What?"

"It's bad, isn't it? This thing you want to tell me. It will make me sad. Or angry. And I'm telling you no. Whatever it is, it can wait. For one damn day it can wait." She tilted her head, her fierceness fading into something beseeching. "Can't it?"

It was a mistake; I get it. I should have fought harder. Been stronger. But not telling her about Max. About Rabbit. About the danger she was in because of me . . . it was a fucking relief.

It was like a boulder got rolled off my back.

"It can wait," I said.

You really are a coward, aren't you? the voice said, loud and clear, and I couldn't argue with it.

I stroked her cheeks, pink from the sun despite her hat. The white-blond tips of her hair were damp and clumped together with sweat.

"Good," she said with a smile. "Because I want to have some fun."

"Fun?"

"Yes, Dylan, I understand that it's a thing people have every once in a while. Like squid. Or a stomachache, but better."

I made the mistake of smiling at her and she clapped. The despondent and wrecked woman who'd come to my bed last night was nowhere to be seen. Or if she was, she was very well hidden. She was all light again and I was drawn to her like a moth. And part of me wished I were stronger. That I could resist her a little better, but I couldn't.

She owned me. Despondent and wrecked, smiling and bright—it didn't matter. I was hers.

"Let's go swimming," she said with another one of her heartbreaker smiles, the edge of it pulled taut by the stitches.

"What? Where?"

"Over there." She jerked her thumb over her shoulder to what looked like a bunch of weeds around a tree. "The Flowered Manor Trailer Park and Camp Ground swimming hole!"

"That's where you went skinny-dipping?" I asked. I didn't think Rabbit was watching the campground, but that didn't mean someone wasn't. But the campground was far away and the trees around us were silent. And it felt like we were the only ones around. "Anyone could see you."

"I'm not an expert, but isn't that the point of skinny-dipping?"

"Annie, we can't just pretend everything is normal right now."

Her smile faded a little and I felt bad for doing that to her, taking away some of that light.

But that, I thought, *is what you do. That is the very point of you.*

"Why not?" she asked. "We've done all kinds of pretending together, haven't we?"

I couldn't deny that. Half of what we were to each other was lies. The other half, the hard honest truth I never told anyone.

"Give me today," she said. Plaintive and real. Beautiful and broken. Brave and scared all at once.

I was used to being one thing. And one thing at a time. That's all I could hold. And what she wanted from me, what she was asking, was messy. It was human and fraught with disaster. And I had no idea if I could do it.

And I knew that I really shouldn't. For her sake.

She put the mower's key into her back pocket and cocked her hat over her eyes, like she was some kind of desperado.

"Stay or go," she said. "But I'm swimming."

This was a bad idea. All the way around.

Silent, I watched her go and then, before she got to the edge of the cattails, she lifted her shirt up over her head and dropped it on the ground behind her.

I didn't know what a hero would do.

But the beast followed.

12

ANNIE

HE FOLLOWED.

For a second she really didn't think he would.

Because he was worried. Because he wanted to protect her. Because of whatever secret she was forcing him to keep from her.

Good lord, I've lost my mind. I just asked a man to lie to me.

Whatever. A one-day reprieve. That's all she wanted.

He was here. And she would take him. With a smile, pretending her heart wasn't in play, she would take him.

She hacked through the cattails and the murky mud that sucked at her boots and got to the rocky edge of the beach. The bushes around the swimming hole were dense and intact. No one was here.

The water was completely undisturbed.

It was a solid disk of reflected blue sky, dotted with white clouds. It seemed a shame to ruin it.

But that it would return to this state when she walked away, that was a comfort.

That it would not be changed by her shattering its surface buoyed her.

She could hear Dylan behind her, stepping through the cattails, surprisingly quiet, and she quickly stepped out of her boots. And when she knew he could see her, she unbuttoned her shorts and bent over to push them down.

His quick, hard intake of breath turned her blood to kerosene.

That's right, buddy. I said we were having fun.

She gave him one quick glance over her shoulder and was totally satisfied by his heavy breathing, the way he was clutching her shirt in his hands, like he wanted to be touching her.

The water when she stepped in was cold and bright, and it went straight to her head, clearing out the cobwebs. The confusion. The uncertainty. And it made everything so clear. The sky was bluer. The cattails, bending so slightly in the breeze, were a perfect green, tipped with a deep, rich brown.

When the water was deep enough she dove in, turning underwater so when she came back up she was facing him.

He stood on the shore, in the shadow of the big tree, in jeans and a tee shirt. His arms crossed over his chest.

"You're not coming in?" she asked.

He glanced around like someone might be hiding in the cattails.

"No one is here, Dylan. We're all alone."

Still he hesitated, and she gave him a chicken sound for good measure.

Finally, he pulled off his shirt, too. The sight of his body was a predictable turn-on. The thick slabs of muscle across his chest and stomach. He wasn't one of those super-cut models, he was a man. Who worked. And his body showed all of it.

In the cool water her body warmed.

The bandage was gone on his side and his scar, five inches wide, was pink and dotted with stitches.

"How is your side?" she asked.

"Fine," he said, which was bullshit. When would they stop lying to each other?

"Then, you should try the rope swing." She pointed to the frayed rope hanging off the thick branch of the oak beside the water.

"You think I won't?" he asked.

He shucked off his pants but left on the black boxer briefs.

"Cheating!" she said.

He shot her a caustic look, which made her repeat the chicken sound, and he rolled his eyes before pushing his under-wear down to his feet.

"You know," he said, "if swimming is your idea of fun I can send you to the Caribbean. Or Fiji. You can have your own pri-vate house right over the water. You can skinny-dip all day."

"Are you trying to get rid of me?" she asked.

"I'm trying to keep you safe."

She smiled at him. "I feel very safe right now."

"You shouldn't," he told her. Completely seriously. "Not here. Not with me."

The truth of his words slid right through her, right into some-thing real and vulnerable that she didn't want to think about. He was talking about her body, about her coming to physical harm, but of that she had no fear.

It was her heart's fate that was in question.

"Don't come in just as a favor to me. I don't need any more pity sex." *Ah,* she hadn't meant to say that. To reveal her vulner-ability like that. But there it was, insisting on being dealt with.

You wanted to tell the truth.

"What does that mean?" He ran his hand down his cock, pulling it a little before he took his first steps into the water. She loved that little masculine gesture. Wanted to see more of them. She wanted to watch him brush his teeth and read the newspaper. She wanted to watch him eat his favorite food and get frustrated putting together a bookshelf.

"Last night," she said.

"You think that was a pity?" His eyebrow went up.

"I know it was." He held his arms up as the water came to his waist. "Don't be such a baby," she said and splashed him.

He scowled at her and finally dove into the water, his white back and ass a quick flash before disappearing under the bluesky reflection.

In the middle of the pond it was deep and she could see him swimming beneath her feet. His sturdy legs and strong back. He popped up behind her but she turned and swam away, keeping distance between them.

"Last night wasn't a favor," he said, sucking water off his lips, pushing back wet hair.

Annie made a face at him.

"I don't fuck women as favors," he said.

"We didn't fuck." She threw the words at him and it was thrilling. The electricity between them was thrilling.

"Fine. I don't let women suck my dick so they can feel better about themselves. I'm just worried about you." They were agitating the water, creating little waves between them. A storm.

"Well, stop. You don't own the corner on fucked-up shit, Dylan. You don't get to be the king of crappy childhoods. You can't protect me from what's already happened!"

She waited for him to say something. To reach out and grab her, to respond in any way, but he didn't.

His quiet face provoked her.

Fuck you, she thought. *You can only pretend to be so removed. I know the truth and the truth was last night. The way you touched me and let me touch you.*

She swam over to one of the big rocks and climbed up onto it. Naked and sleek and dripping, she leaned back on her elbows, watching him under lowered eyelids. She had zero practice being seductive, but the heat in his eyes told her she was doing something right.

"Where did you used to go skinny-dipping?" she asked.

"There was a beach my brother and I would go to back home. A kind of locals-only thing."

"You and your brother went skinny-dipping together?"

"Me and my brother did everything together for a while. But there were usually some girls involved in the skinny-dipping."

"Do you miss him?"

He swam toward the rock. "I thought this was supposed to be fun?"

"It is."

"You need a better idea of fun," he said with a leer, but it was practiced and only for show. He was trying to distract her because she'd gotten a reaction talking about his brother. And she wanted more.

Just as he pulled himself up next to her, she jumped back down into the water, splashing toward the middle. When she surfaced he was standing on the rock, grinning at her. He liked this game. This coy bit of pretend. The pursuit and retreat. And that made her like it even more.

"Come on, you know everything about me. I know so little about you."

"I'd say you know more than most."

It wasn't enough. It would never be enough. Not for her. Not with Dylan.

"Your brother," she said. "Tell me one thing."

"He was a shitty car thief. And he made me go to school when other kids were dropping out. There's two things."

"Do you miss him?"

"What do I get if I tell you?" he asked.

Everything. She would give him everything. But that was entirely too much truth for right now.

"What do you want?" she asked.

"To take you away from here. Anywhere you want to go. I'll stay with you and fuck you day and night and I'll leave when you tell me to. Whatever you want."

Water ran down all of his scars. Over his muscles. His face. Those intense eyes. That beautiful mouth, no longer smiling at her.

Desire hummed under her skin. Her heart lurched under its heavy weight. Her lungs shuddered.

"You're beautiful," she said.

"That concussion is fucking with your vision."

She shook her head. "I know what I see."

"You're looking at a beast, baby." He lifted out his arms and turned. The scars on his feet and legs were red and shiny. Hairless. He was muscled and thick. A fighter.

"You're *my* beast," she told him.

He jumped off the rock and walked out toward her. His cock getting thicker as he got closer. She took small steps away. Not serious retreat, just keeping the game going.

Once he was close enough he caught her wrist, yanking her against him. His skin was hot even in the cold water and she gave resistance a token effort, trying to swim away, but he held on to her. Wrapping an arm around her waist to hold her still. Against her leg she felt him, hard and long.

And mine. Mine for as long as he lets me claim him.

"I'm not scared of you," she said. "I'll never be scared of you."

Every breath they took was pulled from the same air. Their bodies nearly fought for the same space. She felt a sudden need to bite and claw and rip and tear, and as if he saw it, too, he grabbed her. He held her head still in his hands.

"Well, I'm sure as shit scared of you," he said.

"Good," she whispered, all bravado and lust. "You should be."

He kissed her with a barely restrained mean edge that didn't bother her in the slightest.

Yeah, she thought, *show me. Show me everything.*

His hands were rough against her skin, her breasts tiny in the palms of those hands. She reached between their legs to cup him in her own. He got hard at her touch and then harder still.

His hands slid around her back to cup her ass and she loved that. She'd said as much at his house days ago. And now, like he did then, he grabbed her with both hands, squeezing her tight. Holding her hard.

And then his finger slid down over her asshole. And stayed.

Her breath stopped and he leaned back just a little so he could stare into her eyes. She was shaking in his arms, her eyes locked on his. Slowly, slowly he pressed in.

"Look at you," he breathed into her open mouth. "So bad. Is that what you want? You want to be bad, little girl?"

She whimpered. Part yes, a little no. Less no every second.

"I want to fuck you there," he whispered, pressing tiny kisses against her lips and cheeks. A sweet counterpoint to the dirty things happening under the water.

"You think I'm going to say no?" she managed to whisper.

His smile was oddly sad. "No, I don't think you're going to say no."

He pushed his finger in farther and she cried out.

"Does it hurt?" he asked.

"No." Her voice shook and he sank in a little deeper, making her cry out again. She closed her eyes. Too much. It was too much.

"Shhhh," he said, putting a hand over her mouth. "Listen to me, Annie. Open your eyes and listen to me."

Her eyelids fluttered open. She felt pinned, by his gaze, by his finger. His hand. Him.

"I haven't had sex with a woman other than you in years. I'm clean."

"C . . . clean?" What was he talking about? She could not think past the burning pleasure he was giving her.

"No STDs. You?"

"What? No." Her eyelids closed again. He was moving his finger inside her and she could not concentrate.

"Open your eyes," he said. "Now."

She had no choice. No will. She was a creature in waiting. Her eyes snapped open. A bird flew across the blue, blue sky, so far away and right there. Everything all at once.

"Look at me," he said, and she could barely focus. Oh, that mouth. That mouth of his was so beautiful. She put her lips against his, tasting him. Salty and sweet. She sucked that fat lower lip into her mouth. Bit it, just a little.

Everything was suspended. Time. Pleasure. Pain. It was like the entire world held itself in waiting.

For her.

But then with his other hand he pushed his cock down so he slid between the lips of her pussy and she leapt into his arms, her face bumping his. She cried out again and his hand came back over her mouth.

His eyes were hot and focused.

"Shhhh," he breathed.

His cock brushed her clit. Once. On the retreat of his hips, it brushed her again. No matter how he moved, or how she moved, her clit got stroked. Again and again. He slipped high and hard against her. She jerked over and over again, feeling like she was being pulled to pieces. His naked skin against hers was soft. Silky. Hot.

"Can you be quiet?" he whispered, his hot breath against her cheek. "Nod, baby. Can you be quiet?"

She nodded. Still he stroked her, more teasing than anything. Too much teasing, it was starting to hurt, the pleasure plateauing, and she reached down and cupped her hand on the other side of his cock, pushing him harder against her.

Surprise flashed through his eyes. And heat. So much heat.

The water around them had to be boiling. How was the water not boiling?

"I want to fill you up," he said. His cheeks were flushed. The scars white hot. "All the way. Do you trust me?"

Trust had long ago stopped being her problem with him. That's what he didn't understand.

She nodded.

His cock pushed inside her. All the way. One long, steady stroke. She nearly screamed, impaled by his cock and his finger. And the orgasm came out of nowhere. She felt like she had to chase it, hold it. Her hips were a piston against his.

"I'm sorry," she whispered, groaning and crying. She wrapped her arms around his neck, buried her face there, her body convulsing. "I can't stop. I can't . . ."

"It's okay. I got you. I got you, baby."

And she came so hard she bit her tongue. She saw stars. The blue sky above them was filled with birds, startled from trees by screams she could not swallow.

The second it was over, the second she was still in his hands, he pulled out. Stepped back. Both his cock and his finger were gone. Unsupported and surprised, her head dipped under the water before he grabbed her and she started to tread.

"You okay?" he asked, holding her up with one hand.

She was a rag doll. Her head full of stuffing. Her body boneless.

"Fuck, look at you. Just . . ." His hand disappeared under the water and she could tell he was jerking off.

"Let me," she breathed, reaching for him, but he slapped her hand away and before she could get outraged he was groaning low in his throat, his lip between his teeth. His eyes clenched hard.

The water was too deep and she pushed away from his hand

until she could stand on her own. If he wouldn't let her help, she didn't want to detract from what he was doing.

He was silent, so alone seeming, with his back turned to her. His shoulders jerked. Once. Again, and then . . . stillness.

Slowly he took deep breaths. He opened his eyes, but still he didn't look at her. She stared at his profile, wondering what he was thinking.

"I'm sorry," he finally said.

Ah, she thought, bitter sadness leaching through her bliss. He was thinking of regret.

"For what?"

"We didn't use a condom—"

"You pulled out. I mean, you didn't come in me."

"Still," he said with a sigh.

She was electrified by what they'd done. His hands on her body made her feel small and huge at the same time. She wanted more. Endless amounts of more.

And he was sorry.

All that good she was feeling since waking up. The brave and strong shit, it fell around her in shambles.

I just keep hurting him. Even when I try not to.

"Is this what sex is going to be like?" she asked. "One person feeling great and the other person sorry?"

His dark eyes touched hers and then looked away. "Let's get dressed."

He walked to the shore ahead of her. And she thought of how she'd taken care of this swimming hole with this very moment in mind. Perhaps not consciously, but subconsciously, she'd made it a place that was private and secluded. Lilac bushes on one side, cattails and the big tree on the other.

It really was a pretty spot. And now it seemed sad.

"We don't have a towel," he said. "But you can use my shirt."

He handed the red cotton out to her, but still didn't look at her.

"Dylan," she breathed, naked and shivering in the sunlight.

"I don't know," he snapped. "Maybe between us, right now, yes, this is the way it is."

"I don't like it," she said.

"Me neither."

She sucked in a reedy, small breath and then another. And still another. She forced herself to pull on her clothes.

You wanted the truth, she thought. *It's your own damn fault for thinking it would be happy.*

13

DYLAN

WELL, THAT WAS JUST FUCKING PERFECT, ASSHOLE.

I stepped into my pants, jerking them up my wet legs. They got stuck, and I swore and wrestled my body into them.

Way to keep your distance. Way to give her time. Shoving your finger up her ass and fucking her without a condom is just an excellent way of making sure she's all right.

"You ready?" I asked, trying not to snap. Trying in fact to sound kind, because I felt like I kept kicking a damn puppy.

Only Annie wasn't acting like a puppy. She was outraged. And stomping through the cattails with her back straight and her head held high.

I was the goddamn puppy.

Her damp clothes clung to her skin, the bright white tips of her hair dripped.

"Annie—"

"Go to hell, Dylan," she snapped.

I think I am already there.

She was across the field and on the mower before I could catch up and I didn't know what I would say to her if I did.

All I wanted to do was help. Keep her safe.

And I couldn't be fucking it up more.

I turned onto the little bridge and headed back over toward our trailers.

"Hey," a man said, and I spun. Standing at the edge of Annie's trailer was a man with blond hair and a jaw like a cartoon superhero.

I was slow, admittedly because I'd had my brain melted by Annie in that swimming hole, but it finally clicked.

Hero Cop was here. From the hospital.

"Hey," I said, trying to hide both my extreme dislike for the guy and my sudden panic that something might have gone wrong in the investigation. "Everything okay?"

"I didn't know you were living here," the cop said. "In your statement you said you lived outside of Asheville."

"I own the trailer park," I said. "That was in my statement, too."

"Right," he said, smiling a little like he'd made a dumb mistake, but I knew a fishing expedition when I saw one. "I'm looking for Annie. Have you seen her?"

I've seen her, asshole. I've seen more of her than you ever will.

"Grant!" It was Annie coming around the edge of the trailer. Her shirt clung to her breasts and she must have known it, because she flapped it away from her body and then crossed her arms over her chest. But I had to give the guy credit; he didn't stare. He didn't even look. He kept his eyes right on hers.

"I mean . . . Officer Davies. What are you doing here?" she asked. "Is there some kind of problem with the case?"

"No. Not at all. The District Attorney is still reviewing it. I heard you were discharged from the hospital and I just wanted to make sure you were okay."

Her face made that kind of stunned, "oh my gosh, aren't you sweet" expression and I couldn't stand there and watch her get charmed by the cop and I couldn't punch him in the face, so I turned away and walked around my trailer, only to find Ben standing next to the opened hood of a twenty-year-old Toyota that was more rust than metal.

"So?" Hero Cop asked, his voice easily carrying to where Ben and I were standing. "Are you okay?"

"What are you doing?" Ben asked.

"Shhhhh," I said.

"I'm fine," Annie answered. "Really. I did a little work and it felt good, you know. Being outside. Getting something accomplished."

"You're like a groundskeeper or something . . . ?"

"Yeah, I guess you could say that. I mowed part of a field today."

"That's good work," he said without the slightest hint of pandering. "Immediate gratification."

"Exactly," she said, like he'd read her mind. A half hour ago I'd stood next to her on that tractor and given her shit for wanting to work. Pretending that I didn't understand the effect of a little honest labor so that I could keep throwing up smoke screens between us.

Useless drama that wasn't going to get us anywhere.

"You spying on your girlfriend?" Ben whispered.

"No," I whispered back. It was such a bullshit, knee-jerk response that Pops rolled his eyes at me. Slowly, he crept past me up to the edge of the trailer.

"What the fuck are you doing?" I whisper-yelled at him.

Pops shushed me.

"Are you five?" I asked him.

"I . . . I uh . . . I brought you something," Hero Cop said, and I stopped pretending and stepped up next to Pops, watching

Annie and the cop through the green leaves of the flowers planted in the pots where the wheels of her trailer would be.

Spying on my girlfriend, for lack of a better word, with my old man. Because I was making nothing but excellent decisions lately.

Hero Cop pulled a book out of his back pocket, sort of folded and dog-eared. Something that had seen some wear. He held it out to her.

With reverent hands she took it, unfolding it to read the cover. It must have been surprising, because her eyes flew up to his.

"I . . . I don't want to sound presumptuous or anything," the cop said. "But two years back, I shot a man. A . . . well, a kid, really. It was an armed robbery and he had a hostage and . . ." He shook his head. "I had to talk to someone afterward, you know . . . a shrink . . . It's kind of protocol. And she told me to read this book."

"Grant," she sighed. The tone of her voice sent nails into my spine. She talked to me that way, with gratitude and affection and just a little bit of grief. I didn't want to be jealous. Jealousy was a stupid emotion and I'd burned through it years ago.

But I couldn't pretend I liked that she talked to Grant that way.

Pops shot me a knowing look over his shoulder and I didn't like that, either.

"And it helped," Hero Cop said. "Like really helped. There's some parts that have notes I wrote down and I highlighted some stuff. You can ignore it. I mean . . ."

"Thank you," she breathed, holding the book to her chest. "So much."

The cop laughed, his face bright red, a bead of sweat creeping down from his ear to the collar of his shirt. "Well, I know you like books. And I put my number in there. Home and cell. If you ever want to talk."

It was awkward and just about the sweetest goddamn thing I'd ever seen.

I walked away until I couldn't hear their voices, giving the two of them some privacy.

A few minutes later I heard Annie's door open and slam shut.

Hero Cop walked past the edge of the trailer and saw Ben and me standing there like the guilty eavesdroppers we were.

"Well, well," he said, putting his thumbs in his belt. He had to be sweating his balls off in that uniform. "It's the Daniels family of felons. You're just missing Max, right?"

Ben and I were silent.

"See," Hero Cop stepped closer to us, "here's the thing, Dylan. Despite all that money of yours, you're still a Daniels. You still come from a family of murderers and scumbags. But you're smart. And because you're smart, you know you're only going to drag her down."

"Fuck off," Ben said.

"Excuse me?" Hero Cop stepped closer.

"No one asked you," Ben said, and I pushed him back toward the car he'd been working on.

"Ignore him," I said. Because the last thing any of us needed was more trouble.

"You're bad for her," Hero Cop said, his blue eyes pinned to mine. "And you know it." He gave us one more long look and then turned and walked away, back to his cruiser parked by the office.

"Well," Pops said when the cop was gone. "You gotta put an end to that shit right there."

I didn't say anything. Because fuck if the cop wasn't right.

"Dylan?" Pops said. "You hear me?"

"I heard you. There's nothing to put an end to," I said. "It's just a book."

"If you really think that, you deserve to lose her."

Pops bent back over the engine of the old Toyota.

I wasn't going to trade paint with Hero Cop.

Because he was the kind of guy she should be with. And that killed me, it fucking gutted me, but it was the truth.

"If you're just gonna stand there with your mouth open, you can help me with your girlfriend's car," Ben said.

"What? This is Annie's?" There were at least twenty things wrong with the thing, and that was just based on glancing under the hood. God, the 93-horsepower engine was so small. Like a toy.

"Barely runs," Ben said, struggling to lift out the corroded battery.

"Here . . . give me that," I said, and took the battery and set it down on the grass beside the driver's-side front wheel. "You sure you should be doing this?" I asked.

"Doing what?"

"Working on cars."

"Do you really care?"

I thought my silence spoke volumes.

"A guy's got to do something," he said. "Ignition coil is shot."

"She'll need a whole new distributor." I didn't need to look under the car to see that.

"Might as well throw in a new starter. And the EGR system needs to be cleaned out."

"You can do that," I said, joking with the old man about the filthy job before I thought better of it. He smiled up at me and I made sure I was frowning.

"She misses church," Pops said. We both stared down at that engine like it was all that mattered.

"Yeah. She said."

"So?"

"So what?"

"So you should take her."

"Is this relationship advice?" I scoffed.

"It's human advice. That's all."

"Yeah? Human advice?" I let the seething irritation out. I let it just pour right on out all over him. "You feel like an authority on that?"

"No," he snapped back, no longer pretending to look at the motor. "I'm an authority on mistakes. On regrets. And I'm telling you, take her to church. Help her get right. Be the guy beside her instead of that fucking blond cop with the chin I'd like to break in half, or you'll lose her. And you will regret that, son. For the rest of your life."

I didn't want to acknowledge that any of his words rang with an implacable truth. And I didn't want to tell him that I was thinking of taking myself out of the race, because I couldn't be the right guy for her.

Pops's opinion, right or wrong, did not matter.

"Forget the car," I told him, angry for some reason to see him working on that hopeless engine. I had every resource in the world. Money, people, time. But I could not give it to anyone here. "I'll have someone bring her one of mine."

"She asked me to fix it," he said, not looking up from the beat-up four-cylinder engine. "I'm going to listen to what she wants. You might consider doing the same, son."

"Oh, fuck you, Pops. You can't fix the past by getting Annie to love you. And don't call me 'son,'" I said, and went back to my trailer.

But the ghosts only followed.

I FORGOT ABOUT MARGARET COMING, AND THE KNOCK ON THE door threw me out of a nap I hadn't meant to take.

"Hey," I said, opening the door to let her in.

She stood there surrounded by a moat of her favorite cloth grocery bags. "This place is a shit hole," she said.

Maybe it was the nap, or the thing with Hero Cop, but I was

inordinately happy to see her and her grocery bags and judg-
mental eye.

"Well, it's *my* shit hole. Come on in." She came inside and
eyed the trailer like it was the scene of a crime.

"Really?" she asked. "All that money you got and you can't
get her out of here?"

"I'm trying." Though my efforts were totally suspect.

"Not hard enough," she muttered, and handed me the back-
pack where I kept my laptop and mobile office things.

I started setting up my office at the dinette table. The guys
were holding down the fort at the garage and sending me the
results on the engine testing, but the software wasn't on my
phone.

Blake had come to the hospital that first night, storming into
my room demanding justice and ice chips and a better room, like
the old friend he was. What he couldn't get done with his
Southern-boy charm, he got done with money. But since I'd
emailed to tell him I'd be staying at the trailer park, he'd re-
verted to frustrated business partner.

I didn't blame him, but there wasn't much I could do. Annie
and her safety came before all things.

Once the laptop was booting up, I opened one of the other
bags to help Margaret unload food.

I could feel her sideways glance. "What are you doing?" she
asked.

"Helping you unload stuff."

"You feeling all right?" she asked.

I ignored her. Was I really such a dick that I'd never helped
her unload groceries?

Probably.

"That one is not for you." Margaret stopped me as I pulled
a book out of one of the bags.

It was a UNC course book. "You going back to school?"

Margaret took it out of my hands and put it back in the bag.
And then, as if that wasn't good enough, she took the bag and
put it over by the door. "That's my granddaughter's course book.
I'm giving it to Annie."

Annie and college.

Damn. Of course. Leave it to Margaret to think of exactly
the right thing.

"That's a real good idea."

Everyone was doing a better job of looking after Annie than
I was.

Annie should go to college. She would soak up education
and knowledge and opportunity like she did everything else. In
fact, Annie and Margaret's granddaughter were probably not
that far apart in age. They could be friends.

Grant the Hero Cop could visit her on weekends.

It was the future she should have.

I took my kit bag into the bathroom, where it was all I could
do not to heave it against the mirror just to see it shatter. Just to
see something break.

Blake's brother, Phil, had done that at the shop, taken a
ratchet set and thrown it against the wall. It had been the final
straw for Phil.

Phil.

Oh shit.

Phil. Blake's brother. Margaret's son. The black-sheep loser
of the family. The black-sheep loser who'd repeatedly hurt Margaret. And I'd asked her to come here, knowing he was here.

So fucking selfish.

We didn't talk about this stuff. Blake did a little, when he'd
asked me to give his brother a chance, for Margaret's sake. But in
the years that I'd known Margaret, in the years that she'd wel-
comed me into her home, taken care of me like one of her own,
we didn't talk about Phil and the destruction he left behind.

Because it was too personal. Too hard. And I didn't want to be witness to Margaret's pain. To anyone's pain.

And because of that I'd brought her here, where she could be hurt all over again.

I came out of the bathroom and watched Margaret try to jigsaw things into my tiny fridge.

"Phil lives here," I said. "Or he did."

Margaret stiffened for just a moment, just a tiny indication that she was surprised or hurt. It gutted me.

"My dad used Phil's phone to call me about Annie, which means he lives here. Or used to."

"Blake told me."

"I haven't seen him," I told her. "I mean I haven't been looking . . ." I had, in all that had happened, totally forgotten about Phil. But looking at Margaret, it was obvious that she hadn't. That she'd driven here thinking she might see him again.

I couldn't imagine how that must have hurt.

"It's okay." I knew she would say that and part of me wanted to let it go, let that little platitude stand. But it wasn't right.

"No. It's not. I'm sorry. I forgot about him and then brought you here where you might see him."

She cocked her head at me and smiled. "I don't think I've ever heard you apologize."

"Of course you have."

"No." She shook her head. "I haven't. It's nice. And Phil . . ." She sighed. Looking at her in the tiny kitchen, her blond-gray hair back in its frizzy bun, her capable hands working, constantly working, like a magician using distraction, I could see her broken heart. "He . . . he never wanted anyone to see all the parts of his life. He kept everything separate. All the time. And that included me. Since he was in grade school he made it clear he doesn't want me in his life. He made that clear when you fired him. If he saw me here, I imagine he'd just look the other way."

"I really wished it had worked out," I said. "The job. I wish we'd been able to give him a new start. Like you and Miguel gave me."

Margaret leaned back against the counter. "I have three children, Dylan. And all of them made mistakes. But Blake and Christine, they're good people who at one time in their lives did bad things. Phil . . . He was always mean. Always a victim. Nothing was ever good enough for him. Certainly not me. And I tried, Dylan. For years I tried, but he is not interested in being my son. And I don't think it will ever stop hurting or I'll ever stop feeling like I could have done more, but at some point you just have to understand you can't make it happen. You can't force yourself on someone who doesn't want you no matter if they're family."

"I know," I said.

"I watched you for that year after you got out of jail," she said. "I watched you trying to stay connected with Max despite how he kept pushing you away. Miguel used to want to try to stop you from doing it. Forbid you from contacting your brother or trying to go and see him—"

I laughed and shook my head. Nothing would have stopped me.

"I know," she said with a smile. "But that was Miguel. He meant well."

"In the end," I said, "it just didn't matter. Max didn't want me around."

"Some people are just poison to other people."

Like you and Annie. You're bad for her and you're just too chickenshit to tell her.

"Are you going to be all right here?"

"Well, I'm living in a trailer park next to my dad, so I can't say I'm moving up in the world." I tried to make it a joke, but neither of us laughed.

"Why can't you just come home?" she asked.

I thought of that cop and his chin and the way he didn't look at Annie's see-through shirt, the pink of her hard nipples. I thought of that book he gave her. Some survivor manifesto bullshit.

Yeah? That voice was getting uglier in the back of my head. *And your method of fucking her into better mental health is going so well?*

There were undoubtedly better people to take care of her. And maybe Annie was right; maybe she didn't need anyone worrying about her. And I didn't know how to live in this place, next to my dad, without going a little crazy. What happened at the swimming hole seemed proof of that.

"I will," I said. But I didn't know when or if I would be alone when I got there.

"Well, your cupboards are full," Margaret said. "And you got some clean clothes."

"Thank you."

"I think you're crazy staying here, but I get it."

I let Margaret cluck over me. Mother me from the far edges of my life, because it felt nice, if not novel, to have someone do that. But there were boundaries. There had always been boundaries, since the moment I got out of jail and ended up in her home.

And I took those boundaries and I made them rules. Iron-clad. For years.

But in this crappy little trailer, on the edge of a swamp, she smashed right through all of them and put her arms around me.

For a second I was stunned. Hugs just didn't happen in my life. But as she squeezed me, careful of my stitches, I slowly lifted my hands and put them on her back. I awkwardly patted her shoulder.

"Thank you," I said, and then it was over. She pushed herself away and picked up her keys and her purse and worked very hard not to look me in the eyes.

Because her eyes were filled with tears.

I didn't have the slightest idea how to ease whatever pain she was feeling.

"I think I got everything you need," she said. "Call if there's anything else."

"I will," I said.

She grabbed the bag of food for Annie and I nearly told her to leave it. That I would give it to her, but I bit the words back. Margaret looked at me, one of her eyebrows raised. "Did you want to take this to her?"

I shook my head. "I've got some work to do. She'll probably be glad to see you."

"Did something happen?" she asked. "Between the two of you?"

"Nothing I'm going to tell you about," I said with a forced and awkward smile that she saw right through.

Margaret left and I sat down with my laptop, pushing thoughts of Annie to the periphery.

Because I wasn't sure if I was a good person who did some bad things or a bad person who'd done some good. I had no damn idea.

But Annie deserved someone good. And I used to think I could be the guy to give it to her. But it looked like that was only a dream.

14

ANNIE

ANNIE TOOK THE BAG MARGARET HANDED TO HER.

"Margaret." She looked down at the overstuffed bag. "This is too much."

"It's hardly enough, but it will get you through the week."

Margaret had a totally overblown sense of how much Annie could eat. But the generosity was awesome and she would not say no. Not when she could see chocolate chip cookies in a big Ziploc bag on top.

"Did you see Dylan?" she asked. "He's right next—"

"I stocked his cupboards," she said. "And brought him some stuff for work."

How does he seem? she wanted to ask. *Was he wrecked? As wrecked as me by what we'd done? By the way we felt?*

She imagined that if he was at all affected, he was very good at hiding it.

And if for some reason Margaret knew that Dylan was wrecked or hurting, she would not tell Annie about it. Not one word. Margaret made it very clear where her loyalties sat.

"Do you want to come in?" Annie asked. "I have coffee."

"No." Margaret shook her head. She seemed very sad today. "I need to head on back. You take care of yourself."

"Thank you."

Margaret nodded and then stepped away, but then she stopped and turned back to face Annie.

"Remember what I said about Dylan," Margaret said, hitching her purse up higher on her shoulder, "when I dropped you off here before?"

"You said to stay away from him. He'd been hurt enough. And that I would only get hurt, too."

I should have listened, she thought. *I wish I'd listened.*

Margaret nodded, her lips pressed tight. "I was wrong," she said. "Keep trying. It will be worth it. A man like him, he'll push away everything he wants because he doesn't think he deserves it."

"Maybe he deserves more than me," Annie said.

Margaret started to sparkle again. Just a little. Like whatever grief had been wearing her down was lifting off of her, one piece at a time.

"I don't think so," she said.

After Margaret left, Annie took the bag inside and set it down on the table. She was still shattered from this morning at the swimming hole. And exhausted by the thoughts in her head.

He's pushing you away with both hands, he's yelling stop at the top of his lungs, and you are ignoring it. And worse, you're angry at him for having made the choice that doesn't happen to be you.

And it was awesome to make choices, after years of having none, but what happens when your choices hurt someone else? she thought. Where is the pride in that? Or if your choice doesn't choose you?

That thing he wasn't telling her . . . she didn't know what it was. But she could feel that it was bad. And the worst thing she could think of was that it was over between them.

Stop, she thought, *you're going to make yourself crazy.*

There was a thick book tucked down the side of the bag and she pulled it out. Something about her had people giving her books these days, and she wasn't complaining.

It was a UNC undergraduate course book.

College.

She sat down on the settee and flipped it open. The pictures of smiling kids smiling at one another didn't do much for her, and neither did courses about comparative political thought.

But Introduction to Developmental Psychology did. And Human Behavior in the Social Environment. And she wasn't totally sure what Racial Justice & Cultural Intersectionality of Oppression was, but she wanted to know.

There were religion courses. Lots of them. She flipped through pages.

She'd always wondered about Buddhism.

College wasn't something she'd ever considered. It had never been an option for her. Ever.

Now, suddenly, it was. It was something she could do.

Annie's plan for the afternoon had been to go into town for groceries, but thanks to Margaret she didn't need to shop. But she would go in to the library and look up some real estate agents back home. She could start selling off the acreage and make a decision about the house later.

With the money, she could go to college.

Law school!

The phone she'd set on the kitchen counter started to buzz and her heart leapt at the sound. *Dylan,* it pounded. *Dylan.*

But the number on the face of the phone was not Dylan's. It said unknown.

"Hello?" she said, holding the phone to her ear.

"Annie? Is that you?"

"Joan?" She collapsed backward onto the settee, excited and comforted by the familiar sound of her friend's raspy voice.

"Well, well, you're back at that shit hole."

Annie laughed and realized all the things that Joan didn't know. About Hoyt and Dylan. Even Ben and the cancer. "And you're not. We have a lot we need to catch up on."

"Yeah, we do. Can you meet me?"

"Sure. Are you still working at The Velvet—"

"Listen, I don't know if you and Dylan are still doing that kinky phone sex shit, but listen to me: do not go there."

"Okay, but—"

"It's dangerous. Like bad dangerous and I'm not kidding. Don't go there. Don't let Dylan go there and try to be a hero."

"A hero?"

"Don't go."

"Fine. Fine, but where do you want to meet?"

Joan gave her the name and address of a diner in Cherokee. "Tomorrow morning?" Joan asked.

"Works for me."

Annie hung up and thumbed through the screens until she got to Dylan's number. But she didn't call. Instinct told her to call him, that whatever Joan had to say would affect him, too.

But in the end, she put the phone down. Afraid of hurting him when she only wanted to be close to him.

ANNIE DIDN'T KNOW WHAT TIME IT WAS WHEN THERE WAS A knock at her door, but she had graduated from reading the course book to actually circling classes. She was creating a course load for a college she had not even applied for.

She put her pencil in the spine so she wouldn't lose her place and ran to her door to answer it.

It was Dylan out there in the twilight and her heart squeezed. Her heart squeezed so hard she felt like it might be breaking. He was freshly showered and she could smell his soap on the breeze.

He had keys in his hands, which he flipped back and forth around his finger.

Flip, flip.

He looked like a man on his way somewhere.

A man who was leaving.

It's okay, she told herself, applying pressure to a sudden internal pain. *You never really expected him to be able to stay here.*

It didn't have to mean they were over.

Except it felt like if he left now, they might be.

"Hi," she said and pushed open the door to step outside. The wide world felt crowded with everything they weren't saying, and she couldn't imagine being in the trailer with him.

"Hey. You all right?"

Annie forced herself to smile. "Fine. Margaret brought over this college course book and I'm just reading it."

"Yeah? Anything good?"

"Did you know you could take archery in college?"

His chuckle forced her to look away, up at the stars. As far away as he was.

"You going to be an archer?"

"I'm thinking about it."

"Anything else in there look good?"

Yes. All of it. Every course looks like an opportunity. A chance I never thought I'd have.

"There are a few things," she said, holding back her enthusiasm, pulling herself away from him one small piece at a time. Just for safety. Just until she knew what was happening. "Psychology. Social work. Law, maybe."

"Law?"

"Well, only if the archery thing doesn't work out."

They both chuckled. And he flipped that key again.

Flip, flip.

"Did you go to school?" she asked, suddenly trying to make him stay. Even if it was just to talk to her.

"College? Hell no. I got my GED in jail."

"Where'd you get so smart about cars?" she asked. "And business."

"When I was a kid, Pops always had something up on blocks. I learned the basics from him. And the first few months of juvie they had a program for guys to learn a trade, and this mechanic would come in and show us how to change oil and rotate tires. He saw that I had a knack and taught me some pretty advanced stuff."

"It stopped after the first few months?"

"You had to be on good behavior. Those fights I was getting in made it so I couldn't go."

"That must have been hard."

"All of it was hard, Annie. Hard is what I know."

And that right there was the truth of Dylan Daniels. Hard was what he knew, so easy was something he couldn't trust. Soft and tender and careful—those things had no place in his life.

"Officer Davies," she said, and his attention on her focused. Sharpened. He watched her so carefully, as if she were something he could read. But she didn't know what he was looking for. "That cop that was here. He brought me a book, too. About surviving post-traumatic stress."

Flip, flip, went those keys.

"That's good. Probably real good."

Every instinct was telling her not to broach this subject with him, that it would not go well. That it would, in fact, be disastrous. It already looked like he was looking for a reason to leave and this conversation would give him that reason.

But after what happened at the swimming hole and last night, she wasn't sure what she was preserving by keeping her mouth shut.

And she was done keeping her mouth shut.

"Maybe you should read it, too."

His silence seemed like a straight arm to her chest. A bright flashing sign for her to stay away. To keep out.

I do not want you here, so stop pushing your way in.

Flip, flip.

"I'm going to The Velvet Touch."

She blinked. "The strip club?"

Her face must have shown her horror, the hurt that sank down deep into her bones.

"It's not what you think," he said quickly.

"Then what is it?"

"You told me you didn't want to hear this. Not today."

Breath shuddered out of her body. "Well, today is almost over, isn't it?"

Flip, flip.

Annie grabbed his hands. Stopping the keys. Her nerves tautened to the point of snapping. The contact felt good, though. His hands were warm and rough. Familiar. And so she kept holding them.

"Yesterday, a guy named Rabbit came to visit Ben."

"His name is Rabbit?"

"No, I think his name is Ryan Abbot, but he's been called Rabbit for as long as I've known him."

"And this rabbit, is he soft and cuddly?" she asked, reaching for a joke, anything to snap this tension between them. Nothing had been right since coming here and she didn't know how to make it better.

"No. He's an unstable sociopath."

"But does he like carrots?"

"This isn't funny, Annie. Rabbit and Max are in the Skulls together and Max has gone missing."

"But your brother was here, at Ben's trailer. Five nights ago."

"And he's been gone since."

"And this Rabbit guy, he's worried?"

"That's one way of putting it. Also, homicidal and unpredictable and fucking nuts."

"What does this have to do with you? You said you haven't heard from your brother in years."

"Rabbit wants me to find him, make him come back." He took a deep breath and pulled his hand from hers. "And if I don't, he's threatened you and Margaret and Blake and everyone else in my life."

For a second the words didn't make sense. Like at school when they'd do a tornado drill and the siren would go off. For a second it was as if the noise paralyzed everyone.

Dylan's words were like that—paralyzing. But only for a second.

"Oh my God, Dylan—" She reached for him, but he stepped back. Away from her. And she stopped. Trembling on her bare feet, she stopped.

"I called Max last night and I think he called me back this morning. Apparently they hang out at The Velvet Touch and I was there last night—"

"Last night?"

"Before . . . you came over. I lied to you. And I'm going again tonight, but . . . I don't want to lie to you. Not after today. And I need you to take this." From the back of his pants he pulled a gun. Annie jerked back so fast she tripped over her feet, but he grabbed her hands and pressed the gun against her palms.

"No," she said. "No, I'm not taking this—"

"I need to know you're safe. And if you won't leave, you have to have this."

"Ben—"

"Is an old man who couldn't protect you the first time."

He curled her fingers around the cold metal and held them there like they might stick with enough pressure. "For me, Annie. Please."

She swallowed. "Okay," she finally said, and he let go of her hands. The gun was heavy.

"Listen," she said, staring down at that gun. "I wanted to tell you I'm sorry."

"For what?"

"For . . ." She swallowed. "For earlier today and for last night. Ignoring you when you said no. For forcing you into something you didn't want."

"Are you talking about sex?"

"You didn't want it. I mean, in the end, I guess, you wanted it. But—"

"You guess?" His smile, crooked and endearing, was a balm to her insecurity.

"Dylan. I'm trying to say I'm sorry for forcing the issue."

"Baby, I'm going to want to have sex with you until the day I die—I just don't know if it's a good idea." He took a deep breath. "That cop . . . Officer Davies? He seems like a nice guy."

Every hair on her body stood up. She knew what he was about to do, could see the words forming in his head. And after what he'd told her about Rabbit and Max, she even understood that it made sense to him.

"Dylan!"

"No, listen to me. You say you care how I feel and what I think, so that means listening to me even when you don't want to. That cop who brought you the book, he's the kind of guy you should be with. The kind of guy who would give you the life you deserve. Treat you the way you should be treated."

"Why aren't you? If you are what I want?"

"Because I'm the guy who fucks you without a condom and shoves his finger in your ass."

Just the words made her crazy. Her body got hot, wet in an instant. For him. Only him. "I liked that. I liked all of that."

"You deserve—"

"What do *you* deserve?" she interrupted.

He blinked as if she'd just punched him. Just stunned him. "What are you talking about?"

"Do you deserve to be happy? To be loved?"

"This isn't love," he said.

Oh, it hurt. It hurt that he might actually believe it. That one day down here with his family and he was sure somehow that there was no more of the two of them. Together.

I think it is love, she thought, but could not say. Not yet. Maybe not ever. She wasn't brave enough in the face of the impassivity he was able to put on and take off at will.

Flip, flip.

"Good night," he said.

Holding his gun, she watched him get into his car and drive away. For too long she'd done what other people told her to do. She'd acquiesced and surrendered.

His brake lights flashed red as he left the trailer park, heading out to the highway and the strip club past that.

Not this time, she thought.

This time she was going to fight.

15

DYLAN

THE VELVET TOUCH PARKING LOT WAS FULL OF MINIVANS AND big rigs. No motorcycles to be seen.

Last night I sat out here, across from the front door, because of Annie. Because it felt wrong to go inside. But tonight, I didn't have time to waste; I had to go in and talk to people. Find out if anyone here had seen my brother.

The minute the doorman looked me up and down I was acutely aware of my scars. And the thing with my scars in this situation, combined with my size and my general anger—they made me a guy to be wary of. A guy to watch.

"Hey," I said to the doorman.

"Two-drink minimum," he mumbled at me, staring at my face like it was magnetic and he had no choice.

"I'm looking for a guy—"

"Then you're in the wrong place," the bouncer said.

"A biker. People call him Logsy."

"Two-drink minimum." That was it. All he said. He took my money, stamped my hand, and I walked into the club feeling like the shit creek I'd somehow stumbled into was way deeper than I'd thought.

Inside, The Velvet Touch was like every second-rate strip club I'd ever been in.

The girls looked the same, so did the chairs and the stage. The bouncers with black glasses and leather jackets with worn gray seams. Their practiced sneers very nearly made me smile.

I knew before I went in that my brother wasn't going to be here. Not now. Maybe not at all.

But I couldn't go back to the trailer park. Not without knowing something.

I stepped up onto the small raised seating area in the back of the club, hoping I had a good angle to watch everything without drawing too much attention to myself.

"Hey, sugar." A woman in red lingerie approached me with a tray of shots that glowed in the black light. Behind her a blonde flipped herself upside down on a pole. "Want a drink?"

"Club soda with lime," I said.

"You bet," she said, the smile turning down at the corners.

A few minutes later the waitress came back with the club soda. "Tab?" she asked.

"No thanks." I gave her a twenty and held up my hand when she began to give me change. "Spread the word, I'm not interested in any company."

"Sure," she said, slipping the twenty into the Hello Kitty pencil case on her tray.

"I'm looking for a guy named Max—they call him Logsy," I said. "Part of the motorcycle club that comes in here."

The girl's face was utterly still. Carefully benign. She shook her head, pursing her lips. "Don't know the guy."

She was lying to me. And not very well. Her hands on her tray were white-knuckled.

"Black hair. Blue eyes? Tall and thin?" I asked, giving her a chance to tell the truth.

"Doesn't ring a bell, baby," she said.

I wasn't going to force the issue. If I was going to have to come back tomorrow night and the night after that, it would be better to have a friend here.

"Thanks," I said.

"No problem. You should think about getting a lap dance."

An hour later she brought me another club soda and my phone buzzed. I pulled it out of my pocket and kept it low under my table. There were a lot of "no cellphone" signs posted around the place and I didn't need any trouble.

It was a text. A picture from Annie.

It took a second, but then I realized the pale objects were her legs. And her arm was stretched down her naked belly, her hand buried beneath that blue underwear of hers. Her wrist created a gap between her belly and the top of her underwear and I could see her hand, her fingers, a blur, against the shaved skin of her pussy.

She was touching herself. Making herself come.

Thinking of you, she texted. Only of you.

I put my phone back in my pocket. Like it was a loaded gun, I put it away.

But that picture was burned into my brain, no matter how I tried to get rid of it.

I was shaking. The urge to get back to her nearly had me on my feet.

I should pay a woman to take off her clothes, to sit on my lap and grind her ass against me. I should pay her more to take me back into that VIP room and suck my dick. Or let me fuck her.

I should do all of that and take it home to Annie. Tell her what kind of guy I am. Let her smell it on my skin. My fingers.

It would work, too. It would hurt her enough to make me pushing her away stick.

I closed my eyes, tired of the music. Of the strange floral/ musky smell of this place.

"Hey, baby. You want something else?" The waitress was back, her red lingerie glaring under the lights. Her skin glimmered like gold, like she'd dusted her whole body with something, and everything about her was carefully constructed to be appealing. To be the most basely sexy. From her tits to her hair to her mile-long eyelashes and skyscraper shoes.

Everything fake, a hard shell of a costume. A disguise.

And I ached for Annie. Deep inside my bones I ached for her.

What the fuck am I doing? I wondered. Finally, I get something real in my life, something totally authentic, and I push it away.

"I'm good," I said to the waitress. I handed her a few more bills and stopped fighting. I headed for the exit.

And Annie.

The bouncer from before was still there, his arms crossed over his chest.

"Good night," I said, giving him another shot to stare at the side of my face.

"Around back," he said as I pushed open the door.

"What?"

"Guys you're looking for, those motorcycle assholes, they just got here and they're out back. But listen, if I was you, I wouldn't go looking for that kind of trouble."

Lucky for me, what was around back was exactly my kind of trouble.

I nodded at the man in thanks and gave him a twenty, hoping that if I needed some help that would be enough to pull him onto my side. I headed left once I was outside. The thumping bass line of the music inside the club could still be heard. I felt it on the bottoms of my feet.

My life would become better if Max was there. I could sleep through the night without worrying about Rabbit and Annie, and the starter ulcer in my gut might go away. But there was a big part of me that did not want to see Max.

Not now. Not ever again.

It had taken a long time for the wound to heal. For the scab to get thick enough that it didn't split open every time I saw a kid riding bitch on the back of an older boy's bike. Or ate hot cornbread with too much butter.

And seeing him again—I didn't know what would happen. What fucking garbage would come spilling out.

The asphalt of the parking lot gave way to loose gravel as I walked to the end of the building. I could hear something happening back there, just around the corner. Men were yelling, some were laughing. I recognized a few of the voices.

Clock and Grapes and BLJ—they'd been Pops's best friends. His "brothers."

I'd grown up with them in my home. Their thunderous hands patting me on the shoulder, or shoving me out of the room.

One of them sold Mom drugs behind Pops's back, at least twice. All of them might have slept with her.

Fucking brothers.

I was getting good and pissed off, which probably wasn't the best head space for walking into a group of stone-cold outlaws, when a man stepped out from around the corner.

A hand-rolled cigarette glowing in the darkness.

I couldn't see his face or his body. Just his hand, the rings on his fingers as he lifted the smoke to his mouth. But I knew.

Max.

The first time Max went away to juvie, I'd been twelve. And it had been hard for me. Not that I didn't understand, because I understood jail. I'd grown up with the people in my life leaving and coming back from jail all the time.

No, it was hard because for my entire life I'd been Max's kid brother. Not Big Ben's son, or Maria's boy. But Max's brother. And when he went away I didn't know who I was. Every night, I climbed the fire escape and shimmied up to the roof of our apartment building and I tried to feel him out there in all the darkness, behind the cement and iron that kept him away from me. And when he came out, I didn't let him out of my sight. I sat outside the bathroom for him.

I followed him on dates. Tagged along when he started stealing cars.

Which was how everything started.

It wasn't until I started racing that I figured out who I was without him.

Then that was taken from me, too.

So then I sat alone on that mountain, so full of holes and hurt I had no idea who I was. Until Annie answered that phone.

"Max?"

The hand paused, the cherry of the smoke went bright red, and then Max stepped out of the shadows and faced me.

He was lean. Like he'd been whittled and worn down to the essentials. To bone and sinew and survival. His eyes, blue like Mom's, were fever bright.

"Dylan?"

I just stared at him, absorbing the reality of my criminal brother. His hair was long and black, tied back at his neck. He had a close-cropped beard that grew into a longer point at his chin. Like one of those drawings of Shakespeare in textbooks. His face was the same, those cheekbones and jawline. He was almost pretty. Elegant.

I looked like a thug with a nice mouth. Max looked like an angel on his way to hell.

Actually, he looked like Mom. Acted like Mom, too. All impulse. No Plan B.

Whatever Rabbit was afraid of, whatever worst-case scenario he envisioned in his little brain, there was a really good likelihood it would happen. Because Max had a burn-it-all-to-the-ground gene.

But he was here. For the first time in nine years, it was my brother standing right in front of me. And I was pissed. I was.

But I was a lot of other things, too. Way too many to count. And the memories, they fucking swarmed. Jumping the fence at the Sixth Street pool so we could go skinny-dipping on hot summer nights. Stealing fireworks from that stand down by the beach and nearly blowing our hands off on the Fourth of July. Sleeping on the couch at his girlfriend's house when shit got bad between Mom and Pops. Or if he didn't have a girlfriend, we'd take blankets out into the woods and build a fire and pretend to be camping.

Stealing cars. Winning races. The weight of his arm over my shoulder and the pride in his voice when he called me brother.

This guy standing in front of me with the tattoos and the silver jewelry, the president patch on his cut. This guy used to make sure I did my homework. And that I got to school on time.

He stepped toward me and I backed up, unsure of what he was going to do.

Max was, after all, the first person ever to beat me up. I'd been eight, he'd been twelve. And he broke my nose.

"Scared, little brother?" He flicked the smoke down into the gravel and stepped on it.

Grinning, he turned toward the wall, unzipped his pants, and had a piss against the building.

I glanced away, and for a second I nearly smiled.

"Where have you been?" I asked, as if a lifetime hadn't passed since the last time we saw each other. I didn't know how to sift through that shit, how to talk about it. So, I didn't.

The now was easier. Simpler. In the now, this guy wasn't my brother. I hadn't loved him, missed him, and mourned him for years.

He was just some asshole complicating my life.

"Road trip," he said, zipping back up.

"And you couldn't let anyone know?"

"I don't need to let anyone know," he said. "It's my life and I do what I want."

"Rabbit thought you split, like, for good. The deal—"

Max took one step closer to me; his eyes narrowed and my bones got cold. "You don't know nothing about any deal. Not one thing. You got it?"

"Yeah."

"I'm not kidding."

"I don't know anything about anything," I said, lifting my hands.

Max took a deep breath and reached into his pockets for another smoke.

Suddenly I wondered how bad things really were here. If he'd left so he could save himself. And I'd pulled him right back in.

But that wasn't Max's style. Self-preservation wasn't a word he understood.

"Where the hell did you go?"

"I went to visit Mom's grave."

"*What?*" Of all the things I might have guessed—three-day bender, drug-running trip to Mexico, torturing a Rotten Bastard soldier in a Smoky Mountain cabin—none of them had anything to do with Mom.

He shrugged and lit his smoke. Took a long pull and exhaled a thick plume.

The now was shattered and the asshole was my brother again.

"Why?" I asked.

"Never been. Have you?"

"No."

It never occurred to me to go. She left when I went to jail and she never looked back. I did the same.

"It's nice. Aunt Louisa shelled out some cash. Tombstone doesn't say 'beloved wife and mother,' though. I guess she was only a sister there at the end."

"It's . . . she's buried in Arizona." He must have gotten there, seen the grave, and turned back around to make it in three days.

Max nodded, kicking a rock up onto the asphalt a few feet away. He did it again. One after the other, each rock landing on the asphalt. "Long days on the road. Not much time for phone calls."

"But you got my messages?"

"Yours. Rabbit's."

"Would have saved us a lot of trouble if you'd just called that asshole back," I said.

Right in front of my foot there was a stone, about the right size. I nudged it with my toe and then kicked it toward the asphalt. It landed about a foot short.

Max grinned at me. "You gotta give it some lift."

The next one I kicked landed on the asphalt.

Max kicked again and I took a step to the left, where there were bigger stones.

"So, I guess Pops called you, too? That's why you're here?" he asked. "Gotta say, I never thought you'd give a shit about Pops and cancer."

"I *don't* give a shit," I said. I kicked two stones at the same time, both of them landed on the asphalt. "I'm here because Rabbit threatened to kill everyone in my life if I didn't find you. Make you come back."

"That's a little extreme, even for Rabbit."

"I'm not laughing, Max." We weren't kicking stones anymore. We were staring at each other. I had about twenty pounds on him, but there was no question who'd win if we got into it. Max fought dirty and I'd long ago lost the instinct.

But I wanted to fight him. I wanted to hurt him.

"Yeah, I got that. Well, good work, Dylan. You found me. Everyone in your life is safe." He stepped away like we were done, like after nine years that was all he had to say to me.

I grabbed his arm and both of us froze.

"Are you safe?" I asked.

"You want to be careful, *hermano*," he whispered, all threat and menace. He would slice me open, brother or not. "Very careful."

"Rabbit says you're going to get yourself killed."

"Isn't that what we're all doing?" he said with that lunatic smile of his. "Some of us are just better at it than others."

"I'm rich, Max. Like richer than you can even believe. I can send you away, so far away from this shit—"

Max took one gliding step toward me, so close I could smell the tobacco and fire on his breath. The burn of whiskey he must have had before. "Get in your fancy car, take that pretty blond girl you're fucking, and go back to your mountain. Go back to forgetting about me."

"How do you know . . . ?" I stopped, suddenly scared of revealing too much. Because while he was my brother, he was also the king of these cutthroats and I couldn't trust any of them.

"About the girl?" he asked. "Rabbit told me—strippers and bikers are all a bunch of gossips. Said she plugged her husband after he stabbed you. That's some hard-core shit, right there."

"It was."

"You like her?" Max asked, revealing another glimpse of the guy I used to know. The brother I loved. And the impulse to tell my brother everything—how she made my heart stop, and she made me wish I were different and she taught me to reach into the world with some care and some grace—was hard to fight. But I did.

And I was glad, too, when he blinked and the glimpse was over and the killer was back. The temptation to unburden myself vanished with him.

"Don't answer that," he said. "Just take her and go, Dylan."

"No," I said. Maybe because I'd never said no before. Nine years ago when he pushed me out of his life for good, I should have said no. But I didn't. Because it was easier. Because I wanted something better for myself. Because I was tired of wanting more from him than he ever wanted from me.

But I was saying no now.

"What the fuck is wrong with you?" he asked. "Shit is happening exactly the way it should. Mom, dead. Dad, dying. You're living large as some hotshot engine builder. Get your head right and realize everything is exactly the way it should be."

"Don't you want something else?"

"No. I got what I want. I got exactly what I deserve."

And then he was gone, back around the corner. I heard someone shout out to him and Max shouted back and the world just kept on spinning.

16

DYLAN

THE WHOLE DRIVE HOME I TOLD MYSELF I WOULD STAY AWAY from Annie.

That seeing my brother had made me raw. Too raw.

Unfit for her.

I walked directly from my car to my trailer. I even kicked off my shoes. But when I went to charge my phone, I could not resist looking at the picture she'd sent.

And looking at it, her pale flesh, her hands between her legs, only made me worse. More . . . dangerous.

But in the end, even while I was telling myself not to, I grabbed two condoms from the stash in the bathroom and walked straight to her trailer door. In the darkest part of the night. The darkest thoughts running through my head.

You're gonna scare her, I told myself. *Knocks on the door in the middle of the night never bring good news.*

Well, I'm not fucking good news, am I?

I knocked and waited, my hands braced on the cool metal of

her RV. I heard a small thump and the sound of her padding to the door, and I hung my head.

Resigned to this dark thing.

The door opened and there she was, rumpled and sweet. Her hair messy, her eyes barely open.

"Dylan?"

"Open the door, Annie."

Something in my voice, some command, some need I was barely keeping in line, must have penetrated and her eyes opened wide. Her mouth, those sweet lips, opened, revealing the wet edge of her tongue. The shine of her teeth.

Fuck. That mouth . . .

"What are you going to do, Dylan?" she breathed back at me. A challenge. She was not scared and she was not unaware.

"I'm going to fuck you."

Her pale hand, hazy through the screen, reached forward and popped open the door. I threw it open and then slammed it shut behind me once I was inside. Both doors, until it was just us in this trailer.

She wore a tank top and underwear. Nothing else.

I was in jeans and my bare feet. Two condoms in my back pocket.

She stepped back. And then again until she bumped into the kitchen counter and stopped.

Our eyes locked in the darkness, the heat around us thick. I kept coming at her until my belly was touching hers. Her breasts, so small and perfect, were against my chest. Her breath in my mouth.

I wedged my thigh between hers, pressing the harsh denim into the soft skin at her crotch. Her underwear didn't even register. I could feel her heat through the fabric. Her wet. I pushed harder, lifting her onto her toes, and her eyelids fluttered.

"You like that?"

She didn't answer and I applied more pressure.

"Answer me."

"Y . . . yes."

I'd had this vision of coming in here and pushing her on her knees in front me. I imagined cupping my hand around her head and forcing her to suck my cock until she took every inch of me. Until her eyes watered and begged me to stop.

But I wouldn't stop.

I would use her, like the whores I used to pay after the fire. That's how I would treat her.

That's what I thought I'd do. That had been my plan walking over here. The thoughts made my cock pound.

You think you deserve this? I would ask her, pushing my cock against the back of her throat. *You think you want this?*

But, looking at her now, her total acquiescence, her utter willingness and trust, I couldn't do it. I didn't even want it anymore.

Looking at her, so ready for me, so damn willing, I didn't know what I wanted.

As if she knew I stood on the brink and didn't have the balls to do anything, she took over.

Her hair fell into her eyes as she unbuttoned my pants, lowered the zipper. I wasn't wearing underwear, and my cock and the dark hair around it sprang up.

She jacked me slowly in her fist and I put my hand between her legs, shoving aside the cotton of her underwear with rough, clumsy fingers, to get to her.

I scraped a blunt nail over her clit, making it hard. Making it stand up against the wet flesh of her pussy.

She gasped, her hand a sudden clenching fist around me.

My eyes met hers and with all that willingness, I saw a familiar darkness. Mine. My darkness. Or at least a darkness that looked like mine.

I couldn't shock her. Not if I tried.

"Get on your knees." I groaned, and she did it with graceful surrender. "Suck me." My hands braced against the counter while she sucked me back into her mouth.

And it wasn't my shitty, mean little fantasy. It was better. Because it was real. And she was giving it to me with her whole damn heart.

She took me all the way, until I could feel her throat. Until I could feel her gag.

I pulled back, not wanting her to really hurt herself.

Her mouth popped off me and a line of saliva went from the head of my dick to her mouth and I was insane for her. "Don't," she said. "Don't pull away." She sucked me back into her mouth, her lips spread wide and pressed tight around me.

I pushed harder, farther. Her blue eyes watered and I pulled back, just a little, just enough.

And then she sucked me back again.

Without words we mapped that dark edge between not enough and too much and then, her hands on my ass, my cock in her face, we blurred the line. We made our own rules.

"You like that." I growled, watching her. "You fucking love it. Touch yourself while I fuck your face." I felt the vibration of her throat as she moaned and slipped her fingers between her legs.

It was too much, and I lifted her up onto her feet and spun her around so her hands were braced against the counter. I yanked down her underwear and popped her hips out. She got the message and braced her hands, stepped wider.

"Yes," she whispered, her voice husky from the abuse I'd given her throat. "God, yes. Please, fuck me."

She was already wet. Already hot.

But it wasn't enough.

I got down on my knees behind her and licked her. Sucked her into my mouth. I found her clit, and I rolled it with my tongue. Her legs started trembling and shaking. But I gave her no break. No chance.

She came once and then again. And she was lying against the counter now, unable to hold herself up with her arms. The muscles in her legs twitched under my hands.

I pulled one of the condoms out of my pocket and kicked out of my pants.

A good guy would take her to the bedroom. Make sure she was all right.

That's what Hero Cop would do.

But Hero Cop wouldn't even be here right now.

I put the condom on, grabbed her hips, and drove into her. As deep and as high as I could, and her hand smacked against the sink as she braced herself to take my thrusts. Immediately, she came again. Her muscles clenched down hard on me, her cries loud in the dark trailer.

Five strokes later I was bent over her back, coming in waves. In great, huge spurts that felt like they were being dredged up from my feet. My legs were numb, our bodies covered in sweat.

Her shoulders beneath my chest were shaking and I stepped back, away from her.

Part of me was convinced I'd hurt her. Despite her willingness. Despite her welcome. I'd been too hard. Too rough.

"Annie?"

She stood and slowly turned around. Her tank top was twisted and one breast was revealed, the dark nipple just peeking out. Her face was totally and completely blissed out.

"Was that a booty call?" she asked.

I didn't want to laugh. It didn't seem right. But I couldn't quite stop it. I laughed and took off the condom, tying the end in a knot.

"Here," she said and opened the little cupboard under the sink. I tossed the condom in the white plastic garbage can she had under there.

"Who knew sex in the kitchen would be so practical," she said. She took a deep breath and then another, before reaching down and rearranging her underwear. She winced.

"Are you okay?"

"Sensitive."

"I didn't hurt you?"

"I'm fine. I may not walk straight tomorrow, but I'm fine."

I zipped up my pants, that second condom burning a hole in my back pocket.

"Do you want to stay?" she asked.

"I should probably get back." Oh, that was a shit lie. Get back to what? "But I wanted to tell you . . . ah . . . my brother is back."

"You saw him?"

"Yeah. At the club."

"Dylan," she sighed, and I could hear a world of sympathy in that sigh. I had no barriers against it. Nothing with which to protect myself. So, I just turned my face away, running my hand over the counter.

"Are you okay?" she asked. Still she didn't touch me, and I wanted her to as badly as I couldn't stand it if she did.

"Fine." A lie so worthless there was hardly any point in it. She could see how not fine I was. How broken and shaken and fucked up I was.

It astounded me sometimes how changeable her face could be. And perhaps it was because our relationship started on the phone, that I got to know her so well, so completely, without ever once seeing her face, that now I was fascinated by it. The fleeting reveal of her moods. Her old soul eyes. The skin like moonlight. I could watch her for days and not tire of it.

She seemed to accept the fact that I wasn't going to talk about Max. That I wasn't ready. That I would never be ready, maybe. And I was grateful.

"Do you really want me to do this with Grant?" she asked, stabbing me right in the heart.

Fuck, the idea of that man's hands on her was unthinkable. It broke my brain.

"No."

"Then stop saying stuff like that."

I had a million reasons why that was a bad idea. But none of them seemed to matter.

You're the only one I want.

I didn't know what to say. How to hold that in my hands.

"Dylan?"

"Okay."

"Okay, what?"

"I won't say that anymore."

"Good night," she whispered, and stepped forward and kissed me.

I had no grace. And very little generosity. But what I had, I tried to give to her in that kiss.

I was not the right man for her, but I wanted to be.

And I was humbled by her choice.

17

ANNIE

IN THE MORNING, SHE LEFT HER TRAILER TO FIND HER CAR'S
engine in pieces on Ben's picnic table.

"What are you doing?" she cried, utterly aghast at the engine
wreckage.

"You wanted me to fix it," he said, wiping his hands off on
a filthy rag. She couldn't see any improvement in the cleanliness
of his hands.

"I thought you would . . . I don't know, change the oil or
something. Not take it apart. I need my car."

"Well, you can't have it," he said, and fished his own keys
out of his pocket. "Take mine. Where you headed?" he asked.

"Into town—I need to run some errands." It was a lie, not a
big one, but still a lie, and she didn't tell it very well.

"Where's Dylan?"

"Sleeping, I imagine." She wasn't sure if last night was a victory for her or not. It felt like it was, like they were inching back
to the place where they should be.

"Well, I . . . I have some errands, too. You care if I tag along?"

It was so obvious what Ben was doing, and she was so touched that she would have hugged him if he weren't so filthy.

"Max is back," she told him, and his relief was obvious. He nearly went white with it. "Dylan saw him last night."

Ben blinked and scrubbed at his hands like getting them clean was all that mattered. "Is Dylan . . . all right?"

"No," she answered truthfully. "But he's trying. And we can all stop worrying about Rabbit."

Ben didn't say anything, just looked over her shoulder at Dylan's trailer before bending back over her engine.

That's all? she thought. *You don't want to say anything else?*

But he remained silent and she got in his truck.

A half hour later, Annie found the diner Joan wanted to meet at on the far side of Cherokee.

Once she was parked, she glanced down at her phone to see if Dylan had texted, but the screen was dark. She'd left him a text, telling him not to worry, that she was only running errands. More of those half-truths they were so good at telling each other.

Somehow she got the sense that he was hitting bedrock. Not rock bottom, but the hard reality of who he was. She'd done it, or was in the process of doing it.

And maybe that was the only way they stood a chance. If they burrowed down through the lies they told themselves, through the doubts and the fears, through the remains of the life they'd been living before—if they got down to the bedrock of who they really were—maybe they stood a chance.

Everything else—it was a lie. Maybe not one that they said out loud.

But one that they lived.

Day in and day out, a series of lies about who they were that made their lives livable.

And clearing that out of the way, getting down to the very heart of their own truth—it was uncomfortable. And it was hard.

But it had to happen.

The Butterfly Diner was one of those places that looked like it had been locked in a time capsule. The waitresses all wore pink polyester dress uniforms with maroon aprons. A pie case rotated slowly by the cash register, showing off about twenty different kinds of pies. It smelled like coffee and fried bacon.

Heaven.

One of the waitresses, a blonde with an affection for black eyeliner and a full pot of coffee in her hand, smiled at her.

"Go on and sit anywhere, hon. Someone will be right with you."

"Thanks," Annie said.

There was no sign of Joan. All of the booths were filled with men in construction gear or hikers fresh off the trail, gobbling down giant plates of food.

"Hey," a voice said, and she turned to find another section of booths down the back wall. An old smoking section. In the far corner was a woman with short brown hair covered with a base-ball cap.

"Yes, yes, it's me," the woman said, waving her over. It took her a second, but then, with a start, she recognized Joan.

"Hey," Annie said, sliding into the booth opposite this new version of Joan. "You . . . you changed your look." It wasn't just the hair, though. She had in colored contacts and her eyes were a strange, muddy brown. And she was all covered up. Annie was used to seeing lots of Joan's skin, between the tiny robes and the cleavage-revealing tank tops. But today Joan was wearing baggy jeans and a zipped-up sweatshirt.

She looked older.

And exhausted.

"Split ends," Joan said in her familiar rough, who-gives-a-shit voice. "You enhanced *your* look." She pointed at Annie's face, the bruises she couldn't quite hide under the big glasses she wore. "Dylan didn't do that, did he?"

"No. It's . . . it's a long story."

"Yeah, well, it's a regular story hour here today, ain't it?"

"Are you . . . okay?"

"Peachy. Fucking peachy."

Annie laughed. "It's good to see you."

Annie could see her fighting it, but then Joan smiled, too. "Glad to see you're still alive," she said.

A waitress came by with a coffeepot.

"The coffee is actually great," Joan said. "And so is the pie. Everything else is shit."

"Can we put that on our advertising?" the waitress asked her. She was young, the waitress. She looked like a college student.

"Free of charge," Joan shot back.

"I'd love some coffee." Annie flipped up her cup. The waitress filled Annie's expertly to the brim without spilling a drop.

"How about me?" Joan asked, though her mug was full.

"Suck it," the waitress said and walked away.

"She loves me," Joan joked.

"You want to tell me what is going on?" Annie took a sip, burning her tongue. But it was great despite that.

"I can't tell you much."

"Because you're undercover?" Annie whispered over the table.

Joan stared at her and then laughed. "You do not have a future as a spy, in case you were wondering. But no . . . I'm not undercover. Not anymore."

"Because of the other night? Because of me?"

"No." Joan was quick to assure her. Joan threw a napkin up on the table that she had folded into a very small, very intricate fan. Annie realized there were at least six other napkins folded the same way stacked next to her plastic water glass.

"Joan?" she asked, the sight of those napkins vaguely concerning. "Are you okay?"

"Fine. I'm on leave." She put her hand down over the napkins like they didn't exist if Annie couldn't see them. Or maybe if Joan herself couldn't see them. "It's a long story."

"I have time."

"I don't." Her fake muddy-brown eyes were dead serious and Annie let it go.

"So why are you still here?"

"Vacation. I'm thinking of going camping."

"Did you bring me here just to make jokes?" Annie asked.

Joan blinked up at her. "Wow, look who found her backbone." She leaned forward across the table. "I brought you here to tell you The Velvet Touch is the central meeting point for a man named Mr. Lagan." Joan said the name with a slightly French accent. "Zo, the owner of the strip club, who frankly is a bit of a psychopath, and the Skulls motorcycle club, which would be Max and his little band of brothers. Including one asshole named Rabbit. Max has apparently split, which frankly is the smartest thing he's probably done in his whole life—"

Annie's heart rate doubled and she tried to calm it down with long, slow breaths.

"He's back."

"What?"

"He came back. Last night."

Joan closed her eyes, as though the news actually hurt her. "Well," she breathed. "What's one more dead biker?"

"What the hell is going on, Joan? You're freaking me out."

"Good," Joan said. "You *should* be freaking out. Everyone should be."

"What are they doing at The Velvet Touch? Who is this Lagan guy?"

"Lagan is a self-proclaimed prophet or some shit. A nut job, basically. And he's got this cult out in the woods, young girls, most of whom he rapes and beats and convinces he's their lord and master."

"Why . . . why are they meeting? Is it like a sex ring? Or prostitution?"

"No. God, no. Lagan doesn't share his wives with anyone. He's got a PhD in chemistry, and for years he's been out in the woods cooking up meth and Molly."

"What?"

"MDMA. A pure form of what used to be Ecstasy. Ring any bells?"

Annie stared at her blankly.

"Good God, you really lived in a cave. Drugs. He's cooking up drugs. And now he's going all international and bringing in small planes full of coke, and he's getting the Skulls MC idiots to distribute for him into Florida and Georgia. But things are not going well between the three parties."

Almost all of this was going over Annie's head, but she got the gist that this was bad. Really bad.

"Who are the DEA after?"

"Lagan. Lagan is the one I want. He's . . . he's the devil."

Annie was a little scared of Joan in that moment. Scared of the light in her eyes. Unholy and fanatic.

"Why are you telling me this?" she asked.

"You need to tell Ben that he has to cut ties with Max. No bullshit this time. He does not want to get pulled in with this shit. And frankly, it would be a good idea for him to move on."

"Move on? Like leave?"

Joan nodded.

"He won't . . . He can't. He's dying."

"What?"

"Cancer."

Joan rubbed her hands over her face for a long minute. "Shit. Dylan can't get him to move—"

"Dylan's there now, too."

"What?" She dropped her hands. "You're all there now? How the hell did that happen?"

"When I got back from Dylan's after that night, Hoyt, my ex-husband, was there."

Joan sat back, her arms braced straight against the table, her mouth dropped open. "Does that explain the eye?"

"Yeah, it explains the eye."

Annie hadn't told this story, and frankly, she didn't know how to start. Or where to start. Nothing felt right in her mouth. It all seemed so stupidly dramatic. Previous to this one night, nothing in her life had much happened, and then suddenly it was as if she'd landed in a soap opera. And now the soap opera had a motorcycle club and a drug-dealing child rapist and—

"I shot him."

The words exploded in the room. No one reacted. No one probably even heard her, but it seemed like she'd screamed it, and she felt the aftershock with her whole body.

"That sounds so crazy when I say it out loud. I shot him." She lifted her coffee cup but it was empty. Probably for the best; her hands were shaking so hard, she'd spill it everywhere. "I haven't talked about it with anyone who wasn't a cop or actually there . . ."

Joan cupped her hand over hers, lowering the mug to the table. Annie had shocked her, and for some reason, that shocked Annie all over again.

"You need to start from the beginning."

Which beginning? Where did Annie McKay start? That farm in Oklahoma? Or in the trailer? Was it a choice she could make? Could she choose her own starting point? Because if she could, she'd pick the trailer. She'd pick the freedom of choice, even with its rough edges.

"Okay, clearly you need a drink," Joan said. "Like a real one."

"Here? Do they serve liquor?"

"Not officially."

Joan looked up and caught the waitress's eye. "A bottle," she

mouthed, and the waitress nodded and brought over more coffee, filling the mugs only halfway this time, and then from her
apron, she slipped Joan a small bottle of whiskey.

"Thanks," Joan said. "Add it to my bill."

"Joy."

Joan poured a shot of whiskey into their coffees and then
tucked the bottle beside her next to the wall.

"Now, tell me what happened."

AN HOUR, A PIECE OF LEMON MERINGUE PIE, AND ANOTHER
shot of whiskey later, the story was out. Every violent and surreal inch of it.

"Holy shit, Annie," Joan said. "You okay?"

"Sometimes more than others."

"And Dylan?"

"We're . . . I think we're figuring things out." That seemed
like a very adult thing to say. Utterly accurate, without revealing
how little she understood about what was happening between
her and Dylan.

"And what about that shit-box Phil?"

"I haven't seen him." She ran the side of her fork across the
plate to get the last of the meringue. Joan had been right—the
pie was awesome. And she stress-ate the whole damn thing. "Or
Tiffany."

"Fucking Tiffany," Joan breathed, pouring more whiskey in
her cup. There was no coffee now; she was just drinking shots
out of a coffee cup.

Silent, Annie pushed the empty plate away.

"You're not jumping to her defense?" Joan asked.

Annie shrugged. "He would have killed me," she said. "And
even if she didn't think that would happen, she knew he'd beat
the shit out of me and she didn't do anything to stop it. She
might have even pointed the way to my trailer, I don't know."

Annie got up from the booth, suddenly tired of thinking and talking about her life. There was only so much reflection a girl could take. "I'm going to the bathroom."

In the restroom she splashed water on her face and checked her messages; still nothing from Dylan.

His silence seemed ominous.

When she went back out to the booth, it was empty. There was a twenty-dollar bill on the table next to a note scrawled across her paper placemat.

Be careful.

That was it.

Annie looked around and caught sight of their waitress outside, standing beside a little blue sedan. The light was reflecting off the windshield, so Annie couldn't see clearly, but she thought it was Joan in the driver's seat.

A woman's hand reached up out of the window and grabbed the waitress's apron, clenching it in her fist. The waitress stumbled as she was pulled forward, bracing one hand against the roof of the car, and then, she bent down and the driver leaned forward—definitely Joan. And the two kissed.

It wasn't friendly. Or see you later. Or thanks for the pie.

Like one of them was leaving and never coming back, that's how they kissed.

The waitress grabbed the back of Joan's head, knocking off the hat. Annie could see them clenching at each other with white knuckles, and then as quickly as it started, it ended. The waitress stood up. Joan reached for her, but she stepped away again. And then she turned, head down, and walked back to the restaurant.

After a long moment, Joan drove off.

Annie stood beside the table like she'd been turned to stone and the waitress came back. Her eyes hard despite the tears clinging to her lashes.

"Your friend is an asshole," she muttered, grabbing up the twenty on the table.

"I know."

"And," she said, her eyes wide and livid, "she's gonna get herself killed."

That was what Annie was afraid of.

18

DYLAN

Don't worry.

That's what her text said.

"Don't worry," I muttered, and knocked on Annie's door again. She'd sent that text almost three hours ago and I was really trying not to worry.

"Jesus, Dylan, you're going to wake the whole goddamn place."

It was Pops, walking up the dirt track from the laundry to his camper. He had a plastic hamper in his hands, half full of white tee shirts, all in a heap.

Weird—I'd never seen my dad do laundry before. I'd never seen him do anything for himself before. Mom cared for him like he was a baby.

"Have you seen Annie?" I asked.

"She left early this morning," he said, still walking toward his trailer. I had no choice but to follow.

"You talked to her?"

"I gave her the keys to my truck because she wanted to run some errands."

That was the same thing she told me. Errands in Cherokee. There was nothing inherently threatening or worrisome about any of that. At all.

But I couldn't stop being worried.

"She told me you saw Max last night."

"Yeah. He's back."

"How is he?"

The wind whistled through the park. "Same old Max," I said.

I braced myself for Pops to ask more. Part of me wished he would so I could take this simmering tension and anxiety out on him, but he was silent on the subject of Max.

"You gonna go looking for Annie?" Pops asked.

"Nope." I took a deep breath. *Don't worry,* she'd said. *I know what I want,* she'd said. *I'm a grown woman,* she'd said.

So, I was going to trust her. And try not to worry.

"We're gonna need some parts for her car," Pops said as he walked on. "I figure you can handle that."

"I don't own an auto parts store. I run a garage that builds high-performance race car engines. I have fourteen patents, Pops."

"You're too important to have one of your guys pick up spark plugs? I guess we can just ask her to buy her own parts. Annie seems like she's got plenty of cash—"

"What does she need?" I sighed.

"Timing belt's shot. Battery is on its last legs. Some spark plugs. All new filters."

He kept talking, but I was distracted by some kind of amazing smell coming out of the little brick oven he had built on the corner of the cement pad.

"What are you making?" I asked.

"Go look."

I peeked inside the top of the oven and saw cornbread in a cast-iron skillet.

The sight sent a wave of memory through me. Mom's cornbread every Sunday, whether she was sober or not. Burnt tongue. Scorched fingertips. Fighting Max and Pops for the last piece.

"I fried up the chilies and put them in there." Pops put his laundry down next to the parts for Annie's transmission. "I made some for Annie last time—she liked it a lot."

There were very few happy times for the family, but Sundays were one of them.

"Mom died, you know." It was mean. And I was trying. "That's where Max was, visiting her grave."

"Yeah. I know. Louisa called me."

"She called me, too. Three weeks after the funeral."

"Louisa never much liked us, did she?" Dad's smile made my stomach turn.

"She told me Mom had been dating a guy. Nice guy, owned a convenience store outside of—"

"Don't do that. You want to hurt me, fine. Do your best. But don't come at me like a pussy."

My head snapped back. "Pussy?"

Pops just stared at me. Until, suddenly, he said, "I'm sorry."

I had no real proof, but my gut insisted that was the first time I'd ever heard an apology from that man's mouth.

"Yeah?" I asked. "For what, exactly?"

"For everything."

"Now who is the pussy?"

Pops chewed on the inside of his lip. "The shit that happened to you in jail. The retaliation with the Rotten Bastards. You weren't a part of the Skulls. You didn't deserve that. And I asked you—"

He cleared his throat and started pulling out those white shirts.

"It was my choice, too," I said. "You got plenty of stuff to feel guilty about, but that was my call."

"You were just a kid."

I watched him make a hash of folding his shirts. "No one is a kid for long growing up with you and Mom."

His lips went tight; I'd made a direct hit. And I couldn't lie—it felt good to get a reaction. It felt good to hurt the guy.

"I deserve that. It . . . wasn't a good way for any kid to grow up."

"You're too late with this, Pops. I don't give a shit about your regret. Or your apologies."

Pops nodded like he knew that. And he probably did.

"Then why are you still here?" Pops asked.

"Because Annie is. Because you haven't ruined her life yet and she thinks she needs to take care of you." That wasn't it. Not all of it. When Max told me to leave last night I said no. And I meant it. Well, the kid in me meant it. But the truth was, it wasn't just Annie keeping us here. I had my own lead-filled baggage keeping me from moving.

"Well, I'll die just as fast as I can," he said.

"It's not fucking soon enough, Dad," I said and stomped away, and then suddenly I was turning around and heading right back toward him. The tide in my chest pushing me back.

"The childhood shit, even jail, I don't care anymore," I said. "I survived. It's over. The thing I want to know is where were you when I got out? Max turned his back on me and you just vanished. You vanished—"

"Because that was the only chance you had that you wouldn't end up back in jail or killed by some Bastard wannabe trying to get his patch."

"And what about after the crash, Pops?" I spat. "After I almost died. I was in that hospital for two months and I heard nothing from you. Nothing from Max. You gonna tell me you didn't know about it?"

"No," Pops whispered. "We knew."

Something shattered. Something very small but very real

shattered. The last of my hope that they hadn't known. That the only reason they were never there was because they didn't know I'd been hurt. Nearly killed.

But they knew.

And it fucking hurt.

"So? Where the hell were you? When the skin came off my feet and the plastic surgeon said they did everything they could for my face and it hurt so bad I screamed. And I was all alone. All those sponsors, all those women, all those hotshots who said they loved me. Everyone fucking left me. Where were you then?"

"You had that Miguel, his whole family—"

"They weren't you!" I yelled.

Pops's lips twisted, his dark eyes dry as a bone. "I'm sorry, Dylan," he said.

"Oh." Sarcasm was dripping off my words. Off my body. Like an oil I couldn't stop secreting. "You're sorry. Well, then. You're forgiven."

"Dylan?" It was Annie's soft, quiet voice, and both Pops and I stiffened and turned toward her. Like we'd been caught burying a dead body. Or maybe exhuming it. Dragging it around, rotting and awful. Numb to the stink.

I was embarrassed by this. By this sudden desire I had to sift through this crap again. To try to make my case with a man who didn't give a shit. Not when it mattered. Not when I needed him to care.

Of all my secrets, of all the things I never showed her, this seemed like the worst. The darkest. That thing I was most ashamed of. So ashamed I didn't even think about it anymore. Now I was nauseous and wanted a shower.

Killing a man—I felt nothing about it anymore.

But this thing with Pops, wanting him somehow to make right a past he was barely a part of, it was a combustion engine waiting for a spark.

Behind me Pops cleared his throat, or choked. Something. And I jerked out of my fugue state.

"You're back," I said, stepping toward Annie. She nodded and approached us slowly, her eyes darting from me to Pops over my shoulder.

There was the sizzling sound of a fire being doused and a waft of acrid smoke.

"Here." The cast-iron pan thumped down on the picnic table, dropped by one of Pops's hands wrapped in one of his clean white shirts. "I made this for you," he said, and then he took his shirt, now gray and black in places with ash, and his basket and went inside his trailer.

I stared down hard at that cornbread, amazed that Pops's hands made it. And that it looked exactly the way I remembered.

Out of the corner of my eye I saw her reach for me and I stepped back. Just a little. I was reminded of how I'd hated being touched after the accident. The only sensation my fucked-up nerves registered was pain. It took the better part of a year for that to change, and suddenly the sensation was back.

"Are you okay?" she asked.

Okay. I looked up at the blue sky above us. The sky on my mountain was framed by the tops of trees. Lots of them. And I missed those trees. There was nothing here. Nothing but big blue sky.

"I've never said any of that," I told her. I felt like she'd seen into some dark crawl space inside of me. A place not even I went to. "Not ever."

"Do you feel better?" she asked. I could tell by her voice that she wanted it to be true. That by letting those words out I'd lanced the wound or some shit. Cleared out the poison.

The world didn't work that way, but I didn't have it in me to tell her.

"How was town?" I changed the subject.

At her silence I looked up and found her staring at Ben's closed door. She'd gotten a sunburn yesterday and her cheeks were pink beneath her freckles.

"Annie?"

"We need to talk."

ANNIE

THEY SAT IN HER TRAILER. THE CHIPPED FORMICA TABLE AND A loaded silence between them. Annie had repeated everything Joan had told her, without much explanation or reason. Largely because she had no idea how to frame everything. Half the words coming out of her mouth felt like code.

"Dylan?" she asked, the silence having extended to some kind of breaking point.

"So, it wasn't errands?" he asked.

"That's what you're worried about? Didn't you hear the part about the cult and the club running drugs?"

"Yes, Annie, and I'm worried about everything. But right now I'm trying to figure out how much you knew before you went to meet Joan."

"I didn't know any of this," she said. "I mean, I knew she was DEA but I had no idea about the cult or any . . ." She had a dim memory of the night she went to the strip club.

"What?" he asked.

"No, I'm just remembering that night I went to the strip club. The men there. Not men watching the women, but a meeting in the back. There was a guy in a suit—it was weird."

Dylan put his head down on the table. "You're killing me, babe. You really are."

"I think your brother was there, too. I mean, there were definitely motorcycle-type guys."

"Motorcycle-type guys?"

"I don't know what else to call them. But Joan thinks Max is in real trouble."

"Max has always been in real trouble. None of that is news."

"I think Joan is in real trouble," Annie said.

Dylan reached across the table and picked up her hand, his rough callused fingers linked with hers. It felt good, that rough yet tender connection.

"You always run with such a dangerous crowd?" he asked, and Annie smiled.

"I never ran with any crowd. Ever."

"Well, you have some kind of beginner's luck, that's for sure." She gripped his hand hard, until her knuckles rose up white against her skin and she thought of Joan and the waitress, the way they clung to each other. In pleasure as much as pain.

It spoke to her, that mix, that dangerous and raw reality that sometimes no matter how hard they try, people cannot help but hurt the ones they love. But that didn't mean they had to be apart. And one did not make the other not exist.

"Your father asked you to go to jail for your brother," she said.

"You heard that?"

"That must have been awful."

"It was what it was, you know. But that's the way the club worked. The way my family worked. I remember I was in county and Pops came to visit me. He told me my mom had left for good and that I needed to do the time for my brother. And I wasn't even mad about that, you know. I knew what I had to do. I just felt . . . fucking shitty for him, sitting there; the wife he loved to the detriment of everything else had left him and he was trying to save one son by sacrificing the other. It sucked."

Of course you did, she thought, *because your heart is so big. So damn big.*

"What was your mom like?" she asked.

He turned his head aside and looked out the window. "You know those animals that eat their young? She was like that."

"Dylan," she sighed.

"You asked. That's what she was like."

"But your dad loved her?"

Dylan nodded. "He'd follow her over a cliff. He *did* follow her over cliffs. All the time. It would have been beautiful if she'd been sober. It would have been a fucking inspiration. But instead it was hell."

He pulled her hands toward him and put them against his face, her fingers in his hair. His two-day-old beard was rough against her palms, and she curled her fingers against him, stroking him. He leaned into her touch, petting himself against her, and she smiled, her heart swelling.

She pushed herself up out of her seat. The table between them was small and she didn't crawl so much as slide across it. He shifted back, his eyes alight, and made room for her on his lap. She straddled him, her hips and belly right up against his.

He sucked in a deep breath through his nose, like he was about to go underwater, and kissed her. Hard. With all his force and confusion.

And she met him with her own.

His hand clenched the back of her neck. She squeezed his face.

"You are seriously fucking with my life," he said against her lips and she arched against him, feeling him getting hard.

"I seriously want to fuck you." She bit his lips. Sucked on his tongue. And he growled, clamping a hand in her hair, twisting her head until he had her where he wanted her.

"Show me," he said. "Show me how you want to fuck me."

19

ANNIE

SHE LEANED BACK, CAUGHT IN HIS GAZE, AND SLOWLY SHE BEGAN
to grind against him. She was trapped between his body and the
table behind her, which bit into her back so she could barely
move. But it was working; the pressure that built up between her
legs, behind her eyes, was intense and powerful and fast.

She clenched the shoulders of his shirt in her hand, feeling
the seams give slightly in her grip.

He leaned back, so they weren't kissing anymore, their fore-
heads pressed together.

"More," she breathed, reaching between them for his pants,
but he grabbed her hands, holding them behind her back.

"I don't have any condoms," he said. "You want to come?"

She nodded, her lip between her teeth.

"You're going to have to do it yourself," he said with an evil
grin.

"Touch me," she whispered. Begged, really, but that kind of
pride had no place between them.

He shook his head, his eyes hard and hot.

She slipped one hand down into her pants, past the cotton edge of her underwear, over the bare skin of her pussy, until her finger slipped into the wet heat between her lips, and there—right there—found the hard knot of her clit.

She ground herself hard against him, and between his cock and her finger the tension couldn't last and it exploded, fast and hot and hard. She jerked against him, wringing as much as she could from the friction. Burying her face against his neck, her mouth open so she could taste his sweat.

She wanted to eat him. Lick him. And when the orgasm faded, she sat back up. She pulled his shirt off, tossing it over her shoulder. Her hands reached for his belt again, and this time he let her.

"No condom," he said, reminding her.

"You really broke your rules yesterday, didn't you?"

"When?" His eyes locked on her hand as she cupped him through his underwear.

"At the swimming hole, when you were inside me without a condom."

"Yeah." He kissed the skin of her bare shoulder, her neck, any skin he could lean down and get his lips on.

She slipped her hand back between her legs, gathering up the moisture there, and she spread it around his dick, using it as lubricant for her hand. It didn't take long; he, it seemed, was just as loaded and ready all the time as she was.

And that, too, turned her on. That he had no defenses against her right now.

It seemed as he shook in her arms, spurts of come splashing against her hand, that that was the way it should be. If she could, she would keep him like this. Open and defenseless. In her arms.

He was still against her and she let go of his softening cock. She could hear his heartbeat against her ear, and her mouth tasted like his breath, and his hands sweeping up and down over her back were impossibly gentle.

Amazing to think this was the same place where Hoyt had hurt her. Terrorized her.

It was as if part of his ghost, or part of the effect of his ghost, had been exorcised.

"I remember thinking," she whispered, staring at the closed curtain of her little window. The sunlight filtered through, making a hash mark design against his shoulder. She traced it with her fingers. His skin was smooth and warm and the muscle beneath it did not give. "When Hoyt was here and dragging me out to his truck, that . . . you were so gentle with me. Even when you were rough." He made a humming noise. "And I didn't know that until I had that contrast of Hoyt's hands on me."

"What are you saying?"

"That, sometimes, maybe we don't know exactly what we have until someone shows us."

He pushed her hair off her face and kissed her lips, but he was silent.

Not that she expected him to say he loved her. She wasn't entirely sure that she loved him. But there was something growing between them, fast and wild, and she didn't know what the smart thing to do was. Rip it out by the roots? Or let it grow over everything, until it changed her entire landscape.

"I need to wash my hand," she whispered. "And my legs are asleep."

Laughing, he wrapped his hands around her waist and lifted her like she was nothing.

Her feet had barely touched the ground when there was a knock at the door.

She winced and quickly washed her hands while Dylan buckled up his pants.

"Does it smell in here?" she whispered.

"Like sex," he said in a loud, clear voice, and she shushed him. Which only made him smile.

Impossible man. Beautiful, impossible man.

Smiling, her heart alight, she opened the door.

Tiffany stood there, a long-sleeved tee shirt pulled down over her hands. Her face pale and wan.

"Annie," she said. Her smile looked like a wince. "Can we talk?"

No, Annie thought. *No, we can't. You've done enough talking.*

"Please," Tiffany whispered. She glanced back over her shoulder, and there was something so scared in that gesture that Annie forced herself to put aside her anger.

She could feel Dylan behind her, his warm, solid presence.

I have enough, she thought. *More than enough. I can be forgiving.*

"Sure," she said, and stepped outside.

"Annie?" Tiffany said, backing up until there was a patch of yellowing grass between them. "You're okay?"

"No thanks to you," Annie shot back. Okay, so she was still angry.

"I didn't know," Tiffany said, her fingers worrying at the watch on her wrist. "I didn't know he would hurt you."

"That's bullshit, Tiffany, and you know it. You saw my face when I moved here. My neck. Those bruises aren't an accident."

Tiffany glanced away, pulling the hem of her shirt down over her hips.

"I know. But Phil—"

"I don't care about Phil," she said. "Your husband wasn't my friend."

"We're not friends, either," Tiffany snapped.

It shouldn't have hurt. Lord knew, people had said worse. And frankly, Annie knew what Tiffany was doing: trying to minimize her guilt. She'd done it herself with Smith.

But it still hurt.

"Fine." Annie crossed her arms over her chest, weak protection and far too late, but it was all she had. "Then what are you doing here? If we're not friends, you have nothing to apologize for."

Annie, more than done with this conversation, turned back toward the camper, but Dylan was there, radiating tension. His eyes on Tiffany.

Tiffany stepped back and away from Dylan and his hard face. His probing eyes.

"Phil, your husband. What's his last name?" he asked.

"Edwards."

Dylan made a sound like a tire with a slow leak.

"And those kids I've seen you with—"

"What about them?" she asked, going very mama bear.

"They're his?"

"What's it to you?" she demanded.

"Dylan?" Annie asked, putting a hand on his arm, and something in her touch must have translated because he took a deep breath, pulled in some of the anger.

"I'm Dylan Daniels. He worked for me."

Tiffany blinked, like she'd just been hit in the face with a pie.

"He quit working for you," she said.

"I fired his ass," Dylan said.

Tiffany flinched.

"What did Phil have to do with Hoyt finding you?" Dylan asked Annie, who didn't have any idea what was happening.

"Phil told him where I was. They met . . . accidentally, somewhere."

"Fucking Phil. Goddamn fucking Phil. Is he here?" he asked Tiffany, pointing toward the trailer on the other side of the rhododendron.

"Yes, he's sleeping," Tiffany said. "We just got back—"

Dylan charged three steps toward the bush and the trailer behind it, but Tiffany got in the way, her shaking hands up to stop him.

"I have kids," she said, her voice sounding like it was being squeezed out of a small, tight hole. "Three babies. You'll scare them. Please . . ."

"Go get him," Dylan said through clenched teeth. She ran toward her trailer and he followed. Annie jogged to catch up, pulled by some unseen rope tied to all this heartache.

"Dylan," she whispered. "What the hell is going on?"

"I have no idea," he told her.

"Stop, Dylan." She tugged on his arm, forcing him to stop his wild charge across the park. "I can't help you if you don't tell me what you know."

"Help me?"

She threw her hands up in the air. "Yes, I can . . . I can help you, Dylan. Just tell me what we're doing."

"Margaret is Phil's mom."

"Wait . . . *what*?" She nearly pitched forward. "Does she know about Tiffany or the kids?"

"What do you think?"

"There's no way she would let her grandkids grow up like this."

"Not if she knew," he agreed. "Her and Blake both."

"Oh my God."

"Right."

They started walking toward the camper again. Slower this time, but Annie could tell that Dylan was still furious.

"Don't . . ."

"Kill him?" he asked. They stopped near the picnic table set up in the rough, weedy lawn. "I'll give it my best shot."

Inside the trailer there was a rattle and thump. A low, loud voice.

"He hits her, doesn't he?" Dylan asked Annie, both of them staring at that door as though the hounds of hell were about to be released.

"Yeah," she murmured.

"Does he hit the kids?"

"I . . . I don't know."

"What the hell!" Phil cried, coming to the door, blinking into the daylight. He looked old, despite his clothes, despite his attitude. Phil looked worn out. Used up.

He stiffened when he saw Dylan. Annie ran a hand over Dylan's fist, hoping it would help him control the anger.

"Dylan? What are you doing here?" Phil asked, all that contempt for the world dialed back in the face of Dylan's implacable, calm rage. He looked like a scared bully who'd been called out.

"I'm kicking you off the property," Dylan said calmly.

"What? You can't do that."

"I own this place, Phil. I can do whatever I want."

"Blake ain't gonna like this," Phil snapped.

"I gotta hand it to you, Phil. It's amazing all the secrets you've managed to keep from your family. Where you live, that you have kids. A wife that you smack around."

"That bitch lies, all the damn time!" Phil said, looking over his shoulder inside the trailer. "Yeah, I'm talking about you."

Dylan took a lunging step toward Phil, who immediately cowered against the trailer. Annie grabbed Dylan's elbow. "There's a family here," she whispered. "Little kids."

Dylan's deep breath made his nostrils flare, and his control, she could tell, was hard to hold on to. "I want you to get off this property now," he said in the calmest, most terrifying voice she'd ever heard. "And never come back. And if you doubt my ability to enforce that, you can take it up with my lawyer."

"This is bullshit, man."

"This is what happens when you hurt women."

Phil's weasel eyes screwed up. "I didn't touch anyone. I didn't know that cowboy dude was going to beat her up. I didn't know—"

Annie didn't see what happened. But one minute Phil was standing in the doorway and the next Dylan had him yanked down, with one knee on the ground. It looked like they were shaking hands, but Annie could see that Dylan had Phil's pinky finger bent back to the very edge of its ability to bend.

"Do I need to break your finger, Phil? Because I would love to break your finger."

"No," Phil gasped. "No, I'm going."

Dylan let go of Phil and he scrambled to his feet, cradling his hand. His face white and sweating.

"Tiff!" he yelled, without taking his eyes off Dylan. "Get the kids. We're leaving."

Tiffany was back in the doorway, her cheeks slick with stress tears.

"You hear me?" Phil cried, when she didn't move.

Annie approached Tiffany, watching the hem of her tee shirt shake because she was trembling so hard. Her hands, with nails ragged and bitten to the quick, clutched at each other.

"The kids," she whispered, glancing back at the trailer. "They're sleeping—"

"Wake them up," Phil demanded.

"You don't have to go with him," Annie whispered to Tiffany, and Tiffany's wide eyes flew to hers.

"What'd you say?" Phil demanded, but Dylan stepped in front of her, between her and Phil.

"You don't even look at her," Dylan whispered and she could sense the thin control he'd had moments ago was fraying. Quickly.

"You are not alone," Annie told Tiffany again. "I know it can feel like it, but you're not. You have choices."

"Choices?" Tiffany gasped.

"So many more than you can see, because that asshole is in the way of all of them."

Tiffany's breath came fast and shuddery, like that of a person gathering up the courage to jump off a cliff.

"I don't have to go," Tiffany said.

Annie shook her head. "You don't have to go."

"Don't listen to that bitch—" Phil lurched toward Annie, but Dylan was there.

"Christ, you are such an idiot," Dylan muttered, and this time he added that ounce of pressure, and the pop of ligaments and bone was audible.

Annie's stomach turned. Tiffany jumped.

"You broke my finger!" Phil staggered back to the trailer.

"I did." Dylan let go of the dangling pinky finger and grabbed onto his thumb instead. "And I'll break all of them if you don't get in your car and go."

"Tiffany, if you don't get in this car with me," Phil screamed, his voice high and reedy, sounding like he was going into shock, "you won't get another penny from me. You and those fucking kids will never see me again."

Annie smiled at Tiffany. "Sounds good, doesn't it," she whispered. "Never seeing him again."

"It does," Tiffany breathed. "It really does."

"Tiffany!" Phil bellowed. Dylan let go of his hand and gave him a shove backward.

"Look at what we did, Phil," Tiffany said. "That Hoyt man is dead, Annie was nearly killed, and Dylan was stabbed! We were a part of that!"

Tiffany must have heard the gossip from around the park.

"We didn't do shit, Tiffany," he sneered. "We told a guy where his wife was living—that's it."

Tiffany shook her head. Color was returning to her face in great red blotches. "I can't live like this anymore. I can't keep pretending that this is okay. You make the world so dark, Phil. And our kids . . ." Her voice broke and she wiped a hand under her eyes, scrubbing away tears. "I'm not going." Tiffany lifted her chin all the way up. "I'm not going and you're not welcome here. If you come back I'll call the cops."

It was hard work not to clap. Not to cheer. All the hair on Annie's body was standing up in ovation.

"My shit," Phil said. "All my stuff is in there."

"Get it," Dylan said, and Phil started to walk back toward the trailer, but Dylan held up his hand. And like a well-trained dog, Phil stopped. "Tiffany," he said, not looking away from Phil's face. "Pack up his things, would you?"

"I'll help," Annie said. And the two of them went inside the trailer.

Tiffany walked down the narrow hallway toward the bedrooms, the walls lined with pictures the kids had drawn, glitter falling off into small piles in the carpet. Tiffany closed two doors as they walked past and Annie got glimpses of the sleeping kids. Thumbs in mouths, blankets clutched in tiny hands.

In the back bedroom, Tiffany seemed to hit a wall. She stood, staring at the unmade bed, the two dressers. She stood there and shook.

"Hey," Annie whispered. "Hey, it's okay. Tell me where his stuff is and you grab a bag for him."

Tiffany pointed to the dresser in the corner with the cockeyed drawers.

Three minutes later, the dresser was empty of his stuff. Then the closet. The bathroom. Within ten minutes, they had wiped Phil out of the trailer. And with each oversized shirt and pair of underwear, Tiffany seemed to gather herself. Pull together strength and purpose.

When they stepped back out of the trailer, Tiffany threw the duffle at Phil's feet.

"Tiff," he sighed, looking up at her like he thought he could still change her mind. Annie knew that look on his face; she'd seen it before on Hoyt's. She'd been suckered by that face more times than she could count.

For a second Annie worried about Tiffany's resolve.

But she shouldn't have doubted.

"Get your shit and get gone," Tiffany told him. "And don't come back."

"Or I'll break more than your fingers," Dylan added, walking forward toward Phil, making the guy retreat. Phil stumbled as he walked backward, until he was pressed up against the driver's-side door.

Yelling a few choice obscenities, he fumbled with the door handle and finally got in and roared off. A hand stuck out the window, giving all of them the finger.

"I should have broken that one," Dylan muttered.

Tiffany put her head in her hands, her shoulders shaking.

"Tiffany?" Annie asked, tentatively touching her elbow. "You okay?"

"You broke his finger," Tiffany said, looking up at Dylan, part horror, part happiness. She was laughing and crying.

"I don't think he'll come back," Dylan told her.

"No. I'm sure he won't," she said. "He's only here when someone kicks him off their couch. He doesn't . . . he doesn't like the kids. Or me."

"Do you care?" Annie asked.

She wanted to say good riddance, but she understood wanting someone's love even if that love was poison.

"For the kids, yes. But he's gone. And I can't tell you how relieved I am."

"Did you know Phil has family? A mom, a brother, and a sister?" Dylan asked, and Tiffany turned to look at him, her brows furrowed. "I mean, did he talk about them?"

"Phil didn't talk much about anything. When I asked, he just said that they were assholes to him. They kicked him out when he was a kid and then he said . . . I think he said they died."

"His father did," Dylan told her. "But his mother is still alive, and so are his brother and sister."

Tiffany's knees buckled and Annie grabbed her and led her to the picnic table.

"What are you talking about?" Tiffany whispered.

"Phil's brother, Blake, is my partner. In my garage. And his mother is like a mother to me. I've known them for years, and I'm telling you, if she knew she had three grandkids living here, she would move heaven and earth to see you safe. And cared for."

In Annie's arms, Tiffany was positively still. If she was breathing, Annie couldn't feel it.

"Breathe, Tiffany," she urged, and Tiffany jerked, sucking in a breath.

"She is a very good woman," Annie said to her. "Really decent. She wouldn't . . . judge you. Or cast you out—"

"Not like my mom?" Tiffany asked, her eyes sharp.

"I'm just saying she's kind. And she would want to help."

Tiffany turned her face away, looking over at the trailer. One of her girls was coming down the steps, dragging a blanket behind her. Her fine blond hair in a rooster tail over her eyes.

"Mommy?" the little girl whimpered. "Is Daddy gone?"

"Come here, sweetie." She sighed, and the little girl climbed up into her lap. "Did the yelling wake you up?"

"No, Sienna peed the bed again."

Tiffany closed her eyes, and as Annie watched, she literally pulled herself together. Reattached muscle to bone, assembled her spine, screwed in her arms and legs. When she opened her eyes they were cold and serious.

"What's her name?" she asked. "This . . . mom."

"Margaret."

"I can't . . . I can't do anything about Margaret right now," she whispered over her little girl's head.

Dylan nodded, everything threatening and brutal, everything dangerous about him so muted in the face of this woman's bravery and fear.

Annie could not hold back the tide of feeling that curled through her, sweeping away defense. Sweeping away reason.

There was only him.

Tiffany's long breath shuddered. "I'm going to get back inside," she said.

She picked up her dozy baby girl and stepped toward the trailer. She sagged slightly, hoisting her daughter up. And Dylan caught her arm and then quickly let her go, but he walked beside her toward the trailer.

Keeping her safe.

The sight made Annie's throat tight. Her chest hurt. It made everything swell inside of her. A feeling not unlike pain. Or lust. But neither of those two things. Or perhaps more than those two things.

"When you're ready," Dylan said to Tiffany, "I'll get you in touch with her."

"Thank you," she said.

"I'm sorry," Dylan said, and Tiffany's head snapped up toward him. "I . . . I should have thought maybe before I did that. You're a family and I made a decision—"

"*I* made the decision," she said. "And it's okay. You're taking care of Annie." Tiffany shot Annie a smile over her shoulder. "And that's a good thing. I'm going to be okay. I got family who can help. Apparently more than I knew about."

"Lock the door behind you," he said, and she nodded.

Dylan helped close the door behind Tiffany, whose hands were full, and then he waited there until they heard the crappy lock on the screen click.

Night was starting to fall and behind him the sky was purple. The trees black. Annie could feel the setting sun on her shoulders.

"We're quite a team," he murmured with that half-smile she'd grown to love.

Right. Yes.

Love.

Bedrock.

"I love you," she said.

20

ANNIE

HIS SILENCE WAS NOT UNEXPECTED. THE WAY HIS MOUTH
dropped from that grin into slack-jawed surprise—that wasn't
unexpected, either.

Saying that—admitting it, before she had a chance to really
think about it. That really was the unexpected thing.

"Don't say anything," she said, suddenly manic. Suddenly
practically vibrating out of her skin. She didn't regret it. No, she
could never regret it, but she just wished she'd been more pru-
dent. More careful with herself. But it was too late. "I've been
thinking that when we were talking on the phone, even though
we were lying sometimes, we were really showing each other
exactly who we are. The parts of us we never showed anyone, or
even . . . maybe forgot we had. We showed each other our bedrock truth, without even knowing it. I mean . . . I know I did.
And I think you did, too. And since we came back here, things
have gotten more confusing. They've gotten harder because
we're not showing each other that truth anymore. We're back to

telling ourselves lies about who we really are and what we really want like we used to. Like we had to before, just to get through the day.

"And I don't want to do that anymore. I want to show you the truth of me. And . . . loving you is a part of that. It's a part of who I am now. And I heard what you said to me in the trailer, about your parents, and I understand that me loving you, me . . . saying that, might make you panic. Or freak you out, but I just want you to know, nothing is different. I just said some words. The feelings were the feelings I've had all along."

He was still silent, and she guessed maybe he needed some room. Some quiet.

"I'll . . . talk to you later," she said.

Annie turned and nearly ran toward the rhododendron bush and her trailer and all that quiet, all that solace. She'd climb into bed and put her pillow over her head and try to pretend she hadn't said that.

Didn't just potentially ruin everything.

"Annie," he said, just before she cleared the edge of the bushes. She stopped, but didn't turn around. She squeezed her eyes shut. "Please, turn around."

She did, reluctantly. His cheeks were flushed, the color above the scars bright. It was charming. He had his hands shoved in his pockets, his shoulders up near his ears.

"That was the bravest . . ." He stopped and shook his head, unable to meet her eyes. "I don't know how to do this."

Her smile was shaky. *Me neither.* "I know," she told him, forgiving his awkwardness. His silence. His inability to return the emotions she'd just vomited out at him.

It was, after all, something she'd been doing her whole life. This was what she was good at, loving people who could not love her in return.

DYLAN

I BOUGHT THE SIX-PACK OF CHEAP BEER AT THE GAS STATION and I headed straight to The Velvet Touch parking lot. I drove past the front door across the asphalt to the gravel and then around the building to the back.

There was a row of gleaming Harleys outside the back entrance, but none of the guys were around. I parked my car opposite those bikes. I got my six-pack and went out to sit on the hood of my car.

And I waited.

Because in the end, despite all my money, despite Blake and Margaret, who I would only allow so close, I was Max Daniels's kid brother.

That was my truth. Or a big part of it anyway. Bigger, perhaps, than I wanted to admit.

And sometimes a guy just needed his brother.

Max was a reminder of who I was before all the bullshit changed me.

I drank a beer waiting and opened another.

A man came out, a tall Viking-looking dude with a Skulls cut and a mustache that made him look like he had a pussy on his face.

"Logsy in there?" I yelled at the guy.

"Who's asking?"

"His brother."

The guy vanished and within a few minutes Max came out, looking pissed. I imagined him as a cartoon with a bunch of smoke coming out his ears.

When Max got close enough I tossed him a beer.

"What the fuck are you doing?" he asked, catching the beer. I thought he might rifle it back at my head, but he only clenched it in that fist of his.

"Trying to have a beer with my brother. Drink up—it's room temperature. Your favorite."

Max just sighed at me, like I was a kid refusing to go home when he wanted to get down to the business of stealing cars. So fucking familiar, that sigh.

"Look, I'm sorry Rabbit got you screwed up in club business. But you have got to go. Now."

I took a sip of beer and didn't move.

"I don't want you here!" he said.

I leaned back against my windshield, stretched my legs out over the hood. Three weeks ago I never would have considered this, but these were different days. Wildly different days.

Annie loved me. She loved *me*.

And I wasn't entirely sure who I was.

"Is this . . . is there something going on with Pops?" Max asked, proving he wasn't such a hard-ass.

"I thought you didn't care?"

"I don't."

"He's fine. A fucking gardener, if you can believe it. Made me some cornbread."

We were silent for a long moment. I had another drink.

This isn't about the club, I wanted to tell him. *This isn't about anything but you and me and what we used to be. I need that for five minutes. I need my goddamn brother for five minutes and you owe me that.*

It seemed as if Max understood, or had read my mind, or fuck, maybe he needed it, too. Maybe whatever shit he was going down with had him wishing he'd done some things differently. Maybe he wished things were simple. Like they used to be. When it was just him and me against the world.

Whatever.

It didn't matter why. He sighed, leaned back against my car, and popped the top on his beer. I hid my smile with my can.

"Was it good? The cornbread?" Max asked.

"Yeah. He put the fried chilies in it."

"Like Mom made."

"Every Sunday."

Max scooched up on the hood. "Sorry about the paint," he muttered when the rivet on his boot scratched the car.

"It doesn't matter."

"Right." He leaned back against the windshield beside me. "Because you're rich as fuck, ain't you?"

"Yes, I am." I toasted him. He toasted me back. We both drank.

"Dad's all right?" Max asked.

"Well, he's dying. But at the moment he's fine."

"You doing the chemo thing with him?"

"Annie is."

Last time I saw Max I'd been unwilling to talk about Annie, scared of more blowback touching her. But this time—now—I was here to talk about her.

The world was a perverse fucking place. Or maybe that was just me.

"Annie's the girl who shot her husband?"

I nodded.

Max eyed me over the can before he took another long drink. "So you in love or something?"

I drained my can and let it roll down the hood before opening another. Max took one, too.

"I know why you left me after jail," I said.

"What's this got to do with your love life?" Max asked.

Nothing. Everything. Somehow this was part of that bedrock Annie had been talking about.

"It hurt, what you did. It hurt a lot, but I get it. You gave me a new life."

Max laughed up at the parking lot lights, with their buzzing halo of bugs. "And yet, here we are, like nothing's changed."

I had this ache. This pain in my chest I couldn't get rid of. "You were out, weren't you?" Out of the life. Out of danger. He'd been free. "You'd gotten out and I made you come back."

Max twisted the pop-top off the can and tossed it into the dirt past the headlights. "Tell me about this girl."

"Max?"

"I came back," Max said. "Because of this girl. Because of whatever it is you feel for her. So fucking tell me."

"She told me she loved me tonight. I broke a guy's finger, terrified a woman and her kids, and Annie . . . she told me she loved me. It was the bravest fucking thing I've ever seen in my life."

"Brave?" Max scoffed. "She know how rich you are?"

"It's not about that," I said.

"Yeah? You sure about that? Has she seen your fancy beach house?"

"You haven't seen my house."

"I saw it in a magazine, once. Pops had all that shit about you."

I didn't press about Pops and the magazine, one of Blake's brilliant ideas. But that was the second time someone told me that Pops had kept tabs on me after I got out of jail. I understood why he left me; I got it. It was brutal and black-and-white, but that was the way Pops lived. All or nothing.

But it was easier to believe he didn't care.

"Annie doesn't care about money."

"Or maybe she's just lying about not caring," Max said. "You were always a shit judge of women."

I laughed, because I knew what he was remembering. "She's not Michelle."

"Or Mackenzie or Shoshonna."

"I had some bad girlfriends."

"You were just stupid grateful when they let you touch their tits."

"Well, Annie's not like any of them. She's . . . real. You know? Authentic. And she doesn't lie."

Except when she does.

But she wouldn't lie about this. Unless she was wrong. Unless what she felt was something else.

That's what I was scared of.

"What happens if she's wrong?" I asked. "Am I just supposed to trust that what she feels is real? What happens when it's not and I'm left out to dry?"

Alone.

Again.

"You're asking the wrong guy, Dylan," Max said. "Trust got rubbed out of me a long time ago. I say watch your back."

"Christ, you're jaded."

"Fine." Max held up his hands. "You're the one sitting out here behind a strip club with your brother instead of . . . doing whatever it is men do with women who love them."

"You don't know?" I asked.

"No fucking clue."

"What happened to . . . what was her name, Drea?"

"Fuck, from like high school?"

"Yeah. She was nice."

"She was, and that's why she dumped my ass."

There was no denying this was weird, and I think we both knew it. There were about a dozen things we needed to really talk about—what was going on in that club at the top of the list—but for whatever reason, this—shooting the shit—it was what we both needed.

My brother is going to die, I thought. *Not sometime. Not in the future. But soon.*

And he knows it.

And I made him come back. In the Daniels family, the scales of justice were evil. And precise.

"You know, it's too bad that you can't remember when Mom was good," Max said.

"I don't remember because I don't think it happened."

Max nodded. "When she was pregnant with you and for, like, four years after. She was sober."

"What was that like?" I asked, laughing, literally unable to imagine it.

"Well," he laughed. "It wasn't like she was Mrs. Garcia." Mrs. Garcia was a woman who lived in the apartment above us. A single mom with two little girls we used to make fun of because they were always clean and did their homework and never got in trouble. We made fun of them because they were fiercely loved and we were so fucking jealous we couldn't stand it. We would steal their lunches because they had things like cookies and leftover meatloaf sandwiches. And no matter what we did, they only pitied us.

It used to make Max crazy.

"But yeah . . . Mom was fun. We'd have picnics on the beach and she'd take me out of school to go to the movies. I mean it was still Mom, so there was always chaos, but there were also bedtime stories and dinner on the table. And she and Pops . . ."

"What?"

"I don't know, man. They were happy. Like really happy. They were solid. It wasn't all bad. It just . . . got that way."

"Why are you telling me that?"

"Because all you knew was the shitty stuff. And the stuff before that was what me and Pops fought so hard for."

We both drank again, but a sorrow had seeped into my bones and they ached.

"So, you're really in some shit," I said and belched. "Drug running for some meth-cooking cult leader?"

Max stared at me hard and then reached over with that big hand of his and started patting me down.

"What are you doing?" I said, dodging his hands.

"You wired?"

"No, I'm not fucking wired. Jeez." Max just looked at me and I spread out my arms, lifted my shirt.

"Pants, too."

I slid off the car, undid my pants, and dropped them to my knees.

Max laughed.

"Fuck you," I said, and jumped back up on the hood of the car. But I was laughing, too.

"How the hell do you know all that?" Max asked.

"Sources, *hermano*," I said. "I've got them, too."

"You need to keep your mouth shut. Seriously."

"Seriously. Who would I tell?"

"It's a goddamn powder keg. This Lagan fucker . . ." He sighed, staring at the back door of the club. He looked old all of a sudden. Older than thirty-two.

"Why are you doing it?"

"Club needs money. The guys want it."

"What do *you* want?"

Max laughed. "You fucking Oprah, now?" He got down from the car. I watched him go, felt him slipping away. "Thanks for the beer, Dylan."

"Thank you," I said. "For what you did for me. After jail, with Miguel and Margaret."

Max nodded and then smiled, the small internal smile of a person who knew he'd done the right thing. "Worked out all right for you, didn't it."

"Yeah, it did."

"Good. That's . . . that's real good."

Max looked over at the door; there were some other guys out there now. Rabbit among them. He watched us carefully.

"You can't come back here," Max said.

"I can see that," I said, raising my beer toward Rabbit. "How bad is it, Max?"

"Bad as it gets."

"I'm sorry," I said. "I'm sorry I made you come back."

"She better be fucking worth it," he said with a grin that came nowhere near his eyes. "Goodbye, Dylan."

There was a hard lump in my throat, covered in barbs, and all I could do was nod. I watched my brother walk away, back to the life he'd chosen. The life I'd forced him back into.

Maybe it was because I'd watched Annie be so brave just a few hours ago, but I suddenly realized that for all his violence, leaving the Skulls was the only brave thing Max had ever done. This life, he didn't choose it; he let it happen to him. Day after day he refused to make a choice, so the Skulls crept up on him like kudzu, until that was all he had.

And I was doing the same damn thing, up on that mountaintop with my money and my work. Day after day, I was making the easy choice. So easy it was barely a choice, it was something that just kept happening. Over and over again.

Annie, I thought.

It was a leap of faith. Scary as shit.

I got in my car.

21

ANNIE

ANNIE KNOCKED ON TIFFANY'S DOOR, THE HANDLES OF THE cloth bag she held digging into her palm. Finally, the metal door opened and Tiffany stood there, backlit by a lamp behind her, her eyes red-rimmed. Annie could hear the kids' voices inside, over the sound of the television.

"Hey," Annie said. "I didn't want to bother you, but I figured maybe you'd want some food you didn't have to cook."

Annie held the bag out toward her.

"What is this?" Tiffany asked, taking the bag like it might hold a bomb.

"It's some food Margaret made for me, but I can't eat it all. It's cookies and stuff—the kids will probably like it. And there's . . . there's a UNC undergrad course book, too."

"College? What's that for?" Tiffany asked, all hard edges. "You think I've got time to go to school with three kids?"

"I think you should just look at it. See what kind of opportunities you have."

"Right," Tiffany said, wiping her hand over her forehead. Her sarcasm was thick. "So many opportunities."

"I've circled some stuff," Annie said. "For me. You can ignore it."

"You're going back to school?" Tiffany asked.

"I'm . . . I'm thinking about it. I can't go back to the farm."

"I can understand that. Right now, I want to get out of this place so bad it makes my skin crawl."

"Margaret and Blake, they could help you with that."

"I keep wondering . . . how did I not know he had a brother? And a mom. I mean, we must have moved here to be closer to them somehow, and his brother must have gotten him the job."

"It sounds like he kept a lot of secrets. It's part of how he kept you here, you know. Kept you under his thumb."

"He never told me lots of things, but I *knew*." She shook her head. "Other girls. Money from dealing drugs he had squirreled away from us. He never told me about that, but I still knew."

"I think it's easier to think about and believe that bad stuff," Annie said. "At least it was that way for me, living with Hoyt. Got so I couldn't even imagine the good stuff, much less see it."

"Yeah," Tiffany agreed. "It's like I've been living in a dark hole for five years. Anyway, thanks for this stuff—the kids will love the cookies." From the side of the bag, she pulled out the bottle of red wine Annie had brought down from Dylan's after that night they'd shared.

"This looks fancy," Tiffany said, reading the label.

"So, it will probably suck," Annie said, deadpan.

"Right, if it doesn't come in a tub—"

"Or have a spigot."

"It's gross."

They both laughed a little into the darkness.

"You want to come in?" Tiffany asked. "Have some crappy

fancy wine and . . . I don't know, tell me about this Margaret woman?"

"And Blake."

"Yeah," Tiffany sighed. "And Blake."

Annie nodded and Tiffany stepped back, but before Annie could enter the trailer, Tiffany spoke.

"If I could change my part in what happened to you that night, I would. Like in a heartbeat."

Annie nodded. "I know."

"Is this . . . Can we start over?"

"Always," Annie said.

Every day, if she had to, was a chance to start over.

A FEW HOURS LATER, TIFFANY WAS COMFORTING SIENNA, WHO'D woken up from a nightmare, and Annie washed the coffee mugs they'd been drinking wine out of. She put the cookies and some of the other food she'd brought in the cupboards.

There was a little bit of red wine left, and she screwed the top back on and set it by the stove.

The phone in her back pocket buzzed, and her heart was in her throat as she fished it out.

Dylan.

Relief. Such sweet relief flooded her.

She let herself out of Tiffany's trailer before answering the phone.

"Hello," she said, trying not to sound too eager. Too relieved. You know, just in case he was calling to tell her it was all a mistake and he'd moved back to his house.

"Hey," he said. "Did I wake you up?"

"No." She walked down the path toward the rhododendron bushes and her trailer behind that. The moon was in the middle of the sky and she'd guess it was barely midnight. "I've been at Tiffany's. You okay?"

"Isn't that my line?" he asked.

He's joking, she thought. It had to be a good sign if he was joking.

"I'm fine."

"Me, too," he said.

"Where have you been?"

"Talking to my brother."

She paused with one foot on her first step. "Max?"

"He's my only brother." She heard a lot of emotions in his voice. Big ones. Hard ones. And she hated to think of him trying to carry them alone. Not when she so badly wanted to help.

"Where are you?" she asked. "Why don't you come over?"

"I'm on the road back to the trailer park."

"How far are you?"

"Twenty minutes." She was inside her trailer now, the dark splintered by moonlight through the windows. "And this is better. I want to talk to you. And if I was there, we wouldn't talk."

Heat spread under her skin. "We could try."

"Right. We both know how that will go."

She didn't know. Not for sure. Not after today. "Tell me how you think that will go."

"With my cock buried inside you."

"Dylan," she sighed, restless and achy. "Drive faster."

"What happened earlier . . . what you said?"

I love you.

"Dylan, if it's easier, we can pretend I didn't say anything," she said, some of that nice achy and restless feeling evaporating under the bright, hot heat of her embarrassment. She'd really done that. She'd really told Dylan Daniels that she loved him. "I don't want to ruin what we have."

"Nothing is ruined," he said. "Did you mean it?"

"Of course. But I don't expect you to say it back. It's just how I feel."

"Your truth," he said.

"Yeah."

Bedrock.

He took a deep breath and she held hers.

"No one has said that to me."

"In a long time?"

"Ever. My mom maybe, when I was young. But not when I got older."

She tried not to pity him. Because there was nothing pitiful about him. Nothing that she didn't respect. But even her mother had told her she loved her. And no matter how terrifying or stifling that love had been, at least she'd had that security. And could not imagine growing up without it.

"This afternoon," he said, "that thing with Phil and Tiffany."

"What about it?"

"We . . . were a team. Kind of."

"You want to get some uniforms?"

He laughed, which was the point, but he quickly sobered. "No one has had my back since my brother," Dylan said.

"Margaret and Blake—"

"Not the same," he said. "I don't know why, but it's not. Well, that's not true—I do know why. Because I never allowed it. After that shit went down with my family, I didn't let anyone in. Not even them. But that thing with you today, I felt like I used to with my brother."

"And that's a bad thing?"

"Well, it didn't turn out so good, did it?"

"I'm not going to hurt you, Dylan," she said.

I love you.

"Do you promise?" he asked. Whispered, really. "Do you promise not to hurt me?"

She closed her eyes, tears hot under her lids. "I promise."

DYLAN

AFTER THE FIRE, RECUPERATING FROM THE BURNS, MY NERVES were so badly damaged that everything was in pieces. I would feel everything, and then I would feel nothing. The slightest touch on one part of my body would make me writhe in pain, and yet a sharp nail being dug into another part wouldn't even register.

I lived like that for the better part of a year, unable to trust what my body was telling me. Unable to believe anything I didn't see with my own eyes. That's how I landed on my mountaintop. In an environment I could control.

Right here, right now, I was fishtailing out of control.

"I'm still ten minutes away," I told her. Which was good—ten minutes would give me time to pull myself back together, so I didn't get to her exposed and wild and end up hurting her.

It was one thing for her to give lip service to taking me any way she could get me, but the reality of that wasn't something I wanted to test. Because I was a stranger to myself right now. Her verbal promises weren't enough, and I wanted sworn oaths from her flesh.

"Keep talking, baby," I said, watching the exits fly by on the highway.

"About what?"

"Anything."

"Okay, Truth or Dare."

"What?" I laughed, changing lanes.

"We're playing Truth or Dare."

"I haven't played that since I was in seventh grade or something."

"Do you need me to explain the rules?"

"No."

"Truth or Dare." The sound of her teasing laughter slowed

me down, evened me out, and the wildness I felt, it settled down a little.

"Well, we've kind of had enough danger for a while, haven't we?" I said. "Let's go truth."

"Ah, you don't know the trick, do you? Truth is always more dangerous than dares."

"And how would you know that?"

"Church lock-in when I was eleven. Very high-stakes game of Truth or Dare. Here comes your question: What did you like about race car driving?"

"I think we played very different games of Truth or Dare. You're supposed to ask me if I think you're sexy. Or if I like you—"

"I know the answers to those questions," she said. Her confidence was a turn-on. "I want to know what you liked about racing."

"Going fast." She laughed, and the sweet sound of it made me smile. "You think I'm kidding?"

"I think nothing is that simple."

"Racing is. I mean, not just going fast, but going faster than anyone else. I liked going faster and being better than anyone else."

"You're such a man."

"I am, honey. I am such a man."

"How did the crash happen?" she asked.

For a moment the physical memory of the car swinging out of my control, the tire destroyed, the force and speed—it rocked me. I felt, again, that horrible tilt, the wild spin.

"I'm sorry," she said. "You don't have to answer."

"Dirty air," I said. "That's the term anyway. Cars going so fast create air turbulence. Really unpredictable turbulence. I was drafting the leader and I adjusted a quarter of an inch, swinging to the outside, and I . . . I just kept swinging. I couldn't get it back. The car behind me drove me into the wall. That's when the explosion happened and I got ping-ponged into the infield."

"I'm sorry," she said.

"It's just part of the life, baby."

"Dylan—"

"So it's my turn. Truth or Dare," I said.

"Dare."

"What?" I cried.

"I think I've told you enough truth." Her voice was soft and it pulled at me, slipped under my skin, softened nearly every last bit of resistance to her I was clinging to.

It was ridiculous that I had even considered, for a moment, that I would let her walk off with that Hero Cop, that I would allow anyone to touch her but me. Anyone to talk to her like this, unguarded and soft and sleepy.

Even if he would give her some kind of idealized life without danger or darkness.

She was a creature of light, and that did not happen without darkness.

And she was mine.

I could not fight it any longer.

"Go to church with me," I said.

"What? That's your dare?"

"Yep. There's a good chance a lightning bolt might be involved. But I'll risk it for you. Next Sunday. Come to church with me."

"Why?"

"Because I want to take you. I want to do that with you."

"You don't have to."

"I know. You're Catholic, right?" he asked.

"I was. I mean, it's not like it was a choice. It was just where we went."

"Got it. Leave it to me. Church next Sunday."

"Where are you?" she whispered. I could hear how turned on she was.

"I am . . ." I braked to take the exit to the campground. "Three minutes away."

"Truth or Dare." She was breathing hard, and that sixth sense of mine kicked into gear. Something inevitable and dangerous was coming my way. But instead of dreading it, I opened myself up to the possibility of it.

"Dare," I said.

"That thing you said . . . at the swimming hole. Where . . . you know . . . the place you wanted to fuck me."

I pushed on the gas. Heart in my throat. *Oh God, baby, don't . . . don't do this to me.*

"Come over here," she said. "And do it."

22

ANNIE

THERE WAS A CIRCUS THAT CAME TO THE COUNTY WHEN ANNIE was a little girl. All the cars in a used-car dealership parking lot had been parked to the side so the tents could be set up. There had been rides—the Zipper, she remembered, and a little baby sort of roller coaster. A midway with glow-in-the-dark posters and stuffed Bart Simpsons for prizes.

But at night there was a proper circus show.

Annie and her mom went, and it was amazing to her how that parking lot was transformed under the big red-and-yellow-striped tent. There was nothing mundane or familiar beneath that circus tent.

There were high-wire acts and jugglers. Clowns. A woman riding on an elephant.

But the thing she remembered best was one year there was an act with a woman in red sequins, a man with a whip, and a tiger. The woman went into the tiger's cage and lay down with him. Used her own hands to open up that tiger's mouth and then rested her head against his teeth.

It was shocking, that trust. The entire crowd gasped. Annie remembered not breathing for a full minute.

The next day in the papers there were articles about how dangerous it was. How other women in different red sequins in other parts of the world every year got mauled by tigers.

Annie convinced her mom to take them the second night and she watched the same show, her heart in her throat, but this time she noticed that before the woman stepped into the black metal cage, for just a split second, her smile dropped from her face and she closed her eyes and took a deep breath.

She's scared, Annie remembered thinking. She hadn't noticed it the first time, blinded by the shabby glamour of the parking lot circus.

Despite her fear, or maybe because of it, it was hard to know how someone got into that kind of situation, yet the woman went in anyway.

And that made it so much more exciting.

Annie didn't know what the word was for that, being trusting and scared all at once. But that was exactly how she felt right now.

She waited in her dark bedroom, having hung up the phone and then unlocked her door. She debated taking off her clothes. Turning on a light. But in the end, she just lay there and waited for him.

Trust.

Excitement.

Love.

Her door opened and her eyelids shut. Her entire body was shaking. Trembling.

Fear.

But not the bad kind. Not the sour despair, the bright, hot light of terror.

This was anticipation. Gleeful and giddy.

She opened her eyes and there he was in her doorway, wearing his familiar jeans and tee shirt. His silky hair and half his face illuminated in the white moonlight coming in through the windows.

He took a deep breath, his wide chest rising and falling, like he was the one about to crawl inside the tiger's cage.

Yes. She liked that much better. Let him be nervous. Or worried. Let him waste time wondering if this was the right thing to do.

She knew what she wanted.

"Take off your clothes," she said, taking her fear in hand.

He smiled and it was part seduction, part boyish happiness, and she felt so much the same way. This darkness and light that would not be separated.

He tossed something down on the corner of her bed and then reached up behind his head to pull his tee shirt off. He undid his belt and pushed his pants down to his feet, stepping out of his boots and his jeans and his underwear at the same time. And then he stood there, naked and sliced to pieces by moonlight.

"You," he said, and she didn't hesitate to shimmy out of her clothes, dropping them beside the bed.

He put a knee on the bed and crawled up toward her, his erection bobbing as he went. He was braced on his hands and knees over her and she luxuriated in his attention. In that glowing heat in his eyes. She would preen if she knew how.

She reached up and cupped his face, the smooth ridges of the burns familiar now. Simply a part of him.

"Do you want to be here?" she asked him.

"Yes."

"Then no regrets, Dylan. I don't plan on having any."

"Me neither," he said.

"Lie back," she said, and he protested, not moving, but she pressed against his shoulder, pushing him until he had no choice but to fall onto his back.

She climbed over him, sitting, not on his cock, but against it.

She could feel him, hard and warm, caught between her body and his stomach. She shifted a little, gliding over it. Making it wet.

"Fuck, Annie," he groaned, reaching for her legs.

She loved the sight of those rough, dark hands against the pale skin of her thighs. Looking at them made her hotter. Wetter.

She ground down against him a little harder.

"You like my hands on you?" he asked, and she nodded. He slipped one down between her legs where she could see the head of his cock. He cupped himself, his knuckles pressing up into her pussy. One slipping slightly inside of her, the other notching against her clit.

It was rough.

It was perfect.

"Harder," she breathed. And he fisted his cock, all of his knuckles against her now, and she rode them. Up and then down, feeling each one against her clit and then down against the entrance of her body. Each one hard and sharp, nearly too much, but somehow not at all enough.

"Come here," he growled, wrapping a hand around her waist and pulling her toward his head.

"What?" she breathed, not wanting to leave this promise of pleasure with his rough fingers and hard knuckles.

"Come here, baby. I want to taste you."

"Taste—"

Carefully, she crawled up his body. Her pussy hit the tough stubble of his chin and he nuzzled it into her. She flinched and shuddered.

"Annie?"

"More."

He chuckled. "That's my girl."

He positioned her over his mouth and she had to look away—the sight of him . . . and her . . . it was too much. Too

raw. Something out of a movie she never got to see. The old stifling modesty came out of nowhere and she pushed it away.

Bullshit, she thought.

There were people every day in all sorts of places having sex
like this. Why should she be embarrassed?

She braced her hand against the wall and looked down, arching forward a little so she could see better.

He sucked her into his mouth, licking against her clit. Holding it still with the hard edges of his teeth. She worried about
whether or not he could breathe with his face up against her like
that, but then his hands pulled her harder onto him and she
realized she was bracing herself away from him.

And he didn't want that.

She settled more of her weight down and he groaned, opening his mouth wider, sucking on her harder. His chin was there
with that delicious stubble and she shifted herself against it. Circling her hips against him, until she found what she liked.

Both hands plastered against the wall, she let him eat her
until it felt like the whole world was in her body. Everything was
in her body. Everything good and sharp and sweet and hot. It
was her. It was in her. Her body coiled and curled and she closed
her eyes feeling as much of him with as much of herself as she
could.

Yes. She slapped the wall, felt the trailer shake. The earth
move.

Yes. His hands squeezed her ass, her legs, slipped up over her
back, pulling her down against him.

Yes. Again. More. More and more. Until suddenly it was
enough and she came, jerking hard against him, finding the right
pressure to make the orgasm last and last. It unspooled inside of
her, around her.

She unspooled. Endlessly. Perfectly.

Finally, she let go of his hair and slumped backward and he

sat up, practically throwing her back onto the bed and then crawling up over her. His face was shiny, his eyes were . . . oh, they were focused and intense. On her. With her.

Despite that orgasm she was breathlessly suspended by pleasure again. The pleasure she'd had. The pleasure she was about to have.

She would have given him everything at that point.

Anything he wanted.

"Look at you," he sighed.

She arched up against him, a tiger, purring.

"More?" he asked.

"Everything you have," she said.

He kissed her and she tasted her come on his lips. His tongue. Sweet and tangy. Salty and bitter. His damp face made her face damp.

She wrapped her hands around his cock where it lay, hot and hard against her hip. He shifted, his legs on either side of her body. No longer crouched over her, he was up on his knees. Calmly he reached behind him and slipped his fingers back between her legs. She jerked, flinched, really, she was so sensitive. But he did not stop. He slipped one finger inside of her and then another.

She spread her legs, letting him in. Letting him have whatever he wanted.

Slowly, she wrapped her hands back around his cock, jacking him slowly, and then she shifted down, he shifted up, and she slipped him into her mouth. The position was awkward, but his eyes said he liked it. Liked what he saw. He braced one hand against the wall and thrust down into her mouth, until she felt him at the back of her throat. She relaxed, breathing through her nose, covered her teeth with her lip, and pushed up when he pushed down again.

"Oh, look at you, baby," he breathed. "Look at you take it.

You fucking love it, don't you? You love my cock in your mouth."

She couldn't move or talk, pinned as she was by his body, so she simply . . . acquiesced. Total surrender. She felt the shudder run through his body and still he kept stroking into her, pulling back so she could get a breath, spit trailing from him to her mouth. She pressed against his ass, pushing him back into her mouth.

Over and over again, he filled her. Choking her. The edge between pleasure and pain beyond blurred.

He pressed into her until her nose was buried in the skin of his belly, until for a moment she could not breathe, and she trusted him totally to pull away when she needed him to. And he did. All the way out and she gasped for air, brushing the tears from her eyes with one hand and reaching for him with the other.

He stopped, though, and pulled her up into his arms, holding her tight and close. Not kissing her. Just hugging.

"Dylan?" she asked.

"I'm just . . . fuck. I'm just so glad you answered that damn phone."

"Me, too," she whispered against his ear. "But . . . you still owe me a dare."

He leaned back, his eyes blazing. His cheeks bright. "You sure?"

In answer she kissed him. Wrapping her arms around his neck, she kissed him with every ounce of yes she had in her body.

He shifted them, rolling them so she was on her back and he was over her. He pulled away briefly and grabbed what he'd thrown on the bottom corner of the bed.

"Your friend Joan had a lot of stuff in her trailer," he said. "I hope she won't mind I grabbed this."

It was a bottle of lube and more condoms.

"She won't mind," Annie said, breathless and strung tight beneath him.

"Roll over," he said, and she didn't hesitate.

She felt him over her, his hands rough and warm against her back, her ass, her thighs. "Lift up a little," he murmured, lifting her hips up and shoving a few pillows beneath her. He spread her legs wider and she realized he was looking at her.

But the embarrassment was all gone.

"We can stop if it hurts," he said.

"I know."

"Just say—"

"Babe." She smiled back at him. Meeting his eyes over her ass. "I know."

He flipped open the lid of the lube and spread some over his fingers. She looked away, putting her forehead down on her hands. She wasn't sure what she expected, but his erection slipping inside her pussy wasn't quite it.

Not that she was complaining.

He groaned and leaned forward against her back, a living blanket of heat. "You feel so good like this," he told her, stroking out of her and then back in as deep and as hard as he could go, making her gasp and then pant.

She pushed against him and felt the slippery pressure of his finger against her asshole. They both applied the slightest thrust against each other and his finger slid right in. She cried out, shuddering against him.

They stayed that way, nearly frozen but for their rasping breaths and shaking limbs. Slowly she adjusted to his invasion. She realized her legs were locked, all the muscles in her back tight, and one by one she relaxed them, until she was melted back into the bed.

"Good girl," he breathed. "So good. So beautiful. I need to get you ready."

"I'm . . . not?"

"Not yet, baby. I'm big and I don't want to hurt you."

There was a slight sting, a burning feeling, and a slow steady pressure as he added another finger.

It was . . . *oh God*. It was so much. So much of him.

"You okay?" he asked.

"Yes," she panted. She didn't move anymore; she felt pinned and full. Breathing felt like too much. Talking was nearly impossible. She could only lie there. Lie there and feel. And accept. And want.

"You want more?"

She nodded. And pushed her head against her hands and he slipped a third finger inside of her. His hand came down near her face as he braced himself. Pushing himself slowly inside of her.

"We can stop—"

"No!" she cried out, grabbing his wrist, digging in her nails. The edge of pain was like a promise, somehow, that there was going to be more. That there was something bigger and wilder than she'd ever dreamed that her body was capable of.

Dylan kissed her shoulder. Over and over again, and she was shaking and sweating. He shook off her hand and shifted, his knees spreading wider to hold his weight. He slipped his hand beneath her and she knew what he was doing.

"Yes!" she cried before he even touched her. And then his fingers brushed her clit, barely touching it, and she shattered.

His fingers left her asshole and she cried out, arching back to find him again.

And then he slipped out of her pussy and she felt him there. The blunt edge of his cock against the taut skin of her asshole.

"Deep breath." He sighed and slowly, with excruciating tenderness, he pushed himself into her. It was more than his fingers. Fuller and sharper and brighter, and she felt her body shaking again.

"Touch yourself, baby," he told her, and she shoved both hands between her legs. Stunned by how wet she was. The sheets were soaked under her. A quick, hard touch against her clit and she was flying again.

He cried out, slipping deeper inside of her. And she pushed herself back and forward, fucking herself against him.

"Oh, baby. God . . . you're . . ."

He fell over her, his hands braced by her face. And she lifted one hand from between her legs to touch his fist. He opened his hand so she could lace her fingers with his, holding them so hard they were locked together. She pressed her lips against his fist and tasted his sweat, felt the edge of his control.

"I'm going to come," he said, and all she could do was nod, wasted and spent.

His thrusts were gentle and slow and deep. He grabbed the blanket in his fist. His other hand was on her hip, holding her still, and she closed her eyes.

Total surrender.

Three more thrusts and he was bent over her, his head between her shoulder blades. His hands in fists near her face.

"Oh God, Annie. Annie," he cried, and then he was shaking. And she was accepting him. All of him. Any of him.

It was the most giving and fulfilled moment of her life.

Slowly, gently, he pulled away from her, but she still flinched when he left her body. She felt him leave the bed but she could not move. There was a chance she would not be able to move ever again.

"Annie?" She felt the bed dip again as he crawled up onto it with her. He brushed some of the hair from her eyes and she barely, just barely, managed to open them to look at him.

"You all right?" he asked. He was smiling at her, because he had to know just how all right she was.

"I'm so good," she breathed through a dry and dusty throat. "You?"

"I'm so good," he said and kissed her forehead.

He left again and brought back water and some Tylenol,

which he made her take for the morning, just in case she was sore. And a washcloth, which he used to clean her up.

"Let me change the sheets," he said. The wet spot beneath her body had only gotten bigger.

"Just get a towel," she said, too tired to care. So he did and then, because he was a gentleman and the best lover a girl ever had, he lay down on the towel over the wet spot.

"Go to sleep," he whispered against her ear, kissing her cheek. Her neck.

Tell me, she thought. *Say it. I know you feel it.*

She wasn't naive enough to think that amazing sex equaled love, but what she and Dylan had, it was so much bigger than the sex. So much more than their bodies.

I love you, she thought. *I love you so much.*

He had to feel it, too. He just had to.

He curled up behind her, one heavy arm over her waist, and as she was slipping down, down, down into sleep she waited as long as she could. Clung to consciousness with both hands hoping . . . waiting, really, for words that didn't come.

23

DYLAN

"You're kidding," Annie said as I put the plate of eggs in front of her. It wasn't much, a cheesy omelet, but damn if it didn't feel good to make it for her.

"Why would I kid about this?" I asked, stepping back to her little stove to make another for myself.

"Because it's too perfect," she said, laughing.

"Well, it was probably the best moment of my childhood. Totally the best Halloween, by a mile."

"So, you were . . . who?"

"I was Michelangelo."

"Which one was he?"

"The red one with the nunchakus. I was all about the nunchakus."

"Okay." Annie took a bite of the eggs. "And who was Max?"

Sunlight behind her highlighted the dust motes in the air and the white-blond ends of her hair. She looked like she was shooting out sparks. Glitter, maybe. The bruising was fading. She'd plucked

out the remaining stitches in her lip this morning; half of them had
fallen out overnight. Sitting there she was totally unadulterated; it
was like getting a bright shot of summer after a long winter.

"Leonardo, he was like the head turtle and he had swords.
Max had a God complex at a young age. Mom almost didn't let
him get the swords because they were stupid expensive, but she
could never say no to Max. Anyway, when we went out to trick-
or-treat we ran into my friend Joey Gibson, who was dressed up
like Donatello with the bow staff and the purple mask, and his
dad had made his shell costume and it kept falling apart, and he
came with us and then we ran into some other kid we didn't
know who was dressed up like Raphael and he came with us. So,
before we knew it we were trick-or-treating as all of the Teenage
Mutant Ninja Turtles."

"And it was totally by accident?"

"Couldn't have gone better if we tried." I slid my omelet
onto my plate and then cranked off the burner on the stove.
"Wait, do you even know who the Ninja Turtles are?"

She shot me some serious side-eye. "I wasn't totally isolated;
we did have a TV."

"Did you get to trick-or-treat?"

She smiled, twirling cheese around the tines of her fork.
"Smith took me for a few years."

My mouth was full of eggs, so I just lifted my eyebrows.

"I think I was five when he first took me. He found some er-
rand for us to run in town, and then when we got there he pulled
out a cheap plastic princess costume from under his seat and we
hit a few neighborhoods."

"What did you do with the candy?"

"Ate most of it on the way home." She smiled down at her
eggs, revealing that the happy memory had sharp edges that
hurt. "He made me give him all the Snickers. He told me it was
a bribe to keep quiet."

"We can find him, you know," I told her, wanting to give her that.

"How?" She glanced up and her blue eyes were damp. Not crying. Not exactly.

"Private investigators. Terrence works with one all the time. You said he was in Wyoming, right? With a sister. We can find him."

She pulled that bottom lip under her teeth, chewing on it. I looked back down at my eggs, because the sight of her doing that made my blood churn and it seemed totally inappropriate to get a hard-on while she was near tears talking about the man who was a father to her.

"Okay," she said.

"Yeah?"

She nodded, tears gone, nothing but smiles again, and I felt like I had pulled down the stars for her. And I fucking loved this feeling. It was better than racing. Better than making money. Better than anything I'd experienced in my life.

I used the side of my fork to cut more of my omelet.

"You didn't tell me what happened last night," she said. "At The Velvet Touch? With Max."

"Not much to say, really. We just . . . talked." I took a deep breath. "I thanked him for taking me to Miguel and Margaret after jail."

"Really?"

"He saved my life, in a way. I mean . . ."

"I get it," she said. I smiled at her. Of course she did. Somehow, she knew all the hard things. The things that kept me separate from the rest of the world only bound us together.

But I didn't know how to say Max was going to die. Sooner or later, he would end up somewhere riddled with bullet holes, bleeding out all alone.

Those were hard words to say, no matter how distant Max was.

And that I'd made him go back. Forced him back into that fate.

For her, for me. For us.

Guilt was an awful burn in my throat. It made me restless. Twitchy.

"You okay?" she asked.

"Fine," I lied. We ate in silence for a few minutes, the scrape of our forks against the plates grating. The silence got thicker, and I realized I wasn't the only one keeping my mouth shut about something. I could feel the weight of something she wasn't saying.

"What?" I asked.

"Nothing." She got back to her eggs like she was starving.

"Bullshit, nothing. You have something to say, say it."

"I'm just . . . How do you forgive your brother but not your dad?"

"Because it's not the same thing."

Again with her careful silence.

"What!" I snapped.

"Stop yelling at me!" she cried.

"Then say what's on your mind!"

"I'm not going to talk about anything if you yell at me."

"Fine," I said and stood up. "Then we won't talk."

I'd hurt her. If I'd reached across the table and smacked her I couldn't have hurt her more. And I hated it. I hated it as much as I was powerless to stop it. My dishes clattered into the sink.

All that anger I felt a minute ago was made worse by shame.

"I told you I don't know how to do this."

Still she was silent, sitting there, watching me. The fucking trailer was too small all of a sudden, and everywhere I looked, all I saw were the ways I could hurt her. And inevitably would.

I was a fucking Daniels. We didn't love, we crashed. We destroyed. We burned everything in fire.

This is a mistake. You and me, we're a mistake.

I almost said it. It would have been a relief to say it. To bow out of this thing we had between us. This thing that required pieces of me I didn't have or know how to use.

But she just sat there, watching me. Like she knew what I was thinking.

Growing up, I watched my parents on a constant cycle: vicious fight, someone leaves, then comes back, weeping and reeking of alcohol; they make up, only to do it all again.

It was exhausting, that cycle. It was bullshit. And I hated it.

This is how you stay, I told myself. *One hard moment at a time.*

I took a deep breath and then another.

I could apologize, but I'd given her too many apologies lately. It was time, maybe, to show her. To be different. To stop giving her reasons for the apologies.

"I'm going to work on your car today." I ran water over the frying pan and it sizzled, releasing smoke in the air.

"I'm going to mow the other half of the field." She stood with her plate and set it in the sink, too. Her body brushed mine. Her soft skin, her feathery hair. I grabbed onto her before she slipped by, having just narrowly stopped myself from pushing her away.

"Does it get easier?" I asked her, my face in her neck so I wouldn't have to see her eyes.

She kissed my neck. My ear. The scars there. "I don't know," she said. Her quiet honesty was so humbling. "I think so. I hope so."

Ah, that word. Maybe she didn't know, but hope was a tricky fucking beast, and she should know better than to say its name or else it would turn on us.

We kissed, slow and sweet. And I pulled her in closer, flush suddenly with survivor's adrenaline, because we'd just barely dodged a bullet of my own making. I shifted her back, stepping toward the bedroom, thinking of having something else for breakfast, when there was a quick, hard knock at the door.

Annie pulled back and I groaned. "Ignore it," I told her, still trying to get her into bed. But she pulled away from me, smacking at my hands that clung to her hips.

"Stop it," she whispered through her delicious, delicious smile.

She opened the door and it was Tiffany there, her hair pulled back in a ponytail, her tee shirt tucked into a pair of khaki shorts. She looked so young. Like a camp counselor.

"Hey," Annie said, stepping down into the fresh morning air. Leaving me in the shadows of the trailer, with the ghosts of our fight. "What's up?"

"I . . . uh . . . I actually came to talk to Dylan," she said, and Annie glanced back at me over her shoulder.

I came down the small steps, too, and the three of us stood in an awkward triangle.

"I'm ready," Tiffany said. "To meet Margaret and this Blake guy. The kids . . ." She cleared her throat, and I recognized all too well the sounds that accompanied a person swallowing her pride. "I haven't told them. But I keep thinking that if they're good people like you say they are, then my kids would be better for knowing them. For having them in their lives."

"That's true," Annie said.

"But I'm not doing this for money," Tiffany said. "Or charity or for their pity. And they can't just come whenever, you know. I need a date and a time. And maybe we don't even meet here, you know. We'll meet in town. Just them and me."

"Understood," I said. But Blake would not. Blake did things on his terms. Not anyone else's.

"Okay . . . so." She was wringing her hands, and Annie stepped forward and put a hand over hers. "What happens next?"

"I'll call them today," I said. "I'll let you know."

"It's going to be okay," Annie said. "You'll see."

Tiffany was convinced and she smiled.

I did not.

ANNIE LEFT TO GO MOW THE OTHER SIDE OF THE FIELD, AND I grabbed my phone and walked over to where Annie's car was parked.

Stock car racing was an endurance sport. It was an extended act of adjustment. Adjustments to the track. To the car. To other drivers. It required a driver to be constantly connected, constantly aware. Vigilant in the assessment of feedback.

But it was also about anticipation. About being able to see the future, in a way.

And this thing with Tiffany, with Blake . . . the future I saw, it wasn't easy.

It had real crash-and-burn potential.

The hood was up on Annie's car, which meant Pops was around somewhere, his hands covered in black motor grease.

How do you forgive your brother but not your dad?

The question was innocent enough. Even logical.

But nothing I felt about it was logical. It was all gut reaction and old bitterness.

Feelings that had been broken and left unset, to wither and die.

There was a list of parts the car needed, written in Pops's barely legible scrawl on the front bumper, held in place by a socket wrench.

I grabbed the list and called the garage, pacing away from the car, putting off the far more important call to Blake and Margaret. Because I was all kinds of chickenshit.

"989 Engines." It was Rebecca, our receptionist.

"Hey, Becs."

"Dylan?"

"Yeah, I have a—"

"Hold just a second—Blake wants to talk to you."

"No, Becs—"

"Well, holy shit, look who is lifting his head." It was Blake and he was not happy.

"Blake, what the hell are you doing there?"

"All the shit you aren't."

More feedback, more debris kicked up on my windshield. "Can I talk to one of the guys? I need a few parts down here."

"The Beamer broke down?"

"No, it's Annie's car."

"Why don't you just get her a new one?"

"She's got this thing called pride, Blake."

"How inconvenient. Give me the list."

"You want to take my shopping list?" I laughed. Talk about beneath Blake's pay grade.

"I want to get you back here as soon as possible," he said. "So we can get back to work."

I rattled off the twenty items. Spark plugs, timing belt. New windshield wipers. Headlights. Brake light cover. Oil. All new filters . . .

"Got it; I'll get one of the guys to bring this down later. And I need a concrete date from you, Dylan, when you're coming back."

"I don't have one."

"I can't run a fucking business like this."

"I know. And I'm sorry. I am. But . . . there's something else I gotta tell you."

Somewhere in the campground a kid started crying. "Shit," Blake said. "I don't like that tone. Spit it out."

I pinched the bridge of my nose. "Did you know that Phil is married?"

"What? Phil isn't married."

"He is. To a girl named Tiffany."

"You know this for a fact?"

"She's been living with him here at the trailer park."

"Well, that I figure is her problem. I told you, Dylan, Mom and me, we washed our hands of Phil. There's nothing we can do for that guy until he decides he wants help."

"Phil has three kids."

The silence on the other end of the phone was complete. And loud.

"Blake?"

"Three kids?" he asked.

"Yeah. Two girls and a boy. All real young."

"And this wife of his—"

"Tiffany."

"Right. Tiffany. She's the mom?"

"They've been married for, like, five years." I heard him suck in a quick breath. "And I just kicked him off the property for some shit he pulled with Annie, and Tiffany stayed here. Decided not to go with him."

"She and the kids are still in that trailer park?"

"Yeah."

Blake swore long and loud. "My mom is going to lose her mind," he said.

"That's why I'm coming to you first."

"So, what does this woman want? Money?"

"No, actually."

"Right," Blake sneered.

"I'm serious, man. She's not like Phil."

"She only married the guy."

"She wants to meet you and your mom, away from the park. Without the kids. She's got a lot of pride."

"Well, she's not meeting Mom at all until I check this woman out. I'll bring down the parts. See you in a few hours."

Damn, Dylan thought, putting the phone in his pocket. The day really had started off so well.

ANNIE

THE TRUTH WAS ANNIE'S HAPPY PLACE WAS ON TOP OF A RIDING lawn mower. And not just because the faint vibrations of the motor made certain key parts of her anatomy tingle, but because all the thoughts in her head quieted down for a few minutes. And it was just her and the sun and the bright blue sky above her.

And Dylan. Dylan in her heart. And in these quiet thoughts.

It had been a precarious moment in her trailer. She'd seen him rearing up, ready to smash what they had, and she sat there, knowing she couldn't convince him if he was not able to convince himself that they could work.

But then he'd controlled those impulses and that moment, that brutal restraint on his part, it said more to her about how he felt than any words he might say.

In her life, Annie had never felt very lucky. She wasn't entirely sure she believed in luck, actually. But the combination of last night and this morning made her feel like she'd won some kind of lottery.

She got insane sex, more pleasure than she knew existed. She got dark and depraved and tender and wild, and then in the morning she got an omelet and Halloween stories. And a man who fought his worst instincts to stay with her. A man who was trying harder every day.

If that wasn't lucky, she didn't know what was.

But is it love? some voice in her wondered. *Is it enough?*

She made her wide left turn at the top of the field, close to the tree line, and came around, lining up with the straight shorn edge of the line she'd already mowed.

And nearly ran into a man.

24

ANNIE

SHE YELPED AND TOOK HER FOOT OFF THE PEDAL, THE MOWER lurching to a stop. She was thrown against the steering wheel and then back against the seat by the shift in momentum.

"Holy shit!" she cried, her hand against her pounding heart. "You scared me!"

The guy wore jeans, faded and perfectly worn to his lanky body. He had on a plaid shirt and over that a leather vest. There were patches on the front of it, over his chest on either side.

His hair was long and black, tied back at his neck, and a trimmed beard covered the bottom half of his face, dark glasses covered the top half.

She realized she'd seen him once before, that night at the strip club—he'd been part of the group of men coming out when she'd been going in.

And then in a crystallized, ice-cold moment, she knew who he was.

Annie turned off the engine. "Max," she said, into the sudden quiet.

"You must be Annie." He was totally unreadable behind the glasses and the beard.

His mouth was the same as Dylan's. Those pillowing lips with the up-curled edges. The perpetual smirk.

"Are you looking for Dylan? Or Ben?" She said the names in part to see if he would react. Dylan, at the mention of Max's name, or his father's, boarded up tight. He stiffened and shut down.

Max did none of that. It was as if the names meant nothing to him.

His impassive face started to make her nervous.

She swung her leg over the side of the mower. "I'll take you to them."

"I'm looking for you," he said, stepping toward her, and she was now caught between the mower and his body.

He's not going to hurt you, she told herself, but her body wasn't convinced. Her heart rate kicked up. Her palms were instantly sweaty.

"Me?" If she'd wanted to sound tough, she just totally failed.

"I'd like to get to know the woman who managed to pull my brother away from his garage. Brought him down into the real world." His smile had a hint of charm that in any other situation might be effective, but right now it just felt threatening. "What's so special about you, I wonder?"

He took off his glasses and his eyes walked over her body, leaving footprints and dirt across the bare skin revealed by her tee shirt and shorts.

"Nothing," she said.

"Looks like you got tuned up recently." He gestured to the slowly fading black eye. "My brother do that?"

"No. Never," she said.

"Never," he laughed. "You don't know him very well, do you?"

"Better than you," she snapped.

"No one knows my brother better than me." His eyes were cold and mean. "Because I am part of the fucked-up mold that made him. And I know that he's got pretty screwed-up instincts when it comes to women. It's not his fault; our mom didn't do him any favors."

Max was so close she could feel the heat from his body against her bare legs and she fought the urge to cower away. It was what he wanted. To scare her. And she was not going to give him the satisfaction.

"I love Dylan," she said, unwilling to play this game.

"That's what he said. But I'm wondering why."

"If you don't know the answer to that then you don't know him. You don't know him at all."

"Is it the money? You got some fucked-up scar fetish thing? Is it because he killed somebody and you've got some kind of guilt complex?"

"Fuck you, Max."

"Is it the sex? An innocent like you—" He reached out as if he was going to touch her hair and she smacked his hand away.

"You don't touch me!" she said through her teeth. If she had the gun Dylan gave her she would have aimed it right at his heart. It was a startling revelation. That she felt such violence toward this man. That she felt such violence at all was unwelcome. Unnerving.

His blue eyes were back on her, something moving in those depths. Something dark and mean and big.

"Go," she said, suddenly scared. Suddenly more scared than she'd been when he first snuck up on her. This man was not like Dylan. Not at all. They might have the same mouth, but their hearts—their hearts were not the same.

"Scared?"

"It's what you want, isn't it?"

"What I want is my brother to be safe. And if you love him, you need to get him out of here—"

"Annie?"

Max flinched at the sound of Dylan's voice, who was running across the field toward them. Max turned away, pushing his glasses down over his eyes, and she thought he was going to leave.

Good. Yes. Please, leave.

Dylan was beside them, chest heaving as he sucked in breath. He pressed a hand to his side, over the knife wound.

"You okay?" Dylan asked Annie.

"I'm fine—" She barely got the words out before Dylan was turning on his brother, stepping between her body and his.

"What the fuck, man!" He shoved Max with both hands. An explosion of force. Max lurched back, his eyes focused on the trees, pretending, like a thug kid, that he wasn't all that interested in what was happening.

"What the hell are you doing here?" Dylan stepped sideways into his sight line. As angry as Dylan was—and he was angry, it vibrated off him in waves—she also saw the little brother he must have been, following Max into places he shouldn't have gone, blinded by hero worship and love.

"Just having a friendly chat with your girl." His eyes flicked up to hers and Dylan got right back in the way, so Max couldn't even see Annie. She shifted slightly sideways so she could see Max.

"You don't look at her," Dylan said. "You don't talk to her."

"So that's how it is?" Max asked.

"That's how it is. You're dangerous, Max. You've got bad shit attached to you. And I don't want you near her."

Max glanced away at the trees mummified in kudzu. They looked like trees, had the shape and size of trees, but they were something else, underneath.

"Stay away from the strip club," Max said, sounding old. Sounding tired and old. "You don't need to go back there. The club will be out of town by Sunday and then you can go get all the lap dances you want." Max put his glasses back on. The conversation was over. "Take your girl, Dylan, and leave. Get out of here. Stop spying on Pops, stop worrying about me. Cut ties like you should have years ago."

He can't, she wanted to cry. *He's not like you. He's not cold and ruthless; he only pretends because you hurt him so bad.*

"What's happening this weekend?" Dylan asked.

"Nothing you need to know about."

"This Lagan guy—"

Max grabbed Dylan's shirt, wrapped it in his fist. "You don't say that name out loud. Not to anyone. You forget you even heard that name. Understand?"

"Yes. I get it."

Max dropped Dylan's shirt, smoothed out the wrinkles and creases he put there.

Max's hand was shaking and she wanted to look away; she wanted distance from this terrible moment. These awful emotions. But she couldn't. She had to watch. Bear witness to the terribleness of all of it.

She owed that to the man she loved.

"What about Pops?" Dylan asked, clearly grasping at straws. Clearly trying to keep his brother here, to give him reasons to care. To stay alive.

Max laughed. "You want to divide up the old man's estate when he's gone? Fine, you get everything. The shitty trailer, the pictures of Mom he cries over every night—have at it."

"You don't care?" Dylan asked. "Not even a little?"

Max clapped a heavy hand on Dylan's neck, a gesture so oddly intimate, so strangely tender, she bit her lip against sudden tears. "Not even a little."

Without another word, Max turned and walked away. He marched across the field and along the tree line, and then he was gone.

Dylan could not hide his pain; it was there like a wound on his body. And she felt wholly responsible for this agony he was feeling. She was the one insisting that they stay, thinking that somehow she could change his past by forcing him into proximity with his father and brother.

How stupid, she thought. *How mean and selfish.*

"We can leave," she said. Blurted, really.

He didn't say anything, his eyes trained on that spot in the silvery green brush where his brother had disappeared. "We'll pack up. Head back to your house. If the police have more questions for me, or want to arrest me or whatever, you said it yourself, Terrence can handle it. And I'll come back down on Friday to help Ben home from the hospital." Finally he turned toward her, looking older. Broken. "We'll get a cab," she amended, doing everything she could think of to erase that look in his eyes. She did not want to abandon Ben, but if it was between Dylan and Ben it would always be Dylan. Always. "A cab can pick Ben up from the hospital and take him home. It's not a big deal. Really. Let's go. Let's just . . . go."

He was silent, still staring off at the kudzu, at his brother's footsteps through the grass clippings.

She launched herself off the running board of the motor and wrapped him in her arms, pulling his head down to her neck, her hands buried in his hair.

"I'm sorry," she breathed. "I'm sorry I made you stay."

"Annie," he sighed. Just that. Just her name, like that was all he was capable of.

"No, no, I should have listened to you. You've earned the right to walk away from your father and your brother. I kept thinking I was right, but I wasn't. I was selfish and stupid and I'm so sorry. I'm sorry. Let's . . . let's go. I want to see that beach house you keep promising me. I want to go skinny-dipping in the Caribbean."

His arms came up around her, but instead of hugging her, he grabbed her shoulders, pushing her away. She clung to him. "I'm sorry," she said again.

"Stop."

"I can't. I can't. This is my fault."

"It's no one's fault," he said. "It just . . . it's my family, and it's always been like this."

"But you were out of it. You'd left—"

"Annie. Stop. I had you spying on my old man for me. I wasn't out of it. I was just . . . living somewhere else."

His smile worked hard at being convincing but didn't quite succeed.

"We can't leave," he said.

"What? Of course we can."

"I made Max come back," Dylan said. "He'd gotten out, he'd left, and I made him come back to keep us safe. You and me and everyone in my life. He came back because I asked him to."

"You don't know that."

The look Dylan gave her was all pain. All heavy and hard knowledge.

Oh, what she would give to take that away from him.

"He made his choices," she whispered, stroking his face, the smooth edges of the scars. *You have paid enough,* she thought. *Do not feel any more guilt. Any more care. You went to jail for him. Sacrificed enough for him.*

"I know," Dylan said. "But it doesn't make my part in it any easier. We're not leaving. Blake is coming to meet Tiffany. Dad has chemo and I promised you church, remember?"

Those things might all be true, but that was not why he was staying.

"You can't stop him, Dylan. You can't save your brother. Even I can see that."

"No, you're right. He's going to get himself killed. Eventually. And I can't stop it. But I can be here."

Why? she wanted to ask. But she knew the answer.

To witness the terribleness of it all.

"You think he's going to come back?" she asked.

He shook his head. No.

Dylan didn't think Max would be back. But he would stay here, waiting. Just in case.

The feelings she had for him expanded in her chest so fast and so hard she couldn't catch her breath. She leaned forward, kissing his cheek, the side of his mouth. "You're the best man," she whispered. He leaned away, but she would not let him go. "The best man." She kissed him again. And again, seducing him to believe if not her words, then the fact that she felt that way.

Finally, with a low groan, he turned toward her. Accepting her kiss.

He was practically vibrating with tension. With emotion. With hurt and anger and love, and the forces were so powerful she felt like her arms were holding him together. The force of her love.

She kissed his mouth, opened her lips over his, and he yanked her hard against him. His mouth opened and the kiss was everything. It was brutal and tender, sweet and filthy.

He lifted her and turned, sitting himself on the metal seat of the mower, and she straddled his hips, her legs pushed and wedged against the metal body. He had her ass in one hand, the other up under her tank top, holding her neck, keeping her still for his devouring kiss.

He was hard beneath her and she arched into him.

His fingers fumbled between them, yanking at her zipper, the button of her shorts, until he could touch her. His fingers speared deep inside of her and she shook against him.

"Get the condom out of my pocket," he said against her mouth.

She fumbled, distracted by his touch, by the fire in her veins, but finally she found it. He helped her stand and pull off the shorts while she slipped the condom on him. They fumbled and were rough. Clumsy. But it didn't matter. No matter how fast they moved, it wasn't fast enough.

"Come 'ere," he whispered, his voice slurred, drunk on sex and emotion.

It was nuts. Frenzied. But she straddled him again and slid down over him, taking him inside.

"So good," he groaned. "So fucking good."

She put her face into his neck, smothering her cries, as she moved against him.

Her pleasure, the rising tide of her orgasm, hit a plateau. The position, the way her leg was wedged against cold metal—all of it stopped her from coming. She tried to shift, to grind her clit against something hard, his belly or belt, but the way they were sitting would not allow it.

Frustrated, she opened her mouth and bit his neck.

He roared. "God. Fuck, yes." His hands spasmed against her ass and he jerked up high and hard against her. *Yes,* she thought, as her clit finally got some action. "Again. Do it again."

And she did. She bit the strong muscle of his shoulder, sunk her teeth in his flesh, testing herself against him.

He grabbed her hips, lifting and pushing her harder. Faster.

There, oh God, there. Yes.

There were sparks on the back of her closed eyelids. Sparks in her body, lifting up, floating through her. Until finally, it all caught and she was swept up in a mighty blaze. Her body, ashes.

"Thank you," she sighed, limp against him.

He kissed her shoulder and held her tight. She was not ashamed of anything in the bright daylight.

Not of her nudity. Not of her love. Nothing.

In that moment she felt like the power of her feelings, the completeness of them, the way there were no gaps, no weak spots—they would be protected by that.

There was no way they could get hurt when she loved him so much.

25

DYLAN

I HAD THIS LIZARD ONCE. A LEOPARD-TAILED GECKO. I HAVE NO clue how or where I got it. In my memory it was just there. Max might have stolen it for me; I couldn't be sure. We used to catch crickets for it in the field behind the school.

But I remember when that thing was shedding its skin, it went from being really chill and riding around on the top of my hat to biting me and lurching away every time I tried to touch it.

Max kept telling me that lizards couldn't feel it when their skin came off, but I never believed him.

After seeing Max, that's how I felt. Like my skin didn't fit and I wanted to snarl and bite at the world. At anything that had the audacity to touch me.

Fucking Max.

I hated everything about what happened in that field. I hated that he even saw Annie. That he was trying to scare her. That after all these years of silence he would try to sort out my life. And he knew it was bullshit—that was why he couldn't look at me. But what I really hated was that I cared.

Max was involved in some kind of crazy dangerous shit and I *cared*.

And that crazy, frantic sex on a lawn mower of all damn things. Even that didn't feel right.

Nothing felt fucking right.

Annie went and told Tiffany that Blake was coming. From the sounds inside her double-wide, she was not happy.

"He's not meeting my kids!" she yelled. "We're not fucking puppies in a pound he can look over to see if he wants them."

Leaning against the picnic table, I winced. Because frankly, that was kind of the way Blake was going to be looking at them.

I heard the soft rumble of Annie's voice and the two of them came out of the trailer a few minutes later.

"Okay," Annie said with a tense smile. "Here's what we're going to do. Blake and Tiffany will use my trailer to talk."

I nodded. Sounded good.

"Where are your kids?" I asked.

"They're all napping. When's he going to be here?" Tiffany asked.

I checked my watch. One thing about Blake—the guy was always on time. To a fault he was on time. "Any minute," I said, which for some reason made her jump up.

"Thanks a lot," she snapped and went back inside, leaving me to stare at Annie.

"She's probably just changing her clothes and stuff."
Right.

I rubbed my face with my hand.

"This is going to be a disaster, isn't it?" I asked Annie.

"She's nervous," Annie said and she settled against the picnic table beside me, her arm and leg and hip brushing against me.

This feeling, this . . . want . . . I had for her. It was like a badly trained puppy on a leash, lurching after every squirrel. And the touch of her skin against mine made me crazy. Made me want to throw her over my shoulder and lock us up in her trailer and forget about everyone else and their stupid drama.

"Are you okay?" she asked.

"Fine."

"You seem . . . edgy."

I didn't want to talk about my goddamn feelings so I kept my mouth shut, and after a few seconds she sighed and I could practically feel her dropping the subject.

Because I don't have any skin, I wanted to shout. *I can feel everything. I feel too fucking much.*

But instead of yelling, I reached over and grabbed her hand. It was the best I could do.

She grabbed mine.

And the best I could do seemed like it might be good enough.

"Is this guy going to be decent to Tiffany?" Annie asked.

"I don't know, babe. He's a decent guy, but he's been cleaning up after his brother for years. And if he thinks Tiffany is trying to take advantage of Margaret, he'll destroy her."

"Destroy? That's a little dramatic, isn't it?" she asked me.

"Family means everything to him."

"She's family, in a way, isn't she?"

"Not yet."

ANNIE

Twenty minutes later, Tiffany and Annie were settled into Annie's trailer, waiting for Blake. Tiffany didn't want Dylan in there, and Annie didn't blame her. The emotions were high enough.

"You want a drink or something?" Annie asked. "Tea? I have tea. Or I could go next door and see if Joan left some booze—"

"I'm fine."

"You sure? Because I'm not sure how to host this kind of event."

"I doubt there are rules. But I'm fine. I'm not thirsty. I'm not hungry."

There was the quiet hum of a motor that slowly got louder, until a Porsche came into sight and parked right beside Annie's car.

It looked foreign and expensive. And fast.

"What's the deal with these guys and their cars?" Tiffany asked. "Are they all compensating for tiny dicks?"

"Dylan's not," Annie said, before she thought better of it. Tiffany glanced back at her and they both started laughing.

"Phil was. He definitely was," Tiffany said, which because of all the tension in the air was extra hilarious and they doubled up, over the table.

A man got out of the car. He was tall and wore a suit. The kind of suit that matched the car. Foreign and expensive. It was black, and he wore a dark purple tie with it and a white shirt that highlighted the darker tones of his skin. He had dark blond hair with a curl to it.

It was very pretty hair on a very hard man.

At the sight of him, all laughter vanished.

"Shit," Tiffany said. "Is that him?"

"I think so," Annie said. That night she was at Dylan's house she hadn't met Blake, and at the moment she was glad.

"He doesn't look much like Phil," Tiffany said.

"Blake must take after his dad. Dylan told me he was Cuban. And big."

"He's big all right," Tiffany murmured. "He'd squash Phil."

Dylan said something and pointed to the trailer, and within seconds Annie's door opened and they both turned in time to see Blake coming in.

Annie jumped to her feet.

"Hi," she said, sounding far too chipper. *Do not,* she told herself, *ask him if he wants tea.*

"You must be Annie," he said with a soft voice and plenty of charm. "You are as lovely as Dylan said." He was even smiling, but those eyes of his, green like glass, they were not friendly.

"Would you like some tea?" *Dummy!*

"No thank you," Blake said with chilling manners.

"I'm Tiffany," Tiffany said, coming to her feet. She held out her hand. After a long, strange pause, Blake shook it.

"My brother's secret wife." He made it a joke, like they were all in this strange situation together. But somehow it wasn't comforting.

"And you are my husband's secret brother," she said back. "Well, my soon-to-be ex, I suppose."

"Right," he said quietly. "Where are your kids?"

"Don't worry about my kids," she said.

"You don't trust me?" Blake asked, his voice dangerously silky.

Tiffany didn't even hesitate. "Nope."

"That seems about right," Blake said, stepping in closer. "I don't trust you much, either." His eyes scanned over to Annie, like he was encompassing her in that statement, too. He was a big man. Tall and wide. Annie pressed her back against the wall, like she was trying to make some room. Trying to put as much distance between her and his barely concealed dislike.

But Tiffany didn't cower. Not even a little. She stood there with her chin up, her mutual dislike battling it out with his.

Annie was inspired and impressed.

"Well, this is off to a great start, isn't it?" Tiffany asked.

"Right, let's just skip to the end." From the inside pocket of his suit, Blake pulled out a checkbook and a pen.

"I've never done this before," he said, his tone faintly mocking. "So I assume you'll let me know if I'm doing it wrong. Will ten thousand be enough?"

"For what?" Tiffany asked through white lips.

"To make you go away."

Annie gasped. "Blake, no, you don't—"

Blake's eyes sliced Annie open. "You've done enough, haven't you?" he asked her.

"What have I done?" she snapped.

"Tell me," he asked Annie. "If I give you ten thousand dollars will it make you go away, too, so my business partner and I can get back to work? I'm assuming you're in it for his money, so how about we just save some time and do this now."

Dylan. He was talking about Dylan.

"You're wrong," she said, her whole body vibrating with anger.

"We'll see, won't we," Blake said and turned back to Tiffany. "Now, for my ten thousand I want assurances from you that you will not try to contact my mother. Should you take my money and contact my mother anyway, after a DNA test to make sure that whatever children you have are related to me, I will take them from you. And you will never see them again."

Tiffany put one hand behind her, bracing herself against the table.

"Get out of here," Annie said, throwing open the door. "Now. I won't have you—"

"No," Tiffany said, her face pale, her eyes bright. "It's okay."

"It's not okay—he's being an asshole. You do not have to stand here and take this, Tiffany!"

"That's the check?" Tiffany asked, pointing to Blake's checkbook.

Blake handed it to her and she took it with shaking hands. She took her time reading it.

Tear it up, Annie thought. *You don't need that money.*

"Make it fifteen," Tiffany said, "and it's a deal."

"Ten's my offer," Blake said.

"Then I guess Margaret will be getting a phone call, won't she? And now I want twenty."

Annie gasped, stunned.

Blake took the check, tore it in two, and wrote her another one. The sound of him tearing it from the book was nearly violent. Tiffany took it, her hands steadier this time, and she tucked the check in her bra.

Blake sneered, his eyes following her movement.

"Pleasure doing business, asshole," Tiffany said, and stepped out of the trailer.

Annie stared at Blake, her mouth agape.

"What about you?" he asked. "I can write you the same check. I won't say a word to Dylan—you can break it off however you want."

"Get out of here," she said, her voice shaking. Her fists ached, they were clenched so tight.

"I've known that man, worked beside him for almost ten years. My dad used to love these backwoods illegal races and that's where he met Dylan. And that's all we heard about for a year—this fucking kid with the driving gift. My dad gave him a job after he got out of jail. Trained him. Helped him. After the fire my mom practically saved his life, nursing him back to life. According to my sister and younger brother, my dad loved Dylan more than he ever loved us. And frankly, I think it's probably true."

"Why are you telling me this?"

"Because he's only ever treated my mom like an employee. And he's only ever treated me like a business partner. We're not friends. We're not brothers."

"You sound jealous," Annie said, just to be mean.

"I was. I was fucking jealous. For years. But then I got wise. And I'm suggesting you get wise now before you get hurt. Because he's broken. His family—Max, his old man—they broke him. And you know that. The sex is good, I imagine. And he's followed you to this shit hole, but that's not about you, is it? Not really. It's about his family. It will always be about his family. And himself. Deep in your heart you know that and you're trying to convince yourself that you can save him. And you can't. There's no saving Dylan Daniels."

DYLAN

WATCHING BLAKE GO INTO THE TRAILER, I HAD TO PUT THE odds of a happy ending for Tiffany and the kids and Margaret at about . . . minus 10 percent.

Blake was going to pay Tiffany off. And then threaten her until she took the check.

That is what Blake did: he bought outcomes. And when it came to his mother and her happiness, no price was too high.

"Have you seen my mom?"

I turned around at the sound of a little kid's voice, and behind me was Tiffany's oldest. Her son. He was rubbing his eyes, and his hair stood up on the back of his head in a crazy rooster tail.

Great. Just what this situation needed.

"She's in Annie's trailer," I told him. "Why don't you go back to bed?"

"I want my mom," he said, and started shuffling toward Annie's trailer.

Crap. No.

"Hey, kid, you ah . . . want to help me fix this car?"

That got him. The little boy whirled around, all sleep out of his face, nothing but excitement now.

"Really?" he asked.

"Sure," I said.

Shit, I thought.

This was Miguel's grandson. Cars were in his blood. And affection softened me. This boy should have been learning at Miguel's shoulder, or Blake's. Not mine.

But my shoulder was here.

"Let's see what we've got, okay?" I lifted him up on the edge of the hood. "Don't fall," I told him.

"No way," he promised. I smiled and bent down to pick up some of the boxes Blake brought with him.

"What's your name again?" I asked.

"Danny. What happened to your face?"

For a moment I just blinked at him and then I laughed. Because goddamn, wasn't there something refreshing about that. "I was in a fire."

He winced. "Did it hurt?"

"Very much."

"Sorry," the kid said. "Sorry you got hurt."

Christ. The kid was sweet. I hoped Blake wasn't in there ripping Tiffany to shreds.

A screen door shut not too far away, and Danny and I both looked up to see Pops step out of his trailer. He caught sight of us and stopped for a second.

Ignore us, old man, I thought. *I've had a shit day and it's about to get shittier, and I can't handle you and your guilt on top of it. I just can't.*

But of course, Pops always had an instinct about doing the opposite of what I wanted him to and he walked our way.

26

DYLAN

"Do you know Ben?" Danny asked.

"Yeah," I said, using my foot to pull my toolbox closer. "I know him."

"Sometimes he fixes stuff in our trailer."

"Your dad didn't do that?"

"Dad's never around. So Ben did it. He's grumpy."

You don't know the half of it, I thought.

"You got an assistant?" Ben asked as he got closer. He had a strange smile on his face, like he was trying to hide the fact that he was smiling.

"I'm helping fix the car," Danny said, lifting his wrench as proof.

"This brings back memories," Ben said. Before I was Danny's age, I'd been handing Pops his tools while he worked on some project car in our driveway. And the memories were good ones. I couldn't pretend otherwise, no matter how much I hated the man. Toward the end, before Max went away the first time and we started stealing cars, Pops and me, we'd gotten so good working together that he didn't have to tell me what he wanted. I just knew.

I just knew the old man's brain.

He was watching me out of the corner of his eye, waiting for rejection. And that much hope directed my way was painful. So I ignored it.

"Help me open these boxes, would you?" I asked Danny, and he jumped down from the car.

"I saw Max today." Maybe it was the memories or all the goddamn hope in the air, but the words just happened. Fell out of my mouth without thought.

"Where?"

"He was sniffing around Annie in the field."

Pops was silent and I glanced over at him. The thought of Max close to Annie bothered him, too.

"She okay?" Pops asked.

"Fine."

"What can I do to get her to leave?" Pops asked. "I mean, I know she's staying because of me and the chemo—"

"She's already said we can leave," I told him, and despite his asking, I could tell he was stung by her willingness to go. But he only showed me that for a second.

"Then what the fuck are you waiting for?" he asked.

"Swearword!" the boy cried from the ground, where he was surrounded by a moat of packing peanuts.

"Come on, kid," I said. "Let's keep this clean." I started shoving the packing peanuts back in the boxes before they could blow away.

"You're waiting for Max, ain't you?" Pops asked. The hair on the back of my neck stood up so hard it hurt. "You think he's going to come back—"

"No," I said. "I don't. I think he's going to get killed."

"And you're going to stop it?" Pops laughed.

"No." I'd given up enough for my brother. I wasn't giving up whatever kind of future I had with Annie. I wasn't going to go to that strip club and try to rescue him. He'd made his way. I just . . . couldn't leave. Not yet.

"Son," Pops sighed, and I didn't have the fight to tell him not to call me that. "What has he done to make you so loyal to him?"

I didn't know how to explain that it wasn't about anything Max had done.

It was that he was Max. I was only given one brother and we just kept sacrificing our lives for each other.

Tiffany came out, stormed out really, leaving a trail of smoke behind her. "Danny," she said to her son, "come on, honey."

"But I'm fixing the car," the little boy said. He held up new windshield wipers as proof.

"We'll have a chance later," I said to him, which seemed to mollify the kid. Solemnly he handed me the windshield wipers.

"Everything okay?" I asked Tiffany, though I knew the answer was going to be bad.

"Your friend is an asshole."

Yes. Yes, he is.

"Mom!" Danny yelled with glee. "Swearword."

"I'm a grown-up," she said, taking his hand, leading him back through the rhododendron. "I can swear."

A few seconds later Blake was out the door, looking unruffled. "What did you do?" I asked him.

"I took care of things," he said. "That's what I do, remember?" He glanced over at Pops. "You must be Ben." His tone was nothing but accusation wrapped up in a sneer.

For a second, brief and strange, I felt the compulsion to defend my father. But it passed. Thank God. "What's wrong with you?" I asked Blake.

"What's wrong with *me*?" Blake asked, looking around the

trailer park. "Dude, you are one of the richest men in the country. What are you doing here? Playing house with some—"

"Don't," I said, taking a gliding step toward my friend. We hadn't fought. Not in years, and I knew Blake was some kind of bare-knuckle boxing lunatic, but if he said one bad word about Annie I would take him apart. "Don't say another word."

"Fine," he said, lifting his hands. "But you've got a fucking company on the edge of a huge breakthrough. And we can't finish the job without you."

He was right. Totally right.

"Monday," I said. "I'll be back by Monday."

"Yeah, how will you be back? Like you were before? Distracted and on your phone all goddamn day or will you be the Dylan Daniels I need you to be?"

"I'll be back on Monday," I said through my teeth. The Dylan Daniels he needed me to be—the workaholic hermit—*fuck,* I wasn't that guy anymore. But I didn't answer to Blake. I would figure this shit out.

He watched me for a long time and then finally pulled his Porsche's keys out of his pocket. "See you Monday." He said nothing to Ben, but got into his car and roared away, spitting dust and gravel into the air.

"Nice guy," Pops said, but I ignored him and went into the trailer to find Annie sitting on the settee, staring down at the cracked linoleum of the trailer.

Christ, I thought, *I am one of the richest guys in the country. How did I get here?*

"What happened?" I asked.

"He gave Tiffany twenty thousand dollars to never call him or his mother again."

I whistled long and low. That was a pretty dick move, even for Blake.

"She talked him up from ten," Annie said.

Well, that surprised me. Or maybe it shouldn't. Tiffany was a survivor. "Then I guess they both got what they wanted."

"He offered me ten thousand dollars to break up with you." Her eyes were narrowed, dry and hot.

"I'm guessing you said no."

"You say it like it's no big deal he tried to buy me off, Dylan."

"You didn't take the money," I said. "I don't know why it needs to be a big deal. Christ, Annie, don't look at me like that. If I'd met Tiffany three months ago I would have written her a check. I would have written her *two* checks so I wouldn't have to spend any time with her son."

Annie gaped at me, her judgment rolling off her in waves. I opened her fridge. There was a bunch of Diet Coke and a plate with Margaret's grilled chicken on it.

"Let's go get a good steak," I said. "With a baked potato with the works. We'll get dressed up and go out."

"How can you say that, Dylan?"

"Because I'm hungry."

"That's not what I'm talking about."

I shut the fridge door.

"Because everything's different."

"What's different about now and three months ago?" she asked, ignoring the steak proposal.

"You. You are what is different. You have changed everything." It was the unvarnished truth. As close to love as I was capable of getting.

But that rigid set of her shoulders did not relax, and she was still looking at me like she didn't quite believe me.

"Did something else happen with Blake?" I asked. There were all sorts of things the man could have and would have said to her to make Annie look at me like she'd never seen me before.

"He said you're never going to love me," she finally answered. "That you can't."

I breathed deep. Immobile and silent.

"Part of me worries he's right," she said, driving her words in deep.

"No," I said. My hands in fists. *No, you just got here. You just gave me this love; you can't take it away. Not yet. Not because of fucking Blake.*

"But I really want to believe he's not," she said. She was looking at me for confirmation. Like I could just say to her that he was wrong. That I wasn't broken, that sooner or later I would be able to love her the way she wanted.

But I didn't have that answer. And what I did have didn't seem like enough, but I gave it to her.

"You changed me, baby," I told her, stroking her cheek. "I barely recognize who I was before you came into my life. And I don't . . . I don't want to go back to being that way."

Is that enough? Please, God, let that be enough.

Some of the anger fell from her shoulders, and though she wasn't smiling, I could feel her beaming at me. It was an internal thing. An awareness thing.

And it was powerful.

Way more powerful than all my money.

"You said something about a steak dinner," she said, and relief rolled through me, making me light-headed.

"I did."

"I don't have nice clothes."

"I can take care of that," I said. It was crazy how meaningless my money was with her, how I had to find ways to spend it on her. To use it on her behalf.

For years I was used to holding the influence with people because I had the money. But Annie had all the power between us and I didn't know how it had happened. Or if she knew.

Or, frankly, if I cared.

This is what Blake didn't know. This feeling. This moment. When the money he held so dear meant nothing.

Annie couldn't be bought, one way or the other, and that made her priceless.

"We could do that here," she said. "Go to the store and get big steaks and potatoes."

Even if her home was a tin-can trailer on the edge of nowhere, Annie was a homebody. Which, frankly, I loved.

I imagined her in my beach house. The glass walls. The hot tub.

That was the kind of house made for never leaving.

I would take her there. As soon as possible.

"Whatever you want," I told her.

"Wine in a box?" she asked hopefully, with no irony.

"Ahhh, a woman of taste. Only the finest wine in a box for you." I leaned over and kissed her lips. Again. And then, because she was so sweet, I did it again. And because she had changed me on a molecular level and in this moment I could not pinpoint the value I added to her. Not my money, or power.

Just my broken and scared self. And that seemed so inadequate in the face of her love.

Within minutes I was over her on the bed in her trailer, stroking in and out of her so slow and so hard that she shook every time I sank into her.

"You feel that?" I asked, deep inside of her. I lifted her hips, shifted her legs, until I was even deeper. Impossibly deeper. I had all of her and she had all of me, and no sex ever in my life had been like this.

"I feel it," she said, clutching my back as if to keep herself from falling.

"Where?" I breathed against her lips. I licked into her and she opened her mouth.

"Everywhere."

Good, I thought. That was exactly where I wanted to be.

ANNIE

DYLAN WENT TO GET PROVISIONS FOR THEIR STEAK DINNER EX-travaganza and she, restless, wandered over to Ben's trailer. His garden was a mess, and she opened the gate and got to work on the weeding around his peppers. The orange tops of carrots were poking up out of the black soil and so she gently pulled them up, stacking their long bodies together.

"You stealing my carrots?" Ben asked, and she glanced up to see him under his awning. He looked thin and wan, but the smile on his face was an incredible antidote for the expressions of the faces of the other men she'd seen today. Dylan excluded.

"Have you eaten today?" she asked.

"Well, hello, Ben," he said in a falsetto. "Good to see you."

She laughed. "Hello, Ben. Good to see you. Have you eaten?"

"Some crackers. My appetite ain't so hot."

"Dylan is going to get steaks and some potatoes. Any of that sound good?"

Ben looked through his lashes at her as he wandered over to the edge of his garden. "Sour cream on the potatoes?"

"Dylan said the works. I'm not sure what that means."

"For Dylan that means sour cream."

She stood with an armful of carrots she'd harvested. "I can cook these up, too."

"Cooked carrots are a crime against nature."

"Then I can peel them and slice them up," she said.

"You go ahead and take them. I was never much of a carrot fan."

"Why'd you grow them, then?"

"Because it's a garden." Ben shrugged. She put the carrots down in a pile and moved on to his potatoes. She'd come here to his garden because she wanted to be close to someone who knew

Dylan. Who at one point had to have loved him, no matter how badly it ended.

"How long have you lived here?" she asked.

"I read an article about Dylan in a magazine somewhere. And it said that after his accident he was recuperating in his home outside of Asheville. That was what . . . four years ago. Five?"

"You moved here to be closer to him?" she asked.

He stared at her with dark, empty eyes and she realized, even if he'd never said it, she'd known that all along.

"How did he find out about you living here?"

He pursed his lips. "It wasn't hard. I sent him a note, just telling him where I was. I thought . . . maybe he'd come down off that mountain and see me. Come yell at me. Break my nose. Something."

"But he didn't."

"Had the guy that lived in Tiffany's trailer at the time spy on me. He was the first one."

"You knew?"

"Not at first; just thought the guy was some kind of weirdo, but by the second spy Dylan hired I caught on."

"I met Max today," she said.

"Dylan said. I wish I could say his bark is worse than his bite, but that's not totally true."

"I got that sense. I met another guy, Blake."

"His business partner. Funny, I don't think his bark is worse than his bite, either."

"Yeah. He told me Dylan was going to remember sooner or later that he was too broken to love me and he'd leave."

Ben's awkward silence seemed proof positive that she needed more traditional friends. The former-criminal estranged father of the man she loved wasn't so great at this kind of conversation.

But Annie didn't have anyone else. Tiffany certainly wasn't going to want to talk about her love life.

"Do you think Dylan is broken?" she asked Ben, looking up from the potatoes to meet his sad eyes. "I mean really know. Not just guess. Not just hope he's not broken?"

Ben shook his head.

"Me neither," she said.

Annie was clinging to faith that there was going to be proof of this at some point. Something more than the sex that bound them together. She'd told him she loved him and Annie understood that he wasn't ready to say it back. That he might not be able to recognize those feelings. Hell, there were moments Annie wondered if she had gotten it wrong somehow.

She even understood that he might never be able to love her.

And how long do I give him? she wondered, thinking of her mom and Smith. *How many months, years of my life do I give to a man who cannot love me back?*

There was no easy answer for that. Not from her and not from the old man with the garden of regrets.

A few minutes later, Dylan's car drove up to the spot next to their trailers and Annie pushed away bittersweet memories and sour thoughts.

We have now, she thought. *We have tonight.* And she was not going to ruin any of it thinking about a future that might not happen.

He will love me, she thought. A wish she had no way of making come true.

"He ain't gonna want to have dinner with me," Ben said, heading back toward his door. "But I'd take a potato if you have extra. And feel free to use the oven for cooking. Steaks taste real good over that fire."

He was gone before she could protest.

Her hands dirty but her heart hopeful, she walked across the grass to meet Dylan.

"You didn't invite him to dinner, did you?" he asked.

"I didn't get the chance. But I'm gonna take him a potato later," she said.

She grabbed the rest of the bags from the back of the car and from the corner of her eye, she caught Dylan looking over at Ben's trailer. He hesitated, just a moment, as if considering asking him to dinner. In the end, he didn't. But the moment had been real. And maybe she was deluding herself. Putting together small moments and clues that pointed her in the direction she wanted to go.

But for the moment she took comfort in it.

Nope, she thought. *Not broken.*

27

DYLAN

Blake's direct hit about how I hadn't been working much and the company was on the edge of a huge breakthrough still stung, so while Annie took Ben into Cherokee for his chemo treatment I sat down at my laptop and got some work done.

Emails were first. Lots of guys were fishing for early demonstrations of the transmission. I shot them all down and started looking at the Dyno testing numbers to see where things could be tweaked.

After a few hours, though, I kept checking my watch, wondering when Annie was going to get back. I finally heard my car pull up beside the trailer. She'd used it because it was so much more comfortable for Ben to ride in. He'd grumbled about it, about everything, until I told him to shut it and get in the car.

I stepped outside to see if there was anything I could do to help and caught her trying to help Pops out of the passenger seat.

"Hey, hey," I said, rushing to help her. "Let me do that."

I edged her out of the way and put Pops's arm over my shoulder. Awkwardly he tried to pull away from me, but I kept my arm around his waist, my hand fisted in the side of his tee shirt.

"Thanks," she said, pushing her hair out of her face. "I stopped by the library and got some books on CD for him. The nurses told me he likes those."

"Does anyone still have a CD player?" I asked, walking slowly toward Pops's trailer, while he took shuffling, unsteady steps beside me. It was easy not to feel him, not to be aware of his shallow breaths and the faint smell of hospital on his skin. I just pulled way back inside of myself, like a turtle in a shell.

"Apparently Ben does," Annie said. "I want to grab some soup from my trailer and some crackers. I bought some ginger ale. The nurses said that might help, too."

"Keep her away from me," Pops breathed, "just . . . just for a few minutes."

I glanced down at him and saw, as much as I didn't want to, how he was barely upright. Barely keeping one foot in front of the other. This wasn't about him being tired of her, or a dick in the face of her kindness. He'd been putting up a brave face in front of her and he couldn't keep it on anymore.

"Go ahead," I told Annie. "I'll get him in his trailer."

"Are you sure?" she asked.

"Yeah. Get what you need. Take your time."

Annie peeled off toward her trailer and Pops and I just kept walking.

"Bathroom," he whispered, and we picked up the pace. I threw open the trailer door and just barely got Pops inside so he could lurch to the toilet. I stood just outside the door and listened to him retch.

Shit, I thought. *Shit.*

I didn't know how to do this.

"You all right?" I asked when the retching stopped.

"Top of the fucking world."

I smiled at the tone. If he could be bitter and sarcastic, things weren't all bad. I leaned in the door to the bathroom only to see the old man sitting back against the wall across from the toilet, his legs splayed out awkwardly in front of him.

"Let's get you up to your bed," I said.

He shook his head, his eyes closed. "I'll spend the next twelve hours like this."

For a second I was helpless, and then almost immediately I was pissed and ready to just let him sit there. Frankly, he probably had a routine worked out for this. He didn't need me telling him what to do. That was just awkward for both of us.

But then I imagined Annie seeing him like this.

"You'll feel better in bed," I said, reaching into the tiny bathroom to pull him to his feet. "I'll get you a puke bowl like Mom used to give us."

The mention of Mom got him to open his eyes and look at me. But he didn't say anything.

This, I realized, all the hair on my arms standing at attention, was a man at the bottom. The very bottom. My old anger for him retreated. It was useless and ugly in the face of his dying.

"Come on, Pops," I whispered, and helped him into the bedroom. Gingerly he sat down on the edge of the bed.

"You want a shower or anything?"

"You don't have to do this," he said, clinging to his pride.

"Well, I'm already doing it. So, what do you want?"

"Clean shirt," he said. He was already in gray sweatpants. He pointed at the top drawer of the cockeyed bureau in the corner and I pulled out a fresh white shirt.

Pops was attempting to pull off his own shirt but was too weak, or too sick, or both, to get it done. It was oddly and terribly humbling to see him like this.

"Here," I said and lifted the shirt up over his head, like he did to me when I was a boy.

The big Skulls tattoo that used to cover his back had been

blacked out. From nearly his neck to the top of his pants and from shoulder blade to shoulder blade was dense black ink. It wasn't done gently, either. There was scar tissue in there.

"Why'd you get kicked out?" I asked, helping him into a clean shirt.

"I didn't. I left."

I blinked, and he started to lean back in the bed. I tugged the gray and blue covers down to help him. "What do you mean you left?"

"Paid my final dues and got out. Should have done it years before." he sighed as he finally got horizontal on the bed.

"When?"

"When I heard about you killing that boy in jail." He took a deep breath, ragged and wet. Awful. "Your mom begged me when we met. I wish I'd listened to her."

I stood there, staring at him. All these years he stayed away and I never knew he'd quit the club.

"I wasted more years than some people get on this earth," he said.

"Why didn't you tell me?" I asked.

"Would it have changed anything?"

No. Yes. "I got out of jail and I thought . . . I thought you just walked away."

"I did. And that's the way it should have been. You were right to hate me, son. Right to keep me at arm's length," he said, watching me, wretched and pale, from the bed. "Can you get me that puke bowl, please?"

Silently I went and got a bowl and put it down by his bed. His eyes were shut and I thought he was sleeping, so I turned to leave him alone.

"Dylan." His dry voice made me pause in the doorway. "I know it's wrong. And it's selfish and I don't have any right to it, I don't deserve it . . . but, I'm glad you're here."

I bit back a lot of words. A lot of old, useless words. Words that wouldn't even make me feel better if I spat them at him.

"Get some sleep," I said into the dark wasteland his words left in me.

It wasn't forgiveness, that I didn't think was possible, but acceptance.

"Hello?" Annie called out and I stepped out of the bedroom, closing the folding door behind me.

"Hey," I said in a low whisper, intercepting her at the door.

"Is he asleep?"

I nodded.

"Oh." She had a slightly stilted look, like her plans had been thwarted. She had an armful of things that I helped her let go of and set down on the counter. A few cans of ginger ale, a CD player with headphones that she must have found in a time machine.

"They're Ben's. He listens to books while he's getting the treatment. You should have seen, Dylan. He looked so . . . old. And all the nurses were so kind and good to him, no matter how grumpy he was."

"That's good," I said, because there was nothing else to say. It was what my brother had said to me the other day outside the strip club. "That's real good."

She took the Discman and the CDs from the library and a can of ginger ale and tiptoed into his room and set them on the table beside his bed. She reached out and stroked his balding head and I glanced away, uncomfortable with the tenderness.

But that's the problem, isn't it? I thought and forced myself to watch. Forced myself to just accept this, too.

She closed the door behind her and walked to me with a tired smile on her face.

"That," she said, putting her arms around me, "was a day. I can't believe he did that all by himself for so long."

"Come on," I said, leading her out of the trailer. The sunlight accepted us with open arms.

"I'm going to make some soup," she said. "Something with rice. Or noodles. Something easy on his stomach."

"Do you cook?" I paused to shut the door behind me and she moved a little bit ahead of me. The other night I'd made the steak, while she sat on the settee and got skunked on boxed wine. It was one of the best nights of my life.

"No. I'm really terrible at it. I probably should not attempt to make this soup." She smiled at me over her shoulder and there was something in that smile that made me stop. Something revealed in her. Or me. I couldn't tell.

I stopped in that dirt track that ran down the center of this trailer park, the small road that led back and forth from Pops's trailer to Annie's.

"I'm not going to let you go," I said.

Pops's voice, those words he said in the trailer, they roared through my head.

I know it's wrong. And it's selfish and I don't have any right to it, I don't deserve it . . . but, I'm glad you're here.

That's how I felt about Annie and I wasn't going to let her go.

"What are you talking about, Dylan?" She turned back and looked at me and I didn't know what she was seeing. What expression was on my face? Whatever it was, it did not feel neutral.

I felt feral and wild.

"I'm not letting you go," I told her. "And it's selfish and wrong and sooner or later you're going to wake up and realize that I can't love you the way you should be loved. Or want to be loved, and it doesn't matter."

She looked slightly stricken and I realized she'd been thinking about this. Actually contemplating the fact that I might not be able to love her the way she loved me, and that filled me with rage and panic.

"Do you hear me? I'm not letting you go."

I'd crossed the distance between us and I was standing so close, the buckle of her belt bit into my stomach. I would cross any distance to get to her. On my knees.

"I don't want to be let go," she whispered.

"You don't want my money," I said. "You don't care about power."

She was shaking her head. "I only want you."

For how long? I wondered. *For how long before you realize you should have more?* The right thing to do would be to let her go, but I was done with that.

"You're mine," I told her, walking her backward toward the trailer.

"No," she said, shaking her head and smiling at me, the kind of smile that women in movies gave to better men than me. "You got it all wrong, buddy. You are mine."

She was saying words she didn't totally believe yet. And maybe I was, too. But I wanted them to be true. For the first and only time in my life, I wanted to belong to someone and have that person belong to me.

And that had to count for something.

"You're not broken, Dylan. I know you're not."

I grabbed her, yanking her into my arms, and she put her strong, strong arms around my neck and held on. She held on as tight to me as I was holding on to her.

And that had never happened in my life before.

28

ANNIE

THE EXPLOSION ROCKED THE TRAILER, YANKING ANNIE OUT OF a dream about being lost on a college campus, wearing corn-detasseling clothes.

"The fuck?" Dylan cried. He dove over her in the bed, squashing her into the mattress.

The silence after the explosion was heavy, and after a long minute the breeze coming in through the screens smelled funny. Acrid.

"What was that?" she whispered against Dylan's shoulder, still trying to sort out reality from dream. His heart thundered against hers.

"Stay here," he said, and rolled off her. He pulled his pants on from the floor. Shoved his feet into his boots. "Annie? Promise me you'll stay."

"Okay." She pulled on her own clothes and shoved the curtains aside, trying to see something through the window. "I'll stay here. For a few minutes."

Dylan left, and she went into the dining room to try to

see something out those windows. But all she saw was black sky and Ben, slowly coming out of his trailer, a flashlight in his hand.

Dammit, she thought. He needed to be in bed. She didn't think he slept much on Friday night and all day today he'd been outside on his porch, smoking joints, trying to keep the nausea away. She grabbed her phone, dialed 911 but didn't hit send, then she went outside.

There was a group of people standing in the middle of the path past the rhododendron, looking up at the sky. On the horizon, over the edges of the tree line, the sky was a shifting collage of purple, orange, and yellow.

"What happened?" she asked, stepping up next to Dylan.

"It's a fire," he said.

"What's over there?" someone else asked, a woman in a robe whom Annie hadn't seen before.

"The strip club," Ben and Dylan said at the same time.

Annie hit send on her phone and lifted it to her ear.

"What are you doing?" Dylan asked.

"Calling 911."

"*What?*" Ben looked at her, too, and she realized they were worried about Max and cops. Once an outlaw, always an outlaw, Annie guessed.

Well, too damn bad.

"People could be hurt," she snapped at them.

"911, what is your emergency?"

She told the dispatcher about the fire and gave her the highway exit number, and within a few moments there were sirens splitting the quiet of the night.

"What do you think happened?" she asked, putting the phone in her pocket.

"Nothing good."

"Do you want to go?" she asked. "I mean, there might not be much you can do, but at least you can see for yourself—"

"Don't go, Dylan," Ben said. "There ain't nothing you can do for him. He's either in there and dead, or he's gone."

"Yeah." Dylan sighed, his eyes on that far horizon. "You're right."

He wrapped his arm over her shoulder and leaned, just a little, into her. As if to say, *Help, I can't hold all this.*

She grabbed his hand and held on, as hard as she could.

"That ship is going down," Ben said, the sky illuminated by flames they could not see mirrored in his eyes. "All the rats will be swimming away."

Ben gave Dylan a look she couldn't quite decipher.

The sirens stopped. A thick column of black smoke was billowing into the air, over the trees, drifting on the wind toward them.

"Pops," Dylan said, suddenly. "You're moving in with me."

"The fuck you talking about?" Ben asked. Ben and Annie both turned to Dylan with their mouths open.

"You're moving in with me and Annie, to my house near Asheville. The hospitals are better." Dylan shot Ben a hard look. "Fewer rats."

"Are you speaking in code?" Annie asked.

Ben sucked his teeth for a second and then nodded. "That makes sense," he said. "Keeps everyone safe."

"Hey," she said, pushing against Dylan. "Not that I'm not thrilled with this, but what rats are you talking about?"

The sound of a car rolling over gravel very slowly made them turn, and a shitty blue sedan came into view on the far edge of Joan's old trailer. The lights were off, and everything about that car screamed trouble.

Dylan pulled Annie behind him and Ben shifted sideways, making the wall of male shoulders complete.

The driver's-side door opened and Annie fought the urge to hide her face in Dylan's back, expecting Max. Or that guy Rabbit, or any of the other players Joan had mentioned that day in the café.

But it was Joan.

In dark jeans and a black sweatshirt. Her face filthy, her hair covered in a dark cap.

"Joan!" Annie cried, stepping past Dylan, shaking off his hand when he tried to grab her wrist. "She's my friend," she said to him, but he looked dubious.

"Are you okay?" she asked, coming to a stop a few inches from Joan. "Are you hurt?"

"Fine," Joan said, her face tense and still beneath that ash and dirt. "I am. Really."

"You were in the fire?"

"Barely got out. Look, I don't have time to talk. I need my bags from my trailer." Beneath her skin, Joan was frantic. A manic terror pulsed out of her.

"Are you in trouble?" Annie asked.

"Not if I can outrun it. Please, get my bags."

"Yeah. They're . . . they're actually in my trailer. Let me go get them."

DYLAN

I watched Annie go, but Joan watched me. The edge of her lips beneath that ash were white and her hands were in white-knuckled fists.

The woman looked about as guilty as an arsonist could.

"You start the fire?" Ben asked her. The old man must have been reading my mind.

"Nope."

Hmmmm. Pops shot me a look that told me he wasn't sure if Joan was lying or telling the truth.

"You sure seem nervous," Pops said.

"Yeah, well, I got Max in the backseat of my car."

I bolted past her and grabbed the passenger door handle, but she got around me, leaning her weight against the door so I couldn't open it without jerking her out of the way. Which I put my hand on her wrist to do.

"Listen to me," she said, hands up. "Rabbit tried to kill him—"

"What?"

"He's been shot. Twice, actually. Flesh wounds. The one in his calf, I need to take the bullet out."

"Get the fuck out of my way!" I jerked her sideways and opened the door. My brother's half-conscious body nearly toppled out onto the ground.

"Jesus," I groaned, catching him before he landed in the dirt. Pops was beside me, useless and frail, but trying. I had to give him that.

"I tried to tell you," Joan said.

This is how it ends, I thought, *with my brother bleeding out in the backseat of some shit car, shot by his own fucking "brothers."*

God, what a fucking cliché.

Annie came back out holding a duffle bag and a half-full black plastic garbage bag. "Oh my God," she cried and then dropped the stuff, bolting across the dirt to help me.

It took some work, but we got him back inside the car. I shut the door and ran around to the other side and opened that door. Pops followed as fast as he could.

Max was bleeding from a head wound and from his calf. The wound on his calf was tied off with a red bandana that was totally saturated with blood.

"Max," I said, crawling as best I could into the car. "Max, are you all right?"

His eyes fluttered open and fluttered shut again.

Pops leaned in beside me. He made a soft groan in his throat at the sight of his oldest boy. The rope that tied this moment, this awful blood-soaked moment, to my father, to the way he raised us and the choices he gave us, was strung tight around his neck. I could say something about the sins of the father, wrap my fist in that rope, and pull. But one look at the old man's ravaged face and I could see that he was already doing it.

"Annie," I said. "Go get some towels." Her eyes wide in a white face, she nodded and darted off again, and I tried to see under the bandana tied around Max's leg.

"The bullet is buried in the muscle. No bones," Joan said. "I can get it out and I can stitch it up. I've got materials in my stuff. But we need to get out of here."

"He needs a hospital," Annie said, arriving with an armful of towels.

"Hospital won't work," Pops said. "It's a gunshot. There will be too many questions."

"And we can't stay here," Joan said, shoving her bags in the trunk. "I'm not sure if anyone survived that explosion, but if they did, they're looking for Max."

"You mean they're looking for you," I said.

"They might be."

"Who did this?" Pops asked.

"Rabbit," Joan said.

"He dead?" Pops asked.

"I don't know," she said. "It's total chaos over there. But Rabbit wasn't alone. He had the whole MC on his side. This wasn't an assassination. It was a coup. You have to believe me. He's not safe here."

"Where are you going to take him?" Annie asked.

"Someplace safe," she said. I stood up and stared at her. "I swear to God."

"What about his head wound?" Annie asked. "He's probably got a concussion. It might be serious."

"I'll cross that bridge when I come to it," Joan said, slamming the trunk down.

Max's legs spasmed and I looked back down into the backseat of the car. His eyes were open but unfocused. He looked like a character out of a slasher movie, covered in blood.

He was shaking his head at me. "D . . . E . . . A. Not. DEA."

"What's he saying?" Pops asked.

" 'Not DEA,' " I said, looking back at Joan. "You taking him in? Gonna make him turn rat? Because he'll be staying here if that's your plan. We can take care of him."

Joan took a deep breath.

"I'm not DEA," she said. "I never was."

Annie gasped. "But the badge?"

"Fake. I got about twenty fake badges in that bag. I'm not DEA, I'm not . . . anything."

Holy. Shit. This drama kept getting worse and worse.

"Then what are you doing?" I asked.

"Trying to stay alive," she said. "And trying to keep your stupid brother alive. Listen to me—we don't have much time. But where I'm taking him, he'll be safe. He'll be away from the club, which," she licked her lips, "you know he wants."

Guilt pierced me.

"How do you know?" I asked. Max wouldn't have walked around broadcasting that fact; it would have gotten him killed even faster.

"Because I do. Because your brother and I are . . . friends. Sort of. You have to trust me."

I knew what kind of friends Max had. Liars. Cheats. Killers.

This woman had proven to be a liar. Was I just supposed to believe she wouldn't kill him?

"We trust you," Annie said, speaking for all of us. She glanced over at Pops and then at me.

Fuck. This right now, this moment, in the backseat of Joan's car. This was the best shot my brother had. If he stayed, he'd be killed or behind bars.

"Go. Go," I said. I looked back down at Max, whose eyes were shut, but he was still shaking his head.

"Sorry, man," I said to him. "But you'll figure this one out. You always do."

I shut the door, and Joan went around to the driver's side. Annie wrapped her arms around Joan before she could get in the car and Joan just stood there. Stunned.

"Be careful," Annie said, and let her go.

"Take care of him," I told Joan, meeting her eyes over the hood of the car.

"I'll try," she said.

And that was the best I could do for my brother: let a con woman drive away in the middle of the night with his body bleeding in the backseat.

I pulled my old man back as I stepped aside and let the car drive away.

Pops sagged in my arms, and for a second I felt like I was the only thing holding him up.

It was me and the old man in the darkness of the wide world.

And then he shook me off and took a lurching step toward his trailer.

"Ben," Annie said, going after him, and I almost told her not to waste her breath, but if anyone was going to get through to him, it would be her. "Let me help you," she said, and reached for him.

Pops stepped away from her touch and turned to face us. I had to look away. The pain, visible and real and crippling, was all too much.

"Annie," he said, his voice gruff. "I beg you, if you feel any affection for me, any . . . kindness. Leave me alone. Go with

Dylan. Live a life that looks nothing like the one you had before. But leave . . . leave me here."

Oh fuck. Annie was crying.

"But you're moving in with us," she said.

"There's no need anymore—you heard Joan. Rabbit is dead."

"We don't know that for sure—"

"It doesn't matter," he cried. "Don't you get it?"

"No!" she yelled back. "I don't get it. Because you need someone to take care of you. I'm going to take care—"

"I'm not Smith," he said, and glanced over at me. "You don't get a second chance. None of us do. This is how I want to die, Annie. Alone. You . . . Dylan . . . Max." An awful sound broke out of his throat, an emotion so thick and wild he couldn't keep it down. "It just hurts too much."

Tears spilled from the old man's eyes. I wasn't sure I'd ever seen him cry. He sucked in a deep breath and shuffled away. Annie looked at me like I should do something, but I didn't know what to do. I had no resources for this.

"Really?" she asked. "You're going to just let him go?"

"For right now I am," I said. "Come on."

I could feel her wanting to resist me. Wanting to punch and smack. And I could give her that place to let that out. I could let her take a swing. As many swings as she wanted.

She could take that anger and that pain and fuck it out of herself. I could be the tool that she used to make her body feel so much that the pain in her heart went numb.

I knew how to do that. I'd been doing that all my life.

The minute I got out of jail I found ways to make the pain in my heart smaller and smaller and smaller. But it never went away. Never. It came back, found new avenues. New ways in. And it was the same old shit, every time. And *fuck*. Fuck if I didn't realize, looking at this beautiful woman, that sometimes you just had to feel it. Sometimes you had to let the terror and the anger and the fear tear you apart.

So you could feel what came next.

And like that, just like that, I was blown open.

"I love you," I said.

She blinked and reeled back. "What . . . what are you talking about?"

"I love you."

Saying it again I only felt it more. This feeling in my chest, wild and fire-breathing, it gained shape. Edges, soft ones that didn't hurt.

"I love you."

That time I smiled.

She glanced over her shoulder at the smoke, and then over at Ben's trailer, where he'd disappeared. "Now? You realize this now?"

"Yeah." I nodded. "I don't know how this usually happens. But this . . . right now, I looked at you and thought of a dozen ways I could help you not feel this. I could fuck you. Or let you hit me."

"I don't want to hit you!" she cried. "Or frankly, at this moment, fuck you."

"I know," I said. "But those are things I've been doing for years so I don't have to feel the shit. All the bad, nasty, awful shit that life brings. And I've gotten so good at not feeling that shit that I don't feel anything. Do you get that?"

"Yeah." She nodded. "I . . . totally get that."

"And I just realized, baby, right now, thinking of how I could take this pain away from you, I just realized that you have to feel it. You gotta make your way through all the bad stuff to get to the good." I was standing in front of her now, my hands in her hair, my thumbs on her lips. Tears were gathered on her lashes and I brushed them with my finger so they fell down on her cheek. A silver trail.

I sucked one off my finger and it was salty and sweet and bitter. Maybe as all the best things were. I didn't know; I was so unfamiliar with the best things.

"I love you."

"I love you, too," she said and wrapped her arms around my neck.

For a few seconds we just stood in the slowly gathering light. It came from the east, from behind pink clouds, and it rose to take over the darkness, to push it back, bit by bit.

"Okay," she whispered. "I guess I feel like fucking you now."

29

ANNIE

THE NEXT MORNING ANNIE WAS CAMPED OUT ON BEN'S FRONT stoop. He'd opened the door about twenty minutes ago and told her to leave. That he wasn't coming out again. And so far he was as good as his word.

She knocked and banged and yelled, but he was totally silent inside his trailer.

And Annie's heart was breaking.

"Hey." Dylan came to stand in front of her, wearing his jeans and a red button-down shirt with the sleeves rolled up.

"Hey," she said resting her head against the hard planes of his stomach.

"He's not coming out?"

"He's not even yelling at me."

He sighed and stroked back her hair. "Well, let's leave him alone a while."

"And do what?"

"It's Sunday," he said, and she glanced up at him in time to see his smile, crooked and endearing. A shot right to her heart. "And you owe me a dare."

For a second it didn't register and then she laughed at him. "You want to go to church?" she asked. "Now?"

"Well, it's church time, so yeah."

Truthfully she didn't need much convincing. Her heart was heavy and the world seemed like a dark and cold place right now. Annie didn't know if church could help. She didn't know if anything could. But she had to try.

So church it was.

She changed her clothes and went where Dylan led. A small Catholic church just outside Cherokee.

And it was . . . everything she remembered. Everything calm and quiet. It was order and community. Sunshine through stained-glass windows and off-key voices singing as loud as they could.

And it was made perfect by Dylan sitting beside her.

She didn't care much for the priest; he had a funny voice, and all she could think about was that priest from *The Princess Bride* who talked about "mawwiage," with that awful lisp.

But Dylan listened. Leaning forward, his hands between his knees, his eyes focused on the pulpit. Dylan listened with his whole body.

Annie smiled, thumbing through the hymnal for the next song. He didn't sing, so she sang loud enough for both of them.

They left the church holding hands.

"What did you think?" she asked.

"Tuuue wuv," he said in perfect imitation of the priest voice from *The Princess Bride*. "You want a donut or something? Mom always used to bribe us with donuts so we'd go to church with her. It's hard to break that kind of association."

She agreed to donuts. Right now, looking at him, she would agree to anything he wanted.

"You worried about Max?" she asked as they drove toward downtown and a bakery on the main strip.

"He made his bed," he said, pulling into a parking spot.

"Yeah, but are you worried about him?"

"I'm always going to be worried about him. I don't think I know how to stop. Or if I should, you know. I mean, shouldn't Max have someone on this earth worried about him, instead of trying to kill him?"

"I can't believe Joan lied," she said. "Is that . . . like is she a con artist or something?"

Dylan laughed, a dry humph. "A survivor, I'm guessing. Just like the rest of us."

Annie stroked back his hair, her fingers tracing the edge of his ear. "How did you get so kind?" she asked him.

He grabbed her hand and kissed it. "There was this girl," he said. "Who answered this cellphone she found in a shitty trailer. She taught me."

Annie doubted that was true, but she didn't argue.

"What are we going to do about Ben?" she asked twenty minutes later, as they got onto the highway heading home to the trailer park. She had a pink box filled with a dozen donuts. Dylan had gotten a little carried away with the cream-filled.

"Hope he's changed his mind," Dylan said, changing lanes. "But if he hasn't, I feel like we need to respect what the guy wants."

"Even if it's alone and awful?"

Dylan nodded and shifted gears. His powerful, capable hand moved from the gearshift to her knee beneath the only skirt she had. She'd caught him admiring the skirt all morning, even in church, which had seemed incredibly sacrilegious. If not incredibly thrilling.

"Do you want to move in with me?" he asked, out of the blue. "I mean . . . is that a choice you want to make? If we strip away all the drama we've lived through, is that what you really want?"

"It's what I really want," she said, leaning across the seat to kiss his cheek. The corner of his mouth. "But," she asked, "what if without the drama we realize we're boring."

"Boring?" he asked, his eyebrows raised. "Do I need to remind you of what you asked me to do to you this morning? Before church?"

She blushed at the memory, delighted and happy and turned on.

"Naughty girl," he said.

"I love you." She expected a delay, a second, while he got his head around the words again. But there was no delay. No pause.

"I love you, too."

"Do you really want me to move in—"

"Yes. That's all I want. Is you with me."

There was no better answer.

At the trailer park there was a police cruiser in the parking area in front of the office. Grant was stepping out of the office, Kevin behind him

"What the hell is that guy doing here?" Dylan asked, lifting his hand from her knee so he could shift the car as they slowed down.

"He must be here about the explosion," Annie said.

"Right." Dylan rolled to a stop. "That cop liked you," he said.

"He asked me out once," she told him. "In front of the library."

"Yeah?"

"He's a nice guy, but I don't like nice guys. I like bad boys with secrets and tons of money and luxurious compounds on mountaintops."

His hand snaked out and caught the back of her head, pulling Annie in for a fierce, thorough kiss. It felt like he was marking his territory, but she didn't mind.

Dylan broke the kiss, leaving both of them panting. "You want to talk to him?"

Talk to whom? Her mind was wiped clean by that kiss. She couldn't remember what they were talking about.

"Hero Cop."

Right.

"You want me to?"

"No," he said. "I don't want you anywhere near the guy, but he's probably going to know more about what's going on. And it would be good to know what happened to Rabbit."

Very true.

She slipped the donut box to the backseat and leaned over to kiss him real quick. And then again because she loved him so much, before jumping out.

Dylan drove away to park near their trailers.

"Hello, Annie," Grant said as she walked closer. He had sunglasses on, so she couldn't see his eyes, and his smile was reserved. He'd seen that kiss and she could feel herself blushing.

"Grant, are you here about the explosion last night?"

"Just asking some questions."

"I called 911," she said. "What . . . what happened?"

"Someone put a bomb in the back room of the strip club. Three dead. A dozen or so injured."

"Oh my God," she gasped.

"Yeah, we've got DEA here and FBI. Apparently this was some sort of drug bust or something. We're still trying to put together some pieces. You haven't seen anyone or anything suspicious, have you?"

"No. I haven't." Annie lied to a police officer and she kept her mouth shut about Max and Joan. "I heard there was a motorcycle gang involved."

"Yeah. An MC out of Florida."

"Were they the ones killed?"

"Annie," he sighed. "I know your . . . boyfriend's family was involved."

She was silent.

"You sure you don't have anything you want to tell me?"

"I don't know anything," she said. "Dylan has been estranged from his family for years."

"And yet . . . ?" He shrugged. "Here he is. Twenty miles away from the explosion."

"Are you accusing him of something?" she asked.

"No," he said, his voice hard. "I'm just letting you know I'm not an idiot."

Grant pulled a white card out of his breast pocket and scribbled something across the back of it. "That's my cell. Call that. Anytime. If you remember something that might help."

"Okay," she said.

"Good luck, Annie. And not for nothing, you're better than that guy. You're better than this."

"You're wrong," she said. "He's the best man I know and I'm just trying to keep up."

She tucked his card in her pocket and walked away.

Smiling.

DYLAN

I PARKED MY CAR AND LOOKED THROUGH THE WINDSHIELD AT Pops's trailer.

Annie was not going to let Pops die here all alone. Anyone could see it. So, I had to either resolve to living in this trailer park or convince Pops to move in with me.

I hoped he still liked Boston creams, because I got him six.

I pulled open the top button of my shirt as I walked across the lawn toward his trailer. I'd forgotten what a drag church clothes were, but it was worth the discomfort to see Annie so at peace. And in a skirt. The skirt was nice.

I knocked on the door and, predictably, didn't hear anything.

The old man had not taken last night well. Though I don't imagine there was a good way to take last night.

"Hey!" I called out. "You there, Pops?"

There was a sound from inside. A heavy thud. And I imagined him face-first on the bathroom floor. I knocked again. "You all right? Pops?"

"Go away!" Pops yelled.

"Come on!" I yelled back. "You're freaking me out."

I knocked again, but this time the door swung open, unlocked.

"How do the doctors feel about donuts?" I asked, stepping into the dim trailer. All the blinds were shut, the curtains drawn, and it smelled . . . off. "Pops?"

It took me a second, I don't know why, but my brain could not process what I was seeing.

Pops was sitting on the settee, slumped over the table. His hand stretched across it.

There was a knife through it, keeping it pegged to the table.

The smell was blood. Rivers of it.

"Well, now, isn't this another happy family reunion."

And there in the shadows, covered in black soot, with a black eye and a split lip and an arm at an unnatural angle, was Rabbit.

30

DYLAN

Jesus. How did I not see this coming?

Because Joan said Rabbit was probably dead and I wanted to believe her. I wanted this part of my life to be over.

"Come in, come in," Rabbit said, lurching toward me and the door. In his good hand was a gun. At that moment I would have done anything to have back the gun that I gave to Annie. "Shut the door. We wouldn't want to draw any attention to ourselves, would we?"

I stepped in and closed the door behind me. I put the box of donuts on the counter. The pink box with its pretty writing and the smell of sugar coming off of it looked ridiculous in here with the blood and mayhem.

"You survived," I said.

"Barely."

"It was a bomb?"

"It was a fucking massacre."

"The cops are here," I told him.

"Exactly the attention we do not want. So, have a seat."

Rabbit pointed to the table with his gun and I went, slowly, taking note of all of his injuries. Bad hand. One black eye. Something was wrong with his foot—he was limping/lurching. And the way he moved made me believe he had a problem with his ribs.

"What the fuck are you doing here?" I asked Rabbit, who sat down next to Pops. The old man groaned, lifting his head just enough that I saw the busted lip and fucked-up nose. Blood dripped from his nose onto the table. "Beating up old, dying men. That's got to be a new low for you, Rabbit."

"Shut the fuck up," Rabbit said, dropping for a moment that weird jovial act he wore like a shit suit. He reached forward and wiggled the knife in Pops's hand and the old man swallowed a scream. I felt my body contract, all my muscles fighting the urge to do something. Anything. "I'm looking for Max."

"He isn't with you?" I asked, keeping my face carefully blank.

"Nope. Not with me. Hasn't been with me in a very long time, Dylan. For years, really. Max lost his shit about the time you got in that accident, fucked up your face."

Do not respond. Give him nothing. Show him nothing.

"He's not here."

"That's exactly what your father said," Rabbit said. "I got to hand it to the old man, I thought he'd cave so much sooner. Loyalty was never his strong suit, was it? But nope. He didn't say a word about Max. Wouldn't tell me where you were, either. Or that sweet bitch—"

I lunged across the table, but Rabbit pulled up that gun and pointed it back in my face.

He tsked and smiled. His teeth actually looked white in his sooty face.

"I think maybe I've figured out a way to find out what I need. Why don't you go get your girlfriend," Rabbit said. "See if she knows where Max is."

"She doesn't know anything."

"I think I can be the judge of that."

I sat there. Unmoving. "Go," Rabbit, said and pointed the gun to Ben's temple. "Or I will kill him and then I'll kill her."

"Don't." Blood poured from Ben's mouth. "Just run, Dylan. Run and don't look back. I'm a dead man anyway."

"Come on now, Ben," Rabbit said, putting his arm around Pops. "We both know Dylan's not going to do that. Seriously, dude, why you're so fucking loyal to these assholes, I will never know. Now, go. Get the girl."

There was no way. No way at all I was bringing Annie back in here.

But then there was a knock on the door.

"Ben?"

Jesus. It was Annie. Of course it was Annie. And in about three seconds she was going to walk in here.

Pops's eyes met mine and it was like when I was a kid, sitting on the edge of some car, handing him tools before he could ask. In the span of a heartbeat, the plan was made.

I reached forward with both hands and yanked the knife out of Pops's hand and tossed it to him. With his good hand he caught it—barely, and with all the strength he had in that dying body jammed it right into the joint of Rabbit's shoulder.

Rabbit screamed. He didn't drop the gun, but he was barely holding on to it, and I grabbed it, wrestling it from his weak grip. Once I had it I smashed it across his face for good measure. He swore at me, spitting blood and reaching for the gun with his ruined body, so I hit him again. And then again, until he slumped unconscious against the settee.

Pops spit on him and leaned sideways against the window, his bleeding hand cradled to his chest, blood all over his white tee shirt.

"Dylan?" It was Annie behind me. I didn't even hear her come in. "What happened? Is Ben . . . ?"

I turned and faced her, got between her eyes and the carnage of my father and the unconscious shithead beside him. I'd done this before. With Hoyt.

God, how many times did we have to live through some nightmare?

"Go outside," I told her.

"What? No, Ben—"

"I've got this under control, Annie."

She shot me a glare that was all fuck-you. "I'm calling Grant," she said.

"No," Ben gasped.

And my girl, my tough girl, she didn't hesitate. She opened her phone, grabbed a card from her back pocket, and dialed a number.

"Grant," she said, into the phone, her eyes locked on mine. "I need you to come back to the trailer park. I have something for you."

She hung up and shoved the phone back in her pocket. "I'm going to go outside and clear off Ben's chair. You bring him out and we'll get him comfortable and away from this mess."

Annie was totally in charge and I was wasted with love for her.

She left, and I turned and grabbed Rabbit's unconscious body and threw it onto the floor. And then, with the gentlest hands I was capable of, I helped Pops slide across the settee and stand up.

"I got you, Pops," I whispered, my arm around him, nearly lifting him as we went down the stairs. Annie was there to help me, and together we got him into his chair.

She pulled the scarf from around her neck, the pretty one with flowers on it that she'd worn for church, and pressed it against Pop's hand, then wrapped it around his fingers, helping the old man keep pressure against the blood.

Her weight rocked the chair forward and his head rested lightly against hers.

My instincts, my memory, my very will told me not to forgive. That forgiveness was the wrong reaction to all the damaging things my father had heaped onto my shoulders. But I could not look at him with the woman I loved and hold on to my hate.

It was that easy.

I loved her.

I had to forgive him.

It wasn't for him so much as it was for me. For her.

For a future free of all this shit.

The sirens behind us wailed and Annie looked up. I don't know what she saw in my face, what horrors or worries. But she reached for me, grabbing my hand with her own bloodstained fingers.

"We're going to be okay," she said, smiling as best she could through tears.

I felt like I had moved the last of the giant pieces, those rocks mysterious and unseen in my future, that I was so scared of, that were so inevitable.

They were gone now. Cleared out.

"Yes," I told her, slipping my fingers through hers, holding on to her with a tether of hope.

Hope, that wild rebellion. That fierce force of nature. That giant raised middle finger in the face of my past.

That was my new truth.

My whole future.

Hope. And Annie.

Epilogue

Three years later

ANNIE

A WOMAN WITH A CLIPBOARD AND A HEADSET, WHICH MADE her official, wandered through the group of students and parents standing inside the student rec center and yelled, "We need all graduates to head toward the staging area for processing to Sherrill Center. Family and friends, please go find your seats or you will miss the ceremony."

This was about the fifth time she'd yelled it, and people started to actually listen.

All around us, parents were hugging their kids, taking their last photos, wiping away tears.

Dylan didn't move. And neither did I.

It was as if those words were for other people.

They did not apply to us. We were in this together. To the very last.

It was my graduation day.

He stroked back my hair. Red, again. And really curly. He said he liked it, but every once in a while I missed Layla's white hair.

"Have I told you how proud I am of you?" he asked, holding my face in his hands. I held his wrists in mine and we were like a closed loop. A complete circuit.

The world went on and on around us, but we were . . . still.

"A thousand times."

He kissed my lips. His smile kissing my smile. "I'm proud of you."

I would take him with me up onstage if I could. Hold his hand while I took my diploma. Because we did this together. These last three years, the hard things, the easy things, the *really* hard things—we did them side by side. Hand in hand. Sometimes screaming at each other, sometimes weeping hard tears, but together.

We'd lost Ben last year. He'd gone into remission after the chemo three years ago. And Dylan had a real good eighteen months with his father.

They fixed a lot of cars together.

But frankly, I think Ben staying alive as long as he did, and fighting as hard as he had, was because of Dylan.

Family. Love. Forgiveness. Those were powerful things.

Bedrock kinds of things.

Dylan found Smith for me, brought him back to me on a private jet for my birthday. I'd fallen into Smith's arms and wept and apologized and wept some more. He forgave me. I was still working on forgiving myself. Smith still lived in Wyoming. He said he needed the sky and the space. But we went to visit, and he came to us at least once a year.

Dylan's phone beeped, and he fished it out of his handsome new suit jacket and checked the text. I straightened his tie. It was a pretty purple tie that reminded me of spring and new beginnings and hopeful stuff. He'd put up a fight at first, but in the end he wore it.

He had a hard time saying no to me, something I tried not to exploit. But it was difficult when a man like Dylan would pull down the stars for me. And my man did look good in a suit.

"Is it Max?" I asked, because my handsome man in a suit was frowning.

"No. Not Max. Max . . ." He trailed off and shook his head. Right, we wouldn't talk about Max.

"Has Blake—"

"Gone out of his mind? Yes. As per usual. But it's Margaret telling me to get to my seat. She and Smith are getting dirty looks from people who want my seat."

He slipped the phone in his pocket but didn't move.

"I suppose it's time," I said, looking around for the clip-board lady.

"I got you something," he said, reaching into his pocket.

"Yeah!" I clapped my hands. Because I did like it when Dylan got me things. He wasn't extravagant, having figured out who I am and what I like. So, when he got me something it was usually small and always perfect.

He took my hand, pressed a kiss to my palm, and then with his wide, rough fingers carefully draped a gold bracelet over my wrist and struggled with the tiny clasp.

"You want some help?" I asked.

"I got it," he muttered.

Finally, on the third try he succeeded. And he dropped his hands. It was a bracelet with a delicate gold chain, but in the center there was a wide flat gold section.

"It's engraved," he said, and I leaned down to see the words.

You and Me was etched into the gold.

"The other side, too," he said. Carefully I turned the bracelet and on the back it said, in big block letters, sturdy and impla-cable. Undeniable, even:

BEDROCK.

You and Me. Bedrock.

Perfect.

I clasped my wrist and that perfect, perfect bracelet to my chest.

"How did we get here?" I asked, full of wonder and love.

"You pulled me out of the darkness," he said. "I had no choice."

But the truth is never that simple. There was darkness in both of us. And light. I could not claim to have saved him. I could only say that the moment I answered that phone, we began to save each other. Over and over again, in big and small ways.

The truth, our truth, was complicated. But it was beautiful. And it was real.

Love was a choice and we made it every day.

Bedrock.

About the Author

M. O'KEEFE can remember the exact moment her love of romance began: in seventh grade, when Mrs. Nelson handed her the worn paperback copy of *The Thorn Birds*. It wasn't long before she was filling up notebooks with her own story ideas, featuring girls with glasses and talking cats. Writing as Molly O'Keefe, she has won two RITA awards and three *RT* Reviewers Choice Awards. She lives in Toronto, Canada, with her husband, two kids, and the largest heap of dirty laundry in North America. When she's not writing, she's imagining what she would say if she ever got stuck in an elevator with Bruce Springsteen.

molly-okeefe.com
Facebook.com/MollyOKeefeBooks
@MollyOKwrites

About the Type

This book was set in Sabon, a typeface designed by the well-known German typographer Jan Tschichold (1902–74). Sabon's design is based upon the original letter forms of sixteenth-century French type designer Claude Garamond and was created specifically to be used for three sources: foundry type for hand composition, Linotype, and Monotype. Tschichold named his typeface for the famous Frankfurt typefounder Jacques Sabon (c. 1520–80).